All the U Shouldnt Say

"I devoured it in like 3 days, super enjoyed it, spotted like a handful of spelling errors nothing really, and would happily read another" – **Zoe, the mum friend**

"Oh my god!!!! Just finished your book. I had only read the first chapter before now but as you can see, I literally couldn't stop reading (really hope this doesn't wake you up). I'm going to need the next book asap. Arghhh, I love it. The characters are incredible, I LOVE Max. Just arghhhh! It's amazing!!! So easy to read and brilliant, funny and sassy and arghhhh!!!" – **Amy, the school friend**

"It's a great book. Is it my genre? No. Did it entice me? Definitely. Did I feel attacked in parts? Yes. But it's wonderfully written, it's a good read and I look forward to hearing about how successful it becomes!" – **Jamie, the gay best friend**

"Max is based on me, right?" – **Tom, the husband**

About the Author

Sophie lives in York, England with her husband and two daughters. As well as writing, she loves reading, videogames, and boardgames. She hates the miscommunication trope and forced third-act break ups. Due to having aphantasia, heavy descriptions and excessive world building do little for her. She's much more interested in well-constructed characters and entertaining dialogue.

If you'd like to follow along with her writing journey, you can find her on social media or sign up to her newsletter at her website: www.sophieoswald.com

All the Words You Shouldn't Say

S. Oswald

x

All the Words You Shouldn't Say

SOPHIE OSWALD

Independently published version 1.0

Cover design by Mr. Oswald

ISBN: 978-1-9194917-0-7 (eBook)
ISBN: 978-1-9194917-1-4 (Paperback)

This is a work of fiction. The events and people described here are imaginary.

No AI has been used in the writing, editing, or design of this book.

For all the people who
love to fall in love.

Thank fuck for fiction.

Playlist
ATW You Shouldn't Say

Sweet Nothing	⁂	Gabrielle Aplin
people pleaser	⁂	Cat Burns
Fly Away	⁂	Tones And I
Shine – Kygo Remix	⁂	Benjamin Francis Leftwich
Trouble	⁂	Iggy Azalea, Jennifer Hudson
Freaking Me Out	⁂	Ava Max
On Mine	⁂	Diplo, Noah Cyrus
Window	⁂	MAGIC GIANT
Sympathy	⁂	Declan McKenna
Almost (Sweet Music)	⁂	Hozier
Green Light	⁂	Lorde
Strategy	⁂	TWICE
Ready For You	⁂	HAIM
Superbloom	⁂	MisterWives
Aurora	⁂	Vexento
Head on Fire	⁂	Griff, Sigrid
Keeps Me Light	⁂	Tall Heights
Shape of You	⁂	Ed Sheeran
TEXAS HOLD 'EM	⁂	Beyoncé
This Feeling	⁂	The Chainsmokers, Kelsea Ballerini
Blank Space	⁂	Taylor Swift
No Promises	⁂	Cheat Codes, Demi Lovato
Lonely Together	⁂	Avicii, Rita Ora
Heartbreak Anthem	⁂	Galantis, David Guetta, Litte Mix
Shivers	⁂	Ed Sheeran
Getaway Car	⁂	Taylor Swift
i wish i knew how to quit you	⁂	sombr
Peer Pressure	⁂	James Bay, Julia Michaels
Ribs	⁂	Lorde
See Her Out (Thats Just Life)	⁂	Francis and the Lights

Playlist available on Spotify

All the Words
You Shouldn't Say

Chapter One

"My name is Cathy. I'm on the better side of twenty, 5'4", 34DD, blonde (kinda), blue-eyed, pretty in an understated way because I'm inherently too lazy to make much effort with my appearance. I'm clever when I want to be, stubborn even when I don't. My life's goal is to be comfortable in every possible capacity. Hobbies *yawn* include reading, pretending to write, baking for sustenance, and thinking of all the animals I'll never get to pet. I'm not much of a drinker but can be persuaded to be fun sometimes. I'm looking for a very underwhelmingly average man to woo, marry, and give me the best (and only) sex of my life because I'm too picky and prudish to sleep with any of the hot guys my amazing best friend suggests—"

Cathy had seen enough. She raised her eyes from the laptop to glare at her 'amazing best friend', wondering what she'd done to make Sara hate her so much.

"What do you think?" Sara grinned from where she lay on her stomach on the bed beside her.

"Erm ... just a couple of concerns." Cathy's eyes scanned back over the unflattering profile. "First, I thought you wanted to get me a boyfriend, not ensure no man would ever go near me?"

"You said you wanted it to be honest." Sara's voice morphed into a bad impression of Cathy. "*I wouldn't want to mislead anyone.*"

"I don't want to! I want to spare myself as many nonstarters as possible. But this—"

"Did I lie?" Sara gave her a firm side eye.

"You ..." Another glance over the paragraph had Cathy's shoulders slumping. It was all true, in a cruel, psychological warfare kind of way. Actually, "That's not my bra size."

"Yeah, I know, but guys like the sound of double D."

"Eww, gross." Cathy sighed. "I'm taking that out. But that doesn't make me a prude."

Sara rolled onto her front and flashed a toothy smile, all the while texting on her phone. "Doesn't make you *not* a prude."

"I'm cautious. And selective."

Sara raised her heavily mascaraed eyes to Cathy. "So cautious you've never selected anyone, hence the prudishness. And you can't even watch a 12A sex scene without getting embarrassed."

"I ..." But there was no point. When Sara used that tone, it was useless to argue otherwise, even though her embarrassment at sexual media was more about witnessing it with company than the content itself. She loved a good sex scene on her own, but she was never going to admit that. "Where are all these supposed 'hot guys'?" She asked instead.

"There was the plumber last week."

"He was like sixty!"

"Hey, we both agreed he looked good for sixty. And you didn't want my brother."

"Because of the opposite. Louis is seventeen!"

"*And* there was that nice guy you work with—"

"Santi is in a long-distance relationship. He's also way too cool for me."

Sara's tongue clicked against her teeth. "Too old, too young, too taken, too cool. There's always something." She shrugged. "What do you want from me?"

With a groan, Cathy fell back against the pillows. It shouldn't be so hard. All she wanted was a twenty to thirty something, single, not too cool man (or Mr Darcy, but she knew that was asking a bit much of the universe). Shouldn't the world be full of men like that? Where were they all hiding? Or maybe it wasn't the men that were the problem. Maybe it was her. Maybe even underwhelmingly average men weren't interested in lazy, shy, conservative girls.

"Maybe it's me," she muttered mostly to herself. "Maybe I am boring. Maybe I am a prude." She turned the laptop away, dismissing that shameful profile from her attention. "But I'm not going to tell the world that." Rather than let Sara see her wounds, she chose to lighten the mood. "With the right guy, I'm sure I could be just as slutty as you are."

Laughing, she caught the pillow Sara threw at her face.

"If you ever need tips, you know where I am," Sara winked. "Anyway, speaking of slutty, I need to head out."

She rolled off the bed and stepped into her four-inch glossy black heels before standing in front of the mirror to check the fit of her bodycon dress. It was a bold look; skin-tight, low-cut, leaving nowhere to hide. Not that Sara needed to hide any part of her body, not with those long legs and that perfect BMI, boobs small enough that she could go braless but still enough to work with when she wanted to draw attention, like tonight.

"How do I look?" She asked, smoothing the fabric over her hips.

"Gorgeous as always," Cathy replied. "But you're not helping my cause for natural beauty."

Not when she had on a full face of makeup, complete with shimmer over her high cheekbones and glitter around her warm honey eyes, black lashes impossibly long. Her highlighted chocolate-brown hair was somehow both smooth and voluminous, tied up in a playful ponytail, precision-engineered curls arranged around her face, while her boobs were pushed up two cup sizes, the rounded flesh appearing almost *dewy.* Clothes and cosmetics were one thing, but when paired with a premium canvas – perfect figure, dainty hands and feet, blemish-free skin naturally the colour of a perfect light-bronze tan – Sara was a beauty, uncut or polished.

"Oh, is that what the low-effort look is about?" Sara rolled her eyes at Cathy's statement. They had always batted for different teams of feminism; Sara wanting to beat men at their own game by weaponizing femininity for her own benefit, while Cathy mostly forgot about the male gaze and lived according to her own truth: everything as easy and comfortable as possible. One of them definitely received more attention than the other, but one also got to live a life without being regularly tortured by high heels.

"A bit of vanity never hurt," Sara continued, eyeing the paint on her nails. "Especially not when it helps you get laid."

"Or make a week's salary in one night," Cathy added wryly.

Sara gave her a wicked smile in the mirror, those perfectly shaped eyebrows arching seductively. "Same thing."

Cathy's stomach no longer sunk at the thought of Sara's occupation. When they'd first met, Sara had been brutally honest about her escort business, having absolutely no qualms about using her body to make a living, while Cathy could only think what a dangerous and unsavoury activity it was, something that happened in films or you'd watch a Netflix documentary on; it wasn't something people in her small, traditional world did. But it quickly became apparent that Sara knew what she was doing and was doing it rather well. The intimate details she kept to herself, though she was happy to reassure anxious friends that she knew how to stay safe, had acquired a select group of lucrative customers, and was able to save so much money that she'd be able to retire her body in about five years' time to live out her dream of being an artist with her very own brick-and-mortar gallery.

Cathy couldn't argue against that. Especially when, comparatively, she had zero plans, zero dreams, and basically zero cash.

"Who is it tonight?" She politely enquired. There was a fine line between taking an interest in her friend's work and giving in to sordid curiosity, so she tended to not ask very much very often. Sara tended to not say very much either. Whether that was just to maintain confidentiality or because there were parts she'd rather not put into words, Cathy couldn't be sure.

"Liam," Sara replied flatly, pouting at the mirror as she reapplied her lipstick, her Cupid's bow plump and kissable.

"The lawyer?"

"The banker."

"I thought Richard was the banker?"

"Richard's the surgeon. And actually a really sweet guy; he just likes to talk and look at me. Liam, though, he makes me work for it." Utterly undaunted at that prospect, Sara finished topping up her makeup and moved to leave, walking seamlessly on those pinpoint stiletto heels. "Later, darling." She blew a kiss in Cathy's vague direction and strutted from the room.

"Stay safe," Cathy replied, astounded as always by her friend's confidence. While Sara could stroll out into the world, tits up and legs out, feasting off the attention, Cathy would much rather stay inside with a good book, comfortable in leggings and an oversized t-shirt ... which was what she usually did ... *always* did.

When she heard the front door bang shut, her chest hollowed, the sudden silence imposing without the buzz of her flatmate's main character energy.

She didn't notice the door being opened an hour later when her ex-flatmate let herself in.

Alison didn't even knock. She quietly opened Cathy's bedroom door and peered through, watching as her friend sat frozen with a book open on her knees while she stared at the far wall and cried.

"Hey," she finally said, coming closer.

"Hey. Sorry," Cathy apologised, half-heartedly drying her cheeks with her sleeves. While Sara would have ordered her to get a grip and stop being so pathetic, Alison sat down beside her and offered a shoulder to lean on, literally and metaphorically. Sometimes she needed tough love; sometimes she needed the space to be sad. Luckily, she had a friend for both.

"Did something happen?"

Cathy shook her head and waited until the rock in her throat loosened enough to have her voice fully under control.

"I'm just fed up. Six months after graduation and I'm still a waitress on minimum wage." She sighed, but the bitterness stayed trapped inside her. "I just had this expectation that after trying so hard at school and university I would walk into a good job. That's what school made me believe."

"You can't walk into a job if you haven't applied for any," Alison gently reminded her.

"They all have ridiculous requirements!" She despaired dramatically. "Two years' experience; I've just graduated, I have no experience! Or they want you to be an overconfident egotist who believes they'd be the best person for the job; I'm never going to be the best person for the job. I could probably be decent at most things but there will always be someone better because there are like seven billion people in the world!"

Alison tamed her smile and tweaked her tortoiseshell glasses. "Eight. But you don't have to take it quite so literally. Adverts are more of a wish list than a checklist most of the time. And regardless, you can still apply."

"It seems pointless to when they have such unrealistic expectations. It doesn't help that I have literally no idea what I want to do. Maybe a postgrad one day, but I need a break from writing essays." She flexed her right wrist, remembering the hours upon hours of pain it had endured. And for what? Just a degree she was probably never going to use and a whole load of student debt she would probably never pay off. "Everyone always asks what you want to be when you're older. I never had an answer. And now I'm older, I *still* don't have an answer, but now I *need* an answer before I waste my life away."

"You don't need to worry about that just yet," Alison reassured, her almond-shaped eyes soft with affection, their blueness warmer than usual. "It will happen. Just spend the next couple of years getting some kind of experience and a bit of money. Just relax. There's no rush getting into a career."

"Says you, Miss Already-Partially-Qualified-Accountant," Cathy teased, her frown lifting into a smile that almost hid her jealousy.

"I knew what I wanted to do, so it's different. You're allowed to slow down for a couple of years if that's what you need. Maybe you could even start writing again ... in the first place," she teased gently.

Cathy frowned at her. "I can't. I have all these stories, all these half-formed characters and plotlines living in my head but I can't, I can't—"

Alison gave her shoulder a squeeze. "I know. Once the job stress is sorted out, maybe you'll be relaxed enough to get into it."

"I've just gotten over the university stress. And the Dad stress. It doesn't matter. There's always something else to distract me ... something else to exhaust my meagre emotional and mental resources ..."

"Now you're being a little melodramatic," Alison chided warmly.

"I like being melodramatic sometimes."

"I know, but we're going to take it one thing at a time, starting with this."

Alison reached into her handbag to retrieve a slightly scruffy piece of paper, which she handed to Cathy to read.

"What is it?" Cathy asked, the lingering moisture in her eyes making the printed words twist and blur.

"An advert for a job at the company I work for."

The words came into focus.

"Administration Assistant?"

"I know it's not a grad job, but I think it could be what you need right now. Easy work, decent pay, office experience, plus we'd be in the same building. At the very least, it would make a change from waitressing. And I can put in a good word for you."

"I'm not sure ..."

"With your brains, you'll learn the job like that." She snapped her fingers. "And then it's easy money and stress-free work."

"But I'm not *confident*, I'm not *enthusiastic* about admin, and I'm definitely not *resilient*," Cathy whined. "Is anyone genuinely enthusiastic about admin?"

"No, but you are a *quick learner* and a *good communicator* and have a *professional manner*," Alison countered, picking out different buzz words from the advert. "Honestly, you're more capable than you know. You're just stuck in a rut at the moment."

"And my self-esteem is stuck in an even deeper rut."

Even Alison, patient, kind-hearted Alison, would only indulge her negativity for so long.

"And we're going to get you out of it. By you applying for this job, and me recommending you to the hiring manager. We can quickly write a cover letter, email it over with your CV and then it's done."

"Erm ..."

But Alison was distracted as she turned the open laptop towards her and the screen brightened. "What's this?"

Cathy couldn't prevent her scowl. "You know how you think a new job will make me happier? Sara thinks getting me laid is the answer. She wrote this dating profile that the internet is *never* going to see."

Alison read it over, her lips curving downwards. "This is awful."

"I know!"

"No, I mean it's awful and *cruel*."

"Well, maybe a little." Cathy chewed her lip. "I don't think she meant it cruelly."

"She didn't mean it nicely! It's in bad taste, even if it was meant as a joke. You should tell her."

"I don't want to ..." What? Cause a fuss? Damage a friendship? Deny she didn't deserve every word? All of the above?

"It's not okay," Alison gave her a meaningful frown. "Besides, as a – what I assume – contentedly single, independent woman, I wonder why Sara thinks a man is ever the answer."

Cathy shifted uncomfortably. "I wouldn't say no ..."

"Cathy?"

"Okay, okay. So, I might have mentioned to her that recently seeing you and Dylan together has been making me feel ... sad. I'm sure it's just because I'm a puddle of generalised sadness," she hastily reassured, wincing at the appearance of Alison's sympathetic frown.

"Sad, why?"

"Because I want that connection with someone ... I want to *be* someone worth a connection, like you."

Her words deflated Alison a little more, the air slowly seeping out of her like a punctured armband.

"You're envious?"

Cathy gawped at her. "Alison, how could I not be? You have your career all planned out, you're living with the love of your life. You're already saving for a house, you're going to get married in like a year ... you're happy," Cathy added, decidedly unhappily. *You have everything I've ever wanted.*

"Cathy ..."

"And I miss you. I miss living with you. Of course, I like living with Sara, but it's not the same. She's out a lot and always has so much energy. I liked being quiet with you. I miss those hours reading together on the sofa. It was just so easy. But, of course, I am so *so* happy for you. I love you, and Dylan is genuinely a great guy. I really am happy that you're happy."

She felt Alison's cynical stare on her for a tense moment. Luckily, her friend wasn't one to brood or probe. After a moment, she cleared the emotion from her throat, tied up her long black hair, straightened her glasses, and swiftly deleted Sara's unfavourable description.

"It's time you were happy too, so let's get you a job *and* a boyfriend," she declared. "Where is your CV saved?"

"Erm ... yeah, about that ..."

"Do you really not have one?"

"Are you really surprised?" Cathy jumped off the bed and skipped across the room. "I think I'll make us some tea and maybe get us some chocolate."

Alison sighed. "We're going to need it."

*

It had been an awful shift. After eight hours, Cathy's feet were sore and her mouth ached from the fake smile she'd had to wear for all the customers who most certainly didn't *always know best.* And it had been a particularly busy day, especially for a Thursday, intermittent showers forcing unexpected flurries of people (mostly tourists) inside looking for shelter, people who were willing to buy food and drink they didn't really need to get it. The rain was starting up again then, droplets sliding down the dark windows, pitter-pattering on the glass. It was going to be a miserable ride home.

She was the only waitress still there. All the tables were empty. Five minutes until the restaurant closed. She put away the last of the glasses, looking between her watch and the door, hearing the manager cashing up by the front desk.

Four minutes ...

Three minutes ...

The door chimed as it opened.

You have got to be kidding me.

Cathy's heart sank as she heard the manager talking to the idiot customers who were going to make them all stay late just because they didn't like to eat at a reasonable time like reasonable people, or couldn't cope with a little water. *Ever heard of an umbrella?* She listened to the soft thuds of footsteps and the scrape of chairs near the front of the restaurant, still not daring to look. It took a good minute for her to tame her expression from *I want to kill you* to *You can have anything you want unless it's a well-done steak, then I'll kill you.*

"Cathy." Karen, the manager, a well-fed, thoroughbred Scotswoman, came up to the bar, handbag already slung over her shoulder. "I'm sorry, my lovely."

Cathy shrugged. "It happens."

"Aye. I've locked the door and cashed up, so I'll head off. You all right to finish up?"

"Sure," she lied brightly, itching to remind Karen of what they both got paid and whose responsibility it really was to stay late.

"You can keep the tip, my lovely."

With a wink and a grin, Karen wandered off out the back.

Fucking managers.

Taming her face for a second time, Cathy stepped out from the safety of the bar and headed up into the restaurant, hearing male voices before she saw them. There was no obnoxious party, no travel-worn family, just two guys. She had to stay late for *two guys!*

Her three second assessment of them – young, laddish, one blonde, one brunette, friends based on the easy back-and-forth banter – was that they were definitely just hiding from the rain. The blonde one was looking at his phone as she came alongside their table in front of the window.

"Good evening. Are you—"

The brunette looked at her for a second before following her surprised gaze to stare out of the window at the sudden downpour. The rain started streaming down the glass, obscuring any view of the street, and thundered on the roof like stomping feet.

"Well, we were lucky," he observed, something bored in his tone.

"Fucking *yes*!" The blonde looked up from his phone, clearly delighted. "She wants me to come over."

"Now?"

"Yes, now, before she changes her mind."

"Do you really think it's a good idea to sleep with your ex?" The brunette raised his brow. "You really want to go out in *that*?"

"I'd go out in a fucking tornado if it meant I got some. Later, man."

Just like that, the blonde one dragged his body from the chair, narrowly avoided bumping into Cathy – since he apparently still hadn't noticed her existence – and barrelled out into the night, the door snapping shut behind him. Cathy's eyes lingered on the door, bewildered and mildly impressed by the guy's commitment to getting laid.

"That was ..."

"Something," her remaining customer helpfully finished for her. "James is nothing if not enthusiastic."

She pulled her eyes back to him, her gaze latching onto his amused smile. After a second, he cleared his throat and she remembered she *still* had a job to do. And this guy didn't look like he was about to run off anytime soon, sitting comfortably back in his chair, legs stretched out under the table. He seemed very relaxed for someone who'd just been left on his own. Where she would have been writhing with anxiety, he apparently couldn't care less.

"Oh, yes, erm ... are you ready to order? The carvery is closed but the kitchen and bar are still open. Unless you fancy running out after your friend ..." *Please go drown yourself outside. Please.*

His smile tipped up to one side, almost as if he could see straight through her non-existent customer service charm.

"I have no desire to follow him to his ex's. So, since I'll be waiting out this apocalyptic weather, I'll have ... a San Miguel and a portion of sweet potato fries." He held the menu up to her, finally raising his eyes to the nametag pinned on her shirt. "Thank you, Cathy."

Her smile held just long enough. As soon as she'd turned away, it disappeared, replaced with a murderous scowl as she cursed him in her head. Staying late, for one guy, for a single bowl of fries!

"Excuse me?"

She stopped, half-glancing over her shoulder to see him staring at her, a thoughtful frown on his face, as if he was doing a cunning piece of mental arithmetic.

"What's the name of this place?"

"Maguire's?"

She wasn't sure why she'd put an inflection at the end.

"You're not sure?" He teased.

Oh, she *really* wasn't in the mood to be belittled. She just wanted to go home.

"No, I'm sure. I get to feel a piece of my soul fly away every time I see it above the door before a shift."

Shit, I shouldn't have said that.

She didn't stay long enough to see or hear a response.

From her refuge behind the bar, she phoned up to the kitchen to let Conner, the chef, know the pathetic order. He was disgruntled but relieved, no doubt bag already packed, unlit cigarette pressed between his lips, all set to leave as soon as the order was done. Then she took her time finding the right bottle in the fridge, before placing it on a tray and reluctantly walking back across the restaurant. She didn't even look at the man as she reached the table, banging the bottle down a little too firmly, and trotting away again to wait by the lift for his stupid bowl of orange-variety fries to come down.

When they arrived, they smelt so good, looked so perfectly crispy, that she was tempted to pinch one but, ever professional, she approached her single patron, his food untampered.

"There you go, sir. Can I get you anything else?"

"No, this is fine." She had already started to walk away when he continued speaking. "I know you're pissed you've had to stay late, but in the interests of your soul, if you'd like a drink and a sit down, I'd appreciate the company."

Well, she'd never had a customer speak to her like that before. She looked at him to assess his intentions, suddenly acutely aware they were the only two people in the building, not that he knew that. But her feet could really use a rest, and Karen wasn't there to tell her off, and yet—

"I'm not sure I'm allowed to," she said quietly, lamely.

"Didn't your manager just fuck off home?"

A surprised huff escaped her at his casual language. "Erm, well ... yeah."

"Then your secret's safe with me." His smile was a wicked, presumptuous thing.

"Okay, thanks ... I'll just grab a drink then."

"Anything you want. It's on me."

How strange, she thought as she eyed the bottles behind the bar. It was too weird. Things like this didn't happen to her. Maybe it was a set-up. Scrap that thought, the whole thing with Blonde Guy was too convoluted to be part of a set-up. Also, even though she'd barely looked at him, she just knew Mr Brunette did not have low enough standards to be interested in her; his rich voice was full of confidence that would immediately find her depleted self-esteem tedious. So maybe it really was just a free drink and a sit down while he waited out the rain. Though, could he not have offered two minutes ago, so that she could have ordered some food, too? Now she got to watch him eat while her stomach hadn't been full since lunchtime. It was a slightly half-hearted attempt at kindness, but her soul had no better offers.

"What's your poison?" He asked as she took the seat across from him.

"Raspberry lemonade. I have to moped home," she explained before he labelled her as boring like everyone did when they learnt she didn't really care for casual drinking. She fidgeted in her seat, suddenly forgetting how to sit. With his legs under the table, she turned her chair towards the room, crossed her legs, and held her glass to give her hands something to do.

Of course, he'd been watching her while she'd been figuring out how to human, that smug smile still on his face, as if the world existed just to amuse him.

He brushed a hand over his chin before reaching for his drink, and took a long swig from the bottle, eyes keenly assessing her.

"Help yourself." He nodded towards the fries.

"Oh, are you sure?" She squeaked, fingers already moving towards the bowl.

She took his shrug as a yes.

Chip in hand, she leaned back in her seat, chewing slowly while she finally bothered to look at him properly. The more she looked, the more she wished she hadn't. Two things were immediately obvious: he was rich and attractive. He had the face of a well-bred socialite – hair a dark walnut brown; astute, permanently amused eyes a captivating hazel – and the designer clothes to match. His suit probably cost more than her moped did, let alone the polished Rolex on his wrist. A tailored jacket was on the back of his chair, discarded silk tie tucked in the pocket. Shirt collar undone, sleeves carelessly pushed up to his elbows, revealing supple, strong forearms, *careless* ... there was nothing careless about him. The relaxed, professional, *I've-just-had-a-fantastic-day-making-a-fuck-ton-of-money* look was deliberate, right down to the tousled hair and lightly tanned skin, from the sun, not a bottle. She knew, instinctively, that the guy didn't *fake* anything, that he didn't need to. Genetic lottery jackpot, gold-tinted childhood from generational wealth, privately educated ego; he knew the world was his for the taking.

Guys like him didn't usually *see* girls like her. And she was fine with that; she had nothing to say to guys like him anyway. But with the sheer lack of other people around, she seemed to have lost her invisibility cloak, and now she had to talk to him. He probably just wanted to mock her, squash her under his designer shoe, and take pleasure in seeing her squirm. Yeah, that was probably it. There was no other explanation why a genuine *male* stranger would choose to talk to her. Well, he'd picked the wrong wallflower. Tonight, she had thorns.

Okay, maybe not thorns, but she was definitely a little more prickly than usual.

"What's a girl like you waitressing here for?" He asked leisurely, wearing a smile that said he'd heard every thought and opinion she'd just made about him and didn't mind one bit.

"What's that supposed to mean?" She threw back, her hackles immediately raised at his choice of words, even if they'd lacked a judgemental tone.

"Pretty, intelligent—"

"What makes you think I'm intelligent?" She interrupted, trying not to blush at being referred to as *pretty*.

His smile curved slightly more. So, she'd passed the first test. Still, it was vaguely surprising that a guy that looked as put-together as he did would value brains over beauty.

"You have a look about you, one that says this job is beneath you."

"I would never judge someone for being a waitress—"

"Of course not," he mollified. "But you know you belong elsewhere. How long have you worked here?"

She frowned at him. "You really want to hear about my sad little life?"

"Beats being left alone to contemplate my sad little life."

Pfft, yeah right, like your life is at all sad or little. But she decided to play along, since there had been nothing mean in his manner so far. He was polite, surprisingly innocuous. And something about him made her feel at ease despite her inexperience at dealing with male attention ... any attention really.

"I've been here a few years but only during university holidays, until recently."

"You've graduated now?"

"Six months ago."

"So why are you still here?"

She shrugged. "I don't know what to do with my life, at least not career-wise. If money wasn't an issue, I'd travel and write but," she shrugged again, "That isn't possible. Most jobs don't interest me, but I need to get out of this place. The pay used to be all right when we got to keep all our tips; I could double what I took home some days. But now it's split between everyone, even the managers, like they don't get paid enough, and we're the ones running around and smiling for eight hours straight. Fucking managers ... I shouldn't have said that."

He laughed quietly; a warm, reassuring sound. "I won't tell. Are you looking for another job?"

"Not as actively as I should be. I have applied for one," she said, as if that was something to be proud of.

"Doing what?"

"Just admin. It will probably be just as soul-destroying as this but at least I could endure my existential dread while sitting down."

He tipped his head back, draining the last drops from his bottle, purposely hiding his expression to her last remark.

"Well, I wish you luck with that," he said, giving nothing away. "If you'd be so kind as to get me the bill, I'll get out of your way."

"Oh, of course ..." She glanced out the window to confirm that the rain had almost stopped. Then it occurred to her that she hadn't moved her eyes from him at all during their conversation. He was very nice to look at.

Slightly startled by the sudden dismissal (she had genuinely forgotten for a moment she was meant to be his waitress), she jumped to her feet, turning back to the table to pick up her glass. He was watching her; an amused, secretive smile on his face.

"You're not a restaurant manager that's just started taking half his waiting staff's tips, are you?" She stammered.

"Why do you ask?" He replied coolly, intrigued and entertained.

"I meant no offence—"

"And none was taken. I also despair at managers that forget what it's like to be at the bottom of the food chain."

Like you've ever been at the bottom of the food chain, she thought, eyes glancing over the designer clothes again, the Rolex glinting obnoxiously in the faux candlelight.

"Cool." *Dammit, did I just say cool?* "Erm ... I'll go get your bill."

She scurried away before she could embarrass herself any further, returning with the bill a minute later.

"There you go," she placed it on the table and left again, keeping her tired eyes low.

Taking her place behind the bar, she sipped the last of her lemonade, waiting out the five minutes of privacy she'd been taught to give customers while they contemplated their finances. She'd just taken a deep breath, ready to step back over, when she heard footsteps approaching.

"Money's on the table. Keep the change," the man said, walking up to the bar.

"Thank you."

"Have a good night," he added with a smile.

"You too ..."

And he let himself out, the Yale lock slamming shut behind him.

Well, she'd had worse customers.

She headed back into the restaurant to clear the table, her eyes immediately drawn to the small silver tray with a twenty-pound note on it. No, two twenty-pound notes! She looked out the window but Sir Rolex was long gone, lost to the night. Well, he had said to keep the change ...

One twenty she left by the till alongside the order receipt for Karen to find when she arrived in the morning, the second she tucked safely away in her bra.

Maybe not all privileged white boys were so bad. He could come again.

Chapter Two

Cathy worked the afternoon/evening shift at the restaurant because she wasn't, in any capacity, a morning person. As such, she did not appreciate being woken up by her phone ringing at nine thirty *AM*. Who the hell still phoned people anyway?

"Hello?" She grumbled, pressing her phone straight to her ear without even checking the number, rolling onto her side, ready to drift back to sleep at a moment's notice.

"Good morning. Is this Cathy Watson?" A polite, almost robotic, female voice enquired.

Eugh, woken up for telesales, how disappointing.

"That's me." She was all ready to follow up with a *Thanks but no thanks* when the woman continued, her words making any thought of going back to sleep suddenly impossible.

"I'm calling from Atlas Hotels. After reviewing your application, the hiring manager would like to invite you in for an interview. Do you have any availability today?"

What the—

"Today? For an interview?"

She sat up in the bed, pyjamas twisted unpleasantly around her, feeling underdressed for the conversation.

"That's correct," the woman assured her patiently.

"Erm ... I could do one, if that works?" Her mental faculties could *totally* cope with a horribly short notice interview, followed by another gruelling Friday shift at the restaurant, especially when interviews were one of her top five fears, and she would rather be hit by a car and hospitalised than go to work again. Today was looking *great.*

A new job would be pretty great though, if she managed to not screw it up.

Big *if.*

"That's perfect," the nice lady told her.

"Oh, wow. Great!"

"I'll send a confirmation through to the email address on your application with all the details, and we'll see you at one o'clock."

"Perfect, thanks. Bye."

Cathy let the phone drop from her hand as she stared at the far wall, trying not to be overwhelmed, trying not to enter the doom spiral looming in the corner of her mind, the self-destructive part of her very much wanting to jump into it and never resurface ... or resurface at two o'clock when it was too late to change her life and she just had to get along with the devil she knew.

No, she told herself firmly. *You hate the devil you know. Go get a better one.*

Okay, it was happening then. She checked the time on her phone, the minutes creeping towards ten. It was forever and no time at all.

"Sara!" She cried as she barrelled into her friend's room. Upon reflection, there really hadn't been much reason to wake Sara up just then, and definitely not so loudly but, at the time it, had felt important. "Sara!"

"What the fuck?" Sara rolled over in bed onto her stomach where she stretched out like a cat, claws and all, and glared at Cathy. At the lack of obvious blood or protruding sharp objects, she yawned (Sara was also very much not a morning person, hence the evening/nighttime job.) "Why are you screaming?"

Cathy's feet stopped in the middle of the room. "I have an interview."

"Oh, nice." Sara closed her eyes again, nuzzling the pillow with her silk-wrapped head, getting comfy again.

"And I need your help."

"I've never had an interview before and I never plan on having one," Sara told her, still preparing to go back to sleep, present company be damned. "Ask Alison for help."

"I can't. She's at work."

"She won't always be at work, you stupid mare."

"It's today! At one." Cathy finally shared that crucial piece of information.

Sara snapped awake, pushing the duvet off as she sat up and got to thinking. "Today? *Shit.* No, forget that, you'll be fine. Great, even."

"Have you met me?"

Sara managed not to laugh. "It's an entry level admin job, right? They won't be too mean. Tell me about a time you've worked as a team and all that crap. Easy."

Cathy's eyes drifted vacantly up, working through her memories to try and find one that involved teamwork and collaboration and other polysyllabic words employers liked.

After an awkward two minutes, Sara finally sighed, and got to her feet.

"You're a bloody waitress, Cathy. You are literally part of a team."

"Oh, yeah, you're right."

Sara's hands were on her shoulders. "You can do this. Just don't panic. What do you know about the company?"

Oh God, she hadn't even gotten round to researching the company.

"Erm ... I know they run hotels, obviously. And there's one here near the train station that I've walked past numerous times but would never be able to afford to go into. Looks very nice though."

Sara's lips puckered appreciatively. "Perfect. You've totally got this. But, just in case they might like to hear a little more, you've still got time to get on Google while I find you an outfit."

That plan worked well, Cathy researching on her phone while Sara scrutinised her wardrobe, until she sighed and threw a black ball of fabric at Cathy's face.

"Seriously, how is eighty percent of your wardrobe black jeans and black t-shirts?"

"It's my work uniform—"

"And the rest is leggings and jumpers. There is one dress and, shockingly, to no one, it's black. I might have to look in my—"

"The dress will be fine," Cathy quickly decided.

She was familiar enough with Sara's wardrobe to know that there wasn't anything interview appropriate in it –

think very short skirts and low necklines – nor anything she would fit into. Sara's thighs didn't touch; Cathy's were best friends. (Cathy liked to ignore the fact that this had a lot more to do with the genetics of fat distribution than with Sara being a size 8 and her a size 12).

The dress was fine. So were the black tights and black ballet pumps. A playful high ponytail and bright yellow floral scarf tactically made it look a little less like she had a funeral to attend afterwards ... she hoped.

Winter coat on, Sara hugged her goodbye and sent her on her way. After short bus ride into the city centre, she was stepping up the wide stone steps of Atlas Hotels' UK headquarters. The building was imposing – tall, modern and mostly made of dark glass – and corporate, far more corporate than anywhere else she'd ever been. She felt it immediately as she stepped through the automatic door, a huge lobby surrounding her, engulfing her; the feeling that she didn't belong. It was all smooth lines and pristine presentation, bright abstract artwork on the walls contrasting to the whites and greys of the furniture. It felt exactly how the offices of an international luxury hotel empire should: impressive, imposing; exclusive. There was just nothing luxury or empire-y about her.

She forgot all about her sense of smallness at the sight of Alison sitting on one of the huge grey sofas arranged either side of a glass coffee table, a bowl of glazed ceramic fruit in the centre.

"Alison ..." She whispered but her friend was already on her feet and coming towards her, folding her into a hug that didn't come naturally to either of them but felt right in the moment. "I guess you got my message."

"I don't hang around in reception for fun," Alison said, letting go to look at her. "Deep breath. You're going to be okay. Just tell reception who you are and someone will come get you. You can do this." Her voice was low and serious, trying to command the universe to give her a break. "I'll come over tomorrow and we can debrief?"

Cathy could only nod, as if her voice had decided it needed saving for later.

Alison gave her one more firm look before turning away, low heels tapping quietly as she crossed the room, approaching the lift on the far wall. After swiping her card, the doors opened and she disappeared inside. Suddenly alone, Cathy felt twice as vulnerable as when she'd first entered, but she forced a smile, reminding herself this was still the *easy* part, and stepped up to the reception desk.

"Hi, I'm Cathy Watson. I'm here for an interview?"

Again with the inflection? Don't I know anything anymore?

The receptionist gave her a polite smile that didn't quite match her discerning, hard-to-please eyes.

"I'll let them know you're here. If you'd like to take a seat, someone will be through shortly."

"Thank you."

She absently heard the receptionist speak into her headset before a nearby door opened and closed and a man walked into the room, directly towards her, and suddenly the world didn't make sense anymore.

She hadn't even made it to the sofa, which was a shame because she felt like she was about to fall over, so she had to somehow concentrate on staying vertical and on the impossible singularity heading her way.

It was him, Mr Brunette, Sir Rolex, Lord Confidence, from yesterday at the restaurant. The customer she'd sworn in front of, insulted her managers to. Someone, somewhere, was having a good laugh at her expense right then. The interview was doomed.

What kind of bullshit serendipity was this?

While her expression melted with disbelief, his gave nothing away, remaining impersonal almost to the point of rudeness, even as he stood directly in front of her, hand outstretched in formal greeting.

"Miss Watson," he said, in the same richly deep voice she remembered. "Thank you for making it on such short notice."

Maybe he didn't recognise her, even though she looked exactly the same, just in a different outfit of near pure black.

Who really remembered what their servers looked like anyway? Maybe it would all be okay? Maybe she wasn't completely deluded?

A subtle tightening around his eyes pulled her back into the moment, to the interview, to the hand waiting awkwardly long for her to take it.

"Oh," she breathed, reaching out, feeling their palms press together, thumbs lightly locking. While her skin was hot and (mortifyingly) damp, his was cool and dry, his grip firm, confident with nothing to prove. He held on a moment longer than she was expecting, giving her hand a light squeeze before letting go. Then, while her (disgustingly) damp hand dried in the air, she realised she still hadn't said anything.

"Thank you for having me," she fumbled.

Even that seemed to amuse him, just a whisper across his eyes.

"This way," he said, turning around and walking back the way he came.

He stepped back beside the open doorway, letting her enter the plain meeting room first. There was a large oval table in the middle, surrounded by black synthetic office chairs. Along the back wall was a sideboard with a large clock above it and a tidy arrangement of paper, pens, and refreshment facilities – coffee machine, cups, a jug of clear water – on its polished surface. A full glass was already waiting for her on the table. The door clicked closed.

"Please take a seat and get comfortable," he said, before stepping around the table and making himself comfortable on the other side, jacket button undone, hand absently playing with a heavy silver pen while he waited. Suddenly behind in the choreography, she moved quickly, taking off her coat, scarf, and bag, dumping them on one seat before sinking down into another directly across from him.

"Who died?" He asked, his tone far too light for the context. Less interviewer, much more colloquial customer ...

"I'm sorry?"

He nodded in her direction and she looked down.

Ah, balls, should have left the scarf on.

"Oh, no one. Unless you count my job prospects here."

That didn't seem to amuse him. "What makes you say that?"

Was he only capable of asking questions? It suddenly occurred to her that she hadn't found out a single thing about him last night, beyond what his appearance – her prejudices – had told her.

"You must recognise me," she blurted, anxiety making her bold.

"Of course."

"Do you want your twenty pounds back? Is that why I'm here?"

Finally, a smile. "No, I don't. And you're here for an interview for a job *you* applied for." He looked down to write something on the thin stack of paper in front of him. "I take it you still *want* to be interviewed?"

She'd never *wanted* to be interviewed; she just wanted a new job and an easy life. Was that too much to ask for? She definitely hadn't wanted to be interviewed by her overly familiar customer turned potential future ... *Wait* – she still didn't have a clue who he was.

"Probably—"

He scoffed. "*Probably.* I can promise you this job will be better than your current one in every measurable way. Salary, benefits, working conditions—"

"Sorry, just *who* are you?"

He raised his eyes to her, his brow creasing as he recognised how odd it was that he hadn't already introduced himself... or that it was odd *she* didn't already know who he was.

"Maximilian Cannavale, CFO of the European Division. I'm the hiring manager for this role."

Something about the way he said it made her quite sure she was meant to know that already.

"So, you would be ..."

"Your future line manager. Though you will be supervised by my assistant day to day. Your training and workload will be overseen by her. She'll be your primary point of contact."

The second person, future tense had not gone unnoticed. But before she could address it, he asked another question.

"Anyway, the interview. What do you know about the company?"

Okay, she knew this one. "It was founded in the 1970s, with the first hotel opening here in York. The first decade focused on UK expansion, then Europe, America, and Asia. You now have almost two hundred hotels across the world. You focus on luxury but also on creating a cultural experience for your guests, with décor and food tailored to the region." Her mouth hung open for a second before she realised she'd run out of words. Suddenly, it didn't sound like much.

"Good," he acknowledged, writing a few comments in the first box of the form. His eyes moved onto the next question before he dropped his pen and pushed the sheets away.

"Aren't you supposed to ask me those?"

He shrugged. "HR would say so, but it's not necessary. I don't think it's particularly fair to barrage you with questions when you've had so little time to prepare. Unless you'd like to tell me about a time you had to prioritise your workload under pressure?"

"I'm happy to be spared," she said. "Speaking of having so little time to prepare ..."

"What about it?" He crossed his arms over his chest and watched her oh-so expectantly.

Shit. He'd seen right through her plan to get him talking. Fine, if he wanted her to call him out, then she would.

"I'm just trying to figure out what's going on," she answered more lamely than she would have liked, but she was suddenly feeling impossibly awkward with his eyes on her.

"What do you think is going on?"

She met his stare. "I don't know. But I think it's odd how I served you last night and now I'm here having a hasty interview that doesn't feel like an interview at all."

"You got me," he smirked. "This isn't really an interview."

"What—"

"Why did you study English at university?"

He was giving her whiplash. Maybe a mouth ulcer too.

"It combined two of my favourite pastimes; reading and overthinking things."

"*That* is why you're here," he professed as if it revealed everything.

"I don't understand."

He looked at the ceiling as if she'd disappointed him. "Fine," he whispered at the light fitting, before fixing his gaze back on her. "While at the restaurant yesterday, I realised that you were one of the applicants for this position. What I saw from you there, combined with your friend's personal recommendation, convinced me to get you in for an interview. And today hasn't changed my mind. The job is yours if you want it."

Wait, it had never been an interview, not really. It was a job offer.

She felt like laughing. It was absurd, ridiculous. Was she dreaming? Hallucinating from a carbon monoxide leak? *What's in this water?*

A giggle escaped her, followed by another at his widening eyes. "Okay, you can turn the cameras off now. Let me know if I get TikTok famous."

"This isn't a joke."

"You can't seriously be offering me a job after my behaviour yesterday."

"I can and I am."

Her disbelief vanished at the seriousness in his expression, her giggles popping like bubbles until there was nothing left.

"Shit. Why?"

"You intrigue me," he said, as if that explained everything, before glancing at the clock over his shoulder.

"Anyway, a formal job offer and contract will be emailed over to you this afternoon. Read them over, see what you think. If you accept, sign the documents, and we'll see you Monday."

"Monday? As in three days' time, Monday?"

"Yes, that one," he confirmed wryly, suddenly getting to his feet.

She mirrored his movements, collecting her coat and bag where he gathered pen and paper, while her brain struggled to make sense of everything. It settled on saying, "But I have a job."

"That you will need to quit if you want to come here," he replied blandly, almost as if he was beginning to lose patience with her. "Unless you want to work two jobs."

"Absolutely not," she blurted, her innate laziness deeply offended at the idea. "But I'll have to give notice."

"Fuck giving notice."

She staggered at the swear word. "I don't think that would help me get a good reference."

He turned back to face her from where he stood in front of the door, and something about him made her hold her breath.

"You don't need a good reference," he told her, promised her. "They will provide dates of employment and job title; that's all we require. If you gave them notice today, that's still more than they deserve. I'm tempted to file a complaint on your behalf."

"Complaint?" She whispered.

"Your manager left you alone last night, with two male customers. Lone working should be avoided at all costs, yet she deliberately, knowingly, put you in an unsafe environment. You would be well within your rights to make a formal complaint against them. You want leverage for not working your notice, there it is."

She frowned, knowing what he said was true, that she'd felt the wrongness of it last night. Strange but reassuring that he had recognised it too, that he was fighting her corner when she was nothing to him. Well, nothing yet.

He must have thought she was frowning at him, as he grumbled something to himself and ran a hand through his hair before saying his final pitch.

"Just look over the contract. It's a fair offer and we're a good employer."

"You would say that," she quipped, all the while appreciating the effort he was going to.

He scoffed. "I would. Just consider it. I don't think the job will be as soulless as you're expecting but, if it is—"

"At least I'll be able to sit down."

"Exactly."

Suddenly, the door was open and she was following him back into the reception area. His eyes were on her, his hand outstretched. This time she didn't leave him waiting.

"I'm not interviewing anyone else until next week. Hopefully I won't have to." He released her hand, moved to stand alongside her shoulder, and offered her one final leading smile. "Until Monday, Miss Watson."

And then he was striding away, disappearing into the lift a moment later, without another glance in her direction. Gone.

Alone in the reception, she felt far too exposed, her temporary welcome at an end. Until Monday, potentially. *Monday.* It was madness. It made no sense.

What the actual fuck had that been, Mr Cannavale?

Chapter Three

No part of her wanted to go to work.

Even though it was a family-owned small business, there had never been a familial feel to working there. When she'd been on a zero hours contract during university holidays, there had been days where she'd turn up for a shift and half an hour later be sent home because it was too quiet for the gaggle of waitresses there: no hours worked, practically no pay, just her day disrupted. And then they'd taken her tips. And then they'd left her to work late, alone. Maybe her new boss was right: she didn't owe them anything.

New boss. Yep, as bizarre as the whole thing was, it was happening.

While she walked down the street heading towards the city centre, the early winter air crisp in her throat, she turned her mind to thoughts of her new desk, new stationery, new predictable number sliding into her bank account each month, an actual pension (how grown up), and knew it was the right decision. She didn't give herself time to reconsider before the phone was ringing. The call connected a moment later as Peter, the restaurant owner's son, Mr Main Manager, answered with his usual bluster.

"Yes, hello, Peter speaking."

"Hi Peter, it's Cathy." She closed her eyes and bit her lip, pushing back the anxiety that wanted to keep her life shitty.

"Right," he said, clearly not knowing who he was talking to. That settled it. If she was going to make anything of herself, she had to stop being quite so nameless and faceless.

"I just wanted to let you know I'm not coming in today." She took a deep breath. "Actually, I resign. Immediately."

Her feet stopped, expecting anger, frustration at the very least, but Peter just sighed. "Right. Okay. Thanks for letting me know. I'll get your outstanding pay to you shortly."

"Thanks." She waited a moment, but that seemed to be it. "Bye then."

Forget notice periods, it was obvious Peter didn't even expect people to let him know they were quitting. There was something terribly sad about him waiting for a server or a chef to arrive for a shift, giving them an hour, trying to call them, and then resigning himself to the fact they weren't going to show. Another one gone.

She was sad for all of a minute, acknowledging the passing of a (generally detestable) era, before her mind turned firmly back to the future. Because through some wizardry, it had happened. She could tick *new job* off her list and now life was just guaranteed to get better.

Riding her modest high, she bought herself some treats and caught the bus home. With Sara out and Alison not expected until the morning, she shut herself in her room with all her favourite things – chocolate, tea, blankets, books and films – and quietly celebrated her new beginning.

*

"Sara, no! We shouldn't wake her up ..."

"Don't you want to know how it went?"

"Of course, I do, but waking her up won't change anything."

"It will change how bored I am."

Blinking her eyes open, she saw Alison and Sara stood in her bedroom doorway, quietly fighting over the door handle. She grumbled to let them know she'd been thoroughly disturbed, Alison surrendering the door to Sara, who charged through, throwing herself onto the bed beside Cathy. Sara lay on her stomach, wearing her usual lazy clothes: shorts that barely covered her bum and a loose camisole. It was always the same, even in winter. The woman ran hot.

"So, how'd it go?" Sara began, propping her head against her hand, while Alison drifted into the room, finding a perch at the end of the bed.

"What time is it?" Cathy asked, rubbing her palms against her eyes and forcing herself upright even though sleep was still heavy on her shoulders.

Sara checked her phone, which was never far from her fingers. "Just gone nine."

"Eugh, why so early?"

"Because we're nosy bitches."

Nosy? Oh yeah: the job interview.

Her brain finally woke up, fast-forwarding through the memory of an interview that was nothing like an interview, with a man who was nothing like any boss she'd ever had before. While the images came easily, words were much harder to find.

"I'm pretty sure it's real. Maybe there's like a ten percent chance I'm being pranked."

Her unhelpful start was met with blank stares.

"What *are* you on about?" Sara asked, looking at her like she needed psychiatric help.

"The interview."

"Can we have some context please?" Alison prompted, infinitely more patient.

"Right ... Okay, so the guy that interviewed me yesterday was also my last customer at the restaurant the night before. Weird right? It gets weirder because his friend ditched him, so he bought me a drink and invited me to sit with him. We just talked—" She hastily added, trying to mitigate the inappropriately suggestive rising of Sara's brow. "Turns out he was the hiring manager for the job at Alison's company, the one I'd applied for. He realised who I was, got me in for an interview, which was barely an interview, and offered me the job then and there."

"You got the job?" Alison leaned towards her.

"Way to bury the lede!"

"Well, yes, but that's not really the lede. He is."

"Who?" Sara had slipped into attention-deficit mode and was now looking at her phone.

"Maximilian Cannavale."

"*Max* interviewed you?" Alison, in comparison, was hyper-attentive.

"Who is he? Is he hot?"

"Google him and judge for yourself." At Alison's suggestion, Sara got to work. "He's the CFO. I wouldn't have thought he'd normally conduct interviews, unless it was for a director or senior management."

"What is a CFO?" Cathy asked, distracted by Sara holding up her phone.

"This guy?"

Her mouth went dry at the sight of her magnanimous new boss eternalised in a flattering corporate photo. He really did wear a suit well. "Yeah, that's him," she remembered to say as Sara started scrolling, the odd appreciative hum sounding from her now and then.

"Can he really just offer me a job? He barely asked me anything." She wondered absently. Oh, he was actually smiling in that one, while shaking someone's hand, obviously a PR shot. He had a nice smile.

"He's the Chief Financial Officer. He can basically do whatever he wants to," Alison soldiered on in the face of their distractedness. "Put it this way, there's you and me, then supervisors, team leaders, managers, directors, regional chairs, and then the executives, Max being one of them."

"Oh ..." Well, that put it into perspective. They were in drastically different tiers of the food chain, polar opposites in fact.

"Did you research the company?" Alison asked, a little exasperation escaping her.

Cathy crossed her arms over her chest, still keeping half an eye on Sara's phone. "A little." Not enough, clearly. "So, you think it's all genuine?" She very much hoped so, considering she'd already been burning bridges ... and this new job, for all its haste – it felt like the future knocking at the door asking to be let in.

"I don't see why not. You applied for a job, had an interview and were offered the position."

"Isn't there meant to be fair and open competition, or something?"

"Not necessarily. This isn't the public sector. People get headhunted by private companies all the time."

A nervous giggle bubbled out of Cathy. "Me? Headhunted? That's impossible."

"Who cares!" Sara interrupted. "Honestly, it's like you can't let good things happen to you sometimes. If a young, sexy Adonis wants to give you a job, let him. He even has a Wikipedia page!"

Cathy's retort of *When have good things ever happened to me?* never made it out of her mouth, her mind suddenly distracted by the ever-increasing status of her probable new boss. Instead, the words, "He does?" squeaked out of her. She was starting to feel a bit warm; young rich businessmen with their own Wikipedia pages were not commonplace in her life. And she planned on accepting the job, which meant she would get to see him again...

"He's quite well known in the business world," Alison explained, her voice slow and considered as if she was talking to children (she might as well have been). "And thanks to his family, practically a minor celebrity."

"And filthy rich by the looks of it," Sara chimed in.

"How old?" Cathy felt the question slip through her lips.

Sara, very seriously, checked the bio. "Twenty-seven."

Alison ignored their prying. "His grandfather founded the company, but it was his father that made it a global name. As CEO, he moved the company headquarters to America and gave his sons executive roles. Max became CFO of the European division, while his brother became MD of the American division."

"Ah, nepotism," Sara hissed, as if the word was a curse.

"Which they are good at," Alison countered. "Max has a maths degree, and he's a chartered accountant."

"Still nepotism."

Alison sighed. "And he seems nice enough, on the rare occasions I've spoken to him, one of which was to recommend Cathy for the job."

"Wait." Cathy was still two steps behind. "You mean his family *owns* the company?"

"A managing share, yes."

She felt numb all over, weightless, as if stuck in a dream. That was probably why he hadn't thought to introduce himself – why should he have to, when there were pictures of him on the internet, enough to *scroll* through, and the goddamn company she'd been applying to was partly (basically) his?

Well, at least she could cross journalism off as a potential career, since her research skills were apparently pathetic.

"*Fuck* ..." A shaky breath escaped her, as she was suddenly struck by her own inadequacy. It was one thing to feel like a fool but a different thing to *look* like a fool. She'd been brushing shoulders with a giant and hadn't even realised. A giant that wanted her to work for him, for reasons she still couldn't fathom. "What did you say to him?"

Alison watched her warily, as if the expletive had been directed at her. "Nothing much. Just that you were my friend, that you wanted to change industry—"

"Well, whatever you said," Sara muttered, the slight edge to her voice informing them of her impending boredom at their cautiousness, "It worked. And then whatever you said at the restaurant and during your interview, Cathy, must have impressed him too, and now you have a new job. It's all good."

Cathy stared at Alison.

Eventually, Alison shrugged; a very *un*-Alison thing to do. "I guess so. Are you going to accept the job?"

"I kind of have to. I may have slightly, pre-emptively, quit my old one." She winced at Alison's affectionate eyeroll. "Oh, I have the contract too."

She leaned over the side of the bed to retrieve her laptop from where it had been discarded on the floor the previous evening after she'd read the very serious document over and over, hunting for traps. Needless to say, she hadn't found anything nefarious. Logging in, she passed it over to Alison, watching as her eyes darted across the screen, scrutinising every line. Cathy jumped at the touch of Sara's fingers stroking over the bare skin of her leg just below her pyjama shorts.

"Your legs are hairy," she observed.

"Thanks. I'll remember to shave them again one day."

"Maybe for your new millionaire boss ..."

"Stop." Cathy pushed Sara's hand away. "Behave."

"Can I have him then?" The momentary pause apparently told Sara more than even Cathy understood. "Don't worry," she tapped her nose. "Off-limits. Got it."

"What are you on about?"

But then Alison was looking at her over the laptop. She pushed her glasses back up her nose, ready to submit her final report on the whole scenario.

"It all looks fine to me. I think you're good to sign if you want to accept." Alison buffered for a moment at the look of something close to horror on Cathy's face. "Don't worry about the job itself. You could do it with your eyes closed. I really think Max might have just seen something in you. But don't take it if he has made you uncomfortable—"

"He hasn't," she denied too quickly. "I just don't understand the way it's happened. And it's a big change."

"A *good* change. Salaried, annual leave, flexible working, lunches with me—"

Sara growled. "How are we *still* talking about this?"

She rolled onto her knees in front of Cathy, taking her face between her hands, squashing her cheeks as if she could physically squeeze some sense into her. "Alison says it all looks legit, so it's legit. You are not going to refuse a job that is an improvement in literally every. Single. Way. So just sign the damn thing so we can all get on with our lives? Okay? Thanks."

She grabbed the laptop and held it open in front of Cathy.

"Since you asked so nicely ..." She clicked to sign, typing in her name to create the e-signature that would sell her soul to Atlas Hotels LTD and Mr Maximilian Cannavale, BSc (Hons), MSc, FCA, CGMA. Why he wanted her soul, she had no idea, but he was offering more for it than anyone else was. "Done."

"Thank fuck." Sara snapped the laptop shut, threw it onto the bed, and tumbled off the opposite side. "When do you start?"

"Monday," Cathy answered, something similar to dread curdling her stomach acid. "Alison, what's the dress code?"

"Just office wear. Closer to smart than casual," she said, about to expand when Sara's cackle distracted her.

"Have you seen Cathy's wardrobe? She's like a character from a cartoon that only has one outfit."

Even Cathy managed to laugh. "You mean, I won't get away with black skinny jeans and black t-shirts every day?"

"Em, no, probably not," Alison confirmed, utterly straight-faced.

"Guess that's our plan for today." Sara grabbed Cathy's hands, all but catapulting her off the bed. "Put on your one outfit, loser, we're going shopping!"

Chapter Four

The weekend was a retail endurance test. Cathy definitely didn't have enough money to buy herself a whole new wardrobe, so they started by hunting through all the charity and thrift shops the city had to offer. Hours upon hours of flicking through unwanted clothes, fuelled by greasy burgers and hot chocolate from the winter market. They found her a few decent outfits, but they'd had to work for it, especially when her friends were in opposing camps when it came to fashion; Sara advocating short skirts and near see-through blouses, while Alison argued for the classic trouser suit. Cathy was somewhere in the middle, preferring knee-length skirts and dresses, pretty tops, and conservative shirts. Nothing overly formal, nothing overtly *racy*.

Once they'd run out of charity shops, they headed to the retail stores to buy the missing essentials – Cathy *daring* to treat herself to new multipack of knickers and some black tights without holes in the toes. Her bank balance may have been concerningly smaller, but when Monday morning rolled around, far too early – *Eugh, what psychopath decided the workday should start at nine?* – she was grateful to actually have a choice of clothes, some of which weren't black. It was a transformative experience.

Sure, she was still wearing black shoes, black tights, and a black cardigan, but her dress was mostly blue *and* it had a floral pattern. It was progress, even if her rejection of high heels and makeup would have Sara arguing otherwise.

Despite the anxiety dreams that had plagued her through the night, her spirits were moderately high as she carpooled with Alison, holding steady even as she stepped into the building, *her* building. Alison lightly bumped her shoulder and flashed an *I believe in you* smile before leaving her in the reception. The receptionist sorted out her pass, Cathy placing the lanyard around her neck with a juvenile sense of pride at being invited somewhere exclusive.

She was left waiting a good ten minutes before her chaperone arrived. Regrettably, for a couple of reasons, it wasn't Mr Millionaire that came to collect her. One: because she quite enjoyed talking to (and looking at) him. And two: *because* she'd naively been expecting one of the company's most senior executives to take time out of his busy schedule to fetch his new assistant, she didn't notice the woman that had actually come to fetch her until she was stood over her, coughing to get her attention.

"Oh, hello," she said, springing to her feet.

"Cathy Watson?" The woman asked in a deeply unimpressed tone that made Cathy doubt, not just her outfit, but her life choices too. She had a good three inches on Cathy, middle-aged, very obviously dyed blonde hair, and bright red glasses. Oh, bright red, *rhinestone* glasses. *Good lord.* What had she gotten herself into?

A hand reached out towards her, but it felt more like a trap – glossy red acrylic nails poised to scratch – than a gesture of politeness, no hint of a smile cracking those blood-stained lips.

"Yes, that's me. Nice to meet you." She accepted the handshake, if it could even be called that. The woman held her hand for all of two seconds before limply letting go and rubbing her fingers together as if to brush away something unpleasant.

"I'm Sandra. If you'd like to follow me ..."

Not even for a second did those thin lips hint at a smile or any sort of goodwill. As Cathy followed Sandra across the foyer and into the lift, she could almost feel the frost emanating from the woman, leaving her arms pricked with goose bumps, while her suddenly heightened nerves flushed her face and armpits with heat.

"So, what do you do here?" Cathy asked, crossing her fingers in prayer that she was just a human resources representative or some other temporary character in her work initiation.

Red lips puckered moodily, annoyed that she didn't magically already know exactly who and how important she was.

"I'm Mr Cannavale's PA, and you are *my* assistant." Sandra finally smiled but it was more chilling than her scowl. "You would have known that if your interview had been conducted *this* week as originally planned and *not* whilst I was on annual leave. I do wonder what all the rush was all about."

*

"She hates me."

Alison put down her sandwich. "I was about to ask how it was going but I guess that answers it."

Cathy slumped onto the chair across from her. There were quite a few people around, lounging on the grey sofas, feet up on the coffee tables, or in the kitchen area making their lunch. The staff lounge, like the rest of the building, was minimalist but stylish. Only sleek, quality furniture and tasteful fittings, like the chrome bar stools they perched on and the white circular lights in the ceiling, were allowed. It was modern, comfortable and spacious, and luckily, they were far enough away from everyone else that no one would overhear her grumbling.

It had been a long morning of completing mandatory e-learning courses, lots of reading, lots of watching upbeat corporate videos, while Sandra avoided showing her any actual work. She was pretty sure her eyes were a little squarer than they had been when she woke up that morning. She probably also had a hole burned through her forehead from where Sandra had been glaring at her *constantly*.

"You could have warned me she was evil," Cathy said, feeling better for putting that truth out into the world.

"Who?"

"Sandra, the woman I'm working with. For, actually."

"I don't really know her. I'm sure she isn't that bad."

Oh Alison, always so cautious, always prone to thinking the best. It was obvious she hadn't been death-stared *all morning* by a red-obsessed demon.

"No, she hates me. She hates me because I'm young, and therefore utterly inept by default, because I have to share an office with her, and because she thinks I slept my way into this job or something equally unsavoury. I mean, if I was going to sleep my way into a job, I would have gone for something a little better than a bottom of the ladder admin job, don't you think?"

Alison placed a hand to her lips to seal in her laughter. She could only offer a nod of agreement.

"Worst of all, is that I'm *her* assistant. Not Mr CFO's, *hers*." She gave a forlorn laugh. "The woman can't even use Excel for God's sake. And yet *I'm* the incompetent one!"

Alison, finally composed, slid a sympathetic chocolate bar across the table.

"Maybe she'll warm to you."

Cathy scowled back, helping herself to the chocolate. "Maybe she'll die."

A smile tugged up the corner of Alison's mouth. "Is it all right otherwise? Have you seen Max yet? Asked him about the whole hiring situation?"

"The work will be fine, I think. I'll mostly be working with spreadsheets and writing letters based on what I've seen Sandra do, not that she's shown me anything. But no, I haven't seen him yet. It doesn't help that he's put a target on my back by interviewing me without her there. But I can't talk to him because whenever there's a reason to go into his office, Sandra *orders* me to stay put and goes through herself because 'he doesn't like being disturbed'. I'm pretty sure she fancies him."

"She likes feeling distinguished, and you threaten that." Alison sat back, something wicked playing with her usually placid features. "Maybe you should knock her down a peg."

That was fighting talk by Alison's standards. Very aggressive.

"I do have to *cohabit* with the woman for seven hours a day."

Alison adjusted her glasses and checked her fingernails. "I think she's the kind that only has friends or enemies."

"I thought you didn't know her?"

Another slightly sinister smile. "And she's already decided you're not a friend."

Cathy popped another chunk of chocolate into her mouth, mulling the thought over while she felt it melt on her tongue.

She grinned. "Enemies it is then."

*

When she got back to the office, Sandra wasn't there. With a sigh of relief, she stepped in, heading for her desk in the far corner. Her desk faced the window, while Sandra's was directly in front of the doorway, so that her nosy eyes could watch other people's comings and goings all day long, and own the full and immediate attention of anyone who dared to enter her domain. The corner was fine with Cathy. And, yes, she was thoroughly enjoying her new stationery. She even had her own pair of scissors. But that also meant Sandra probably had her own pair of scissors ...

She had just sat down when a rather harassed-looking woman stormed in, glared at Sandra's empty desk, and quickly turned around again.

"Can I help?" Cathy offered, standing up.

Wild eyes turned on her. Flustered hands shoved a letter at her.

"Yes. Can you get Max to sign this and give it back to me as soon as possible."

It wasn't a question. The woman turned on her heels and left as quickly as she'd arrived, leaving Cathy holding a letter she knew nothing about. She didn't even know who the woman was. How was she meant to give it back? She hadn't even said please!

After a deep breath, she remembered that Sandra was still absent, so there was no one gatekeeping the office next door. Suddenly, her irritation at the rude colleague evaporated. She had her ticket in. On tentative feet, she approached her real boss's office.

She waited outside his door for a moment, listening for any voices. The glass wall along his office was opaque, as it had been all day, the blinds pulled down against the peasants' curious eyes. Her hand paused against the door. Suddenly, she was seven-years-old again, waiting to see the head teacher after pushing Lucy Kendall over in the playground. She took a deep breath, reminded herself that she wasn't in trouble and that she had no reason to feel small. Giants were people too, just like everyone else – *Yeah, sure* – except for their fat bank accounts, elite job titles, and excessive number of post-nominal letters.

She tapped her knuckles three times, and let herself in.

It took a moment for her eyes to find him, disorientated by the huge new space. But there he was, sat behind an enormous desk, talking on the phone.

Cathy paused, a rabbit in the headlights, before it dawned on her that she should leave. She rocked on her feet, about to turn around when he gestured for her to stay. Permission granted, she slowly closed the door and stepped in further.

While talking quietly on the phone, silver pen twirling between his fingers, he watched her explore the room. Her eyes took in the glass conference table surrounded by sleek leather chairs at one end, the sofas in the middle, and the desk, longer than she was tall, at the other. It was all silvers and greys, except for the dark blue of the cushions and the browns of expensive books lined up on the shelves behind the desk. Gasping, she noticed the second wall of glass, feet stepping over by their own accord, and gazed upon the city skyline, framed by the greener landscape of the Wolds beyond. And they said money couldn't buy happiness, but she would happily work with a view like that. Give her a comfy chair, an endless supply of breakfast tea and chilled chocolate, and she would write her masterpiece.

The air shifted as a body moved to stand at her side.

"It's quite a view," she commented, still staring at the beautiful grey cathedral and the bright blue sky surrounding its Gothic spires.

"Yes, it is. I'm glad to see you accepted the offer."

She finally looked at him, the sight of him stealing her voice. He was taller than she remembered, slim, lean without bulk, his designer suit fitting him perfectly all over. Her instinct was to talk to him casually as they had before, but she reminded herself firmly that he wasn't her unconventional customer anymore, or even her unorthodox interviewer. He was her young, handsome, ridiculously wealthy boss, who had the whole world at his feet, or at least a chunk of England, quite literally. From the slight amusement brightening his expression, he knew it, and enjoyed it.

It was impossible to be completely formal with him though. His hidden smile seemed to encourage her boldness. And after staring (for longer than she would like to admit) at his photos on the internet, he didn't feel quite like a stranger anymore.

"How could I refuse after you made it all happen so quickly?" She playfully challenged.

His smile widened as he turned away to resume his place behind the desk. She gave him a heartbeat to respond before carrying on, eager to uncover his privately amusing motives.

"Is it common practice to arrange an interview, perform said interview, and offer the job all on the same day?"

"Uncommon but not unheard of." After straightening his jacket, he indicted to the pair of seats across from him, waiting until she'd claimed one before continuing. "After witnessing your clear lack of affection for your previous job, I thought you would appreciate a streamlined recruitment process."

Her cheeks flushed scarlet. "At what point did you decide you would offer me the job?"

"Whilst at the restaurant," he replied, oh-so calmly.

"Why?"

"You impressed me."

All her limbs suddenly felt light and unsteady, and a slight, almost pleasant queasiness danced through her stomach. Invisible needles pricked her skin with heat, while her eyes locked on his teasing smile, powerless to look away. She supposed it was what being weak at the knees felt like.

"I don't understand," she managed to say.

"I liked your CV," he started to explain, relaxing back in his chair. "Well educated, well spoken, with enough hobbies and volunteering to make you a well-rounded individual. You had already been shortlisted before I happened to find myself at your place of work. Whilst there, I saw all I needed to quickly decide the Miss Watson on paper matched the Miss Watson in person. I knew you would be perfect for the role. You still look confused."

"I ..." She shook herself free from the trance she'd been locked in from watching and hearing him talk. "I can't remember doing anything impressive in the slightest. If anything, I behaved inappropriately—"

"Potential, Miss Watson, is what you showed me. And a personality I could get along with," he added wryly. "It may just be admin work for now, but I've given you a foot in the door at a company that likes to invest in people. How far you go is up to you."

"Sandra was meant to interview me too, but you offered me the job, just like that."

"As it was well within my power to," he said a little testily, checking his watch. "If you're so concerned about Sandra's opinion of you, then I have ten minutes. We could bring her in and give you a formal interview, if you'd like?"

And give the witch a chance to get me fired on day one? Absolutely not.

"No," she couldn't decline fast enough. "That won't be necessary. Thank you."

"And yet, you're still not convinced you should be here."

He watched her carefully, the kind of look that went straight through you, that wanted to see you squirm.

She swallowed. "It's not about Sandra's opinion. It about you—"

"Seeing as you don't appear to take compliments well, I'll put it crudely instead." His lazy smile and strangely suggestive tone made her insides simultaneously sink and melt. When he spoke again, his voice became brisk, his smile, smug. "Your academic achievements put you in the top five percent of the population. Include the fact that you're a recent graduate from a Russell Group university, any company would be lucky to have you, especially since you're applying for jobs that you are grossly over-qualified for. I'm sure you have your reasons, but regardless; anyone that hires you is getting a highly competent individual very cheaply.

The fact that you lack clear career goals also, in my opinion, works in your employer's favour; it means they can mould you into anything they need. Essentially, you are a worthwhile investment. And, if one informal interview and decisive job offer is enough to get you off the market, then I consider it worth the deviation from standard recruitment practices."

There was a moment's silence when she tried to figure out if she should be flattered or insulted. It didn't help that she'd switched off halfway through his speech, distracted by watching his mouth move as he talked. The way he was watching her now was equally distracting – firm, amused, arrogant, expectant ... so expectant ...

"I hope I haven't offended you—"

She summoned her voice. "No. I wouldn't say offended. Flattered, mostly, I think."

"That was always my intention." He smiled. "I would like to reassure you that I have no plans to take advantage of the situation. You will always receive a competitive salary and benefits package for your role, and I expect you'll be progressing quicker than most."

"And if I don't?"

"Then I'm going to make the most of having an outstanding administrator."

This man and his backhanded compliments ...

"I guess we'll see," she replied coquettishly. "Thank you for explaining."

"You're welcome, Miss Watson."

He managed to distract her for another five seconds before she decided it really was time to leave. It wasn't until she was halfway to the door, feeling terribly self-conscious walking through the oversized room, imagining his eyes following her every move, that she remembered the papers in her hand. With a grimace, she forced herself to turn back around.

Yep, his eyes were on her, had probably never left her.

She bit her lip.

"Sorry, I actually came in to get you to sign this. I don't know who it's for but I could try and find—"

He held out his hand to silence her.

She handed over the document and watched as his eyes skimmed the contents, narrowing as they found disagreeable words. Abruptly, he ran a hand through his hair and then tore the paper in half.

"Tell Louise I'll read her proposal when there isn't a typo in every other line and her figures add up."

In that moment, he looked impossibly stern, scarily serious, nothing like the quietly amused man he'd been with her only moments ago. It made her voice cower.

With a nod, she took the shredded paper back and tiptoed over to the door, giving that stunning view one last look – the window, not the man – on the way.

"Miss Watson?"

What now? Is he going to snap his laptop in half and make me deliver that to IT too?

She turned back, relieved to find him relaxed again. Pink pinched her cheeks as her consciousness recognised how nice he was to look at. She prayed he didn't notice but those astute hazel eyes didn't seem to miss a thing.

"My door is always open, figuratively speaking, of course."

"Thank you, Mr Cannavale."

"Call me Max."

"Only if you call me Cathy."

Shit, was she flirting?

She only just glimpsed his amused smile before she dashed from the room, the door banging shut behind her.

*

It was a relief to be out of the room, but that ended as soon as she opened her eyes to find Sandra scowling from where she peered out of their office doorway.

"You shouldn't have disturbed Max," she muttered, scurrying down the corridor and snatching the torn paper from Cathy's hands before she had the chance to explain. "If anyone asks you to deal with something that involves him, leave it on my desk and I will sort it once I'm back."

With that, Sandra gave her one final scowl before turning around and walking away.

"No," Cathy accidentally said. Panic set in when it became obvious she'd spoken out loud.

Sandra paused and looked over her shoulder. "Excuse me?"

Well, as much as she'd planned on avoiding drama on her first day (and every other day), Cathy realised that they may as well get the power struggle out of the way early, even if she did loathe confrontation.

"I said no. If someone asks me to do something, I will, because that's my job." She slapped on a sickly-sweet smile. "I'm sure you're only trying to help, and I do find the whole thing a bit daunting since this is my first office job. So, thank you, but I am determined to pull my weight." She held her hand out, praying that Sandra wouldn't resist and turn their disagreement into an actual argument.

With obvious reluctance, Sandra handed back the document before retreating into the office, her face a cunning mask. Cathy breathed out through her nose, releasing the pressure that made her chest feel tight and her head warm. Round one was a win.

"I'm impressed," a voice said behind her.

She jumped round to find Max leaning on his shoulder in the open doorway of his office. He smiled slyly at her glowing cheeks.

"I knew you were a thinker, but I didn't expect you to be a talker too."

She leaned against the wall, trying to look casual when really, she needed to prop herself up.

"Only when I have to be."

"Well, I'm glad to see you have a backbone. If she gets too much though, do let me know. But I'm sure you can take care of yourself," he added in a low purr.

To hide her blushing face, she looked down at the torn document in her hands. Despite her victory, she still didn't know what to do with it.

"Louise's office is just past the kitchen," he whispered in her ear. "She acts tough but really; she's as insecure as they come. Never asks for help, but if it's offered ..."

After a conspiratorial wink, he locked his office and disappeared down the corridor, straight-backed and confident, the dark grey suit fitting him perfectly all over.

She watched him go, breathing out another long, cleansing breath to release a different sort of tension, the image of his smile lingering in her mind ... *No.* She snapped herself back to the present and walked with extra purpose towards Louise's office. After tapping at the door, she let herself in. Louise's fingers quickly stopped pulling at her hair. Soft eyes became hard as they spied an intruder.

"Yes?"

Cathy swallowed her awkwardness, handing over the ruined paper with an apologetic frown. "I'm sorry. Max said there were a few errors with the figures and grammar ..."

The woman snatched the document from her fingers, glaring down at it in anger to hide the embarrassed red of her face.

"If it would be helpful, I could give it a read over before passing it on to Max. I don't mean to speak out of place," Cathy hastened to reassure. "I'm an English graduate, so proof reading is basically fun for me. If you'd like ..."

"Thank you," Louise replied without raising her eyes.

Cathy quickly left, retreating to her desk before she could fall out with anyone else. Sandra gave her the silent treatment for the rest of the afternoon. She was quite happy for the quiet. It let her focus on the never-ending company training that she was *definitely* paying attention to. She *definitely* wasn't mooning over a certain man who wore a suit better than anyone had a right to. Definitely not.

She wouldn't.

That wasn't her.

Her brain didn't care for real men. But Mr Darcy, Edward Cullen, Aragorn, (fanfic) Draco Malfoy, Xaden Rorison ... they were currently nowhere to be found.

Because *he* was there, that privately amused smile looking at her from behind her eyes. *Shit.* Of all the men for her brain to finally pay attention to, it had to be her boss.

And yet, the Max in her mind smirked, enjoying the idea.

Thoughts never hurt anyone, right?

Right?

Chapter Five

Cathy considered day one a success. Not just because she thought she'd made a decent first impression, proved to her boss – and herself – that she did have a backbone, and done everything asked of her without error, but also because Sara had remembered the occasion and made a point of staying in and sorting dinner.

"By sorted dinner, I mean I've ordered a takeaway," Sara said, checking her phone. "It will be here in about ten minutes."

"Not quite dinner on the table but it will do," Cathy cheekily replied.

"There are no standards since I'm not actually your housewife."

"That could be convenient," Cathy mused playfully, as she discarded her bag and poured herself a glass of water.

"Trust me, you couldn't afford me," Sara countered, flopping onto the sofa. She finished writing a text before tucking her phone in her bra and giving Cathy her full attention. "So, how was it?"

Cathy perched on the armrest since Sara's long bare legs took up the entire sofa, and peered into the glass nested between her hands.

"All right, I suppose. It's nice getting a lift with Alison and seeing her at lunchtime, though she does have to travel a bit for her job, so it won't be like today all the time. The woman I cohabit an office with hates me—"

"I don't care about that," Sara whined. "Tell me the good stuff."

"I thought that was good stuff."

"Were there any fit guys there? Any potential boyfriends for you, clients for me? Oh, did you see your millionaire again?"

An involuntary smile pulled at Cathy's lips at the mention of *her* millionaire. "Not everything is about guys, you know. I was really nervous about today."

"I know, I know, but you're overly nervous about everything. It gets rather boring," Sara teased before pressing the subject. "So ..."

Cathy left her in suspense for a moment. "If there were any 'fit' guys, I didn't notice them, but I really didn't meet many people." It was only sort of a lie, since they were already putting Max in a category of his own ...

"You're useless."

"I did see Max again though."

"And?"

"And, what?" Cathy asked, feeling a blush rise in her cheeks at being interrogated.

"What was he like?"

"Well, he's ..." But she struggled to find the right words. "I'm not sure. It's strange, he has this casual, refreshingly authentic way about him, but at the same time I feel like I know nothing about him, like I don't understand him."

Sara stared at her as if she'd gone slightly mad.

"On the surface," she quickly continued, saying whatever came to mind and praying it didn't sound too stupid. "He's this young, attractive, competent, wealthy guy, who seems so at ease wherever he is, but I think there's a lot more to him. I feel like he's secretly laughing at the world but never in a mean way..."

Sara giggled to herself. "Okay, I get it."

"Really?" Cathy was pretty sure what she'd said hadn't made much sense.

"Really. Such a vague yet considered analysis means you're into him."

Cathy's blush turned up a few degrees. "That's ridiculous. I've spent like an hour with him in total."

"Attraction is instant. It's nothing to be embarrassed about." Sara shrugged for emphasis. "He's hot."

"But—"

"I know it's not generally your thing to fancy *real* people, but you are allowed to. I thought you were ready to."

They'd had this conversation many times before. Nothing Sara could say had managed to convince her that fictional men weren't far superior in almost every measurable way – beside the fact they weren't real and therefore fundamentally unattainable, which was a rather severe fatal flaw she had to admit. Even so, Cathy felt far more attraction and affinity to her favourite fictional males than any tangible ones and, for the most part, she was perfectly happy with it being that way. Real people were just too imperfect, and that included herself.

"I am ready to, I think. I'm at least ready to be disappointed by a real man. But Max is utterly unobtainable, which, while fantasising about unobtainable men is my modus operandi, means fixating on him would defeat the point of actually getting to experience something," she finished flimsily.

"So, you do find him hot?" Sara grinned craftily.

Cathy scoffed. "I think it's a truth universally acknowledged that he's easy on the eyes. He's also sickeningly rich and successful."

Sara rolled her eyes at the Pride and Prejudice reference, while Cathy finished it in her head: *a single man in possession of a good fortune, must be in want of a wife*.

Some pretty big assumptions there, Cathy, chill it. But there hadn't been a spouse listed on his Wikipedia page ...

"And?" Sara challenged, pulling Cathy's head out of the clouds. "If you say that makes him out of your league, I'll punch you."

Not just different leagues but different sports entirely. But she wasn't in the mood to try and convince Sara that she was nothing special – prettyish, cleverish, lots of *ishes* – nice enough but nothing special. She was a daisy. A man of Max's calibre had his pick of roses. Sara was a rose.

"*And* when I'm ready, I would like to try and find someone a little more on my level. More relatable," she clarified. "Though I'm really not feeling too hopeful about real people at all."

Sara read her deflated tone and kindly (for once) didn't push her. That didn't stop her dramatic sigh though.

"Fine. It's a start at least, even if it's a pessimistic one. I think you've spent too long living in your imagination. Honestly, the real world isn't that bad and decent guys do exist. You do want to have sex one day, right?"

Luckily, she was saved from having to respond by the doorbell.

As Sara dashed away to fetch their food, Cathy physically and mentally sighed. Of course she wanted to have sex one day, but she wasn't in any rush. With her trusty vibrator and imaginary sex scenes that contained zero awkwardness, ample passion, and always played out exactly as she wanted them to, she was content. From somewhere Max walked into her imagination. She smiled to herself as she slowly stripped the shirt off him, and carved that secretive smile of his onto his face. He prowled towards her, eyes directly on her, wanting only her ... Hmm, she supposed there was no harm adding a new character to her fantasy that night.

The smell of hot Chinese food brought her back to the present. She joined Sara by the table, where the various silver foil containers were scattered. After grabbing bowls and cutlery, they sat down and tucked in.

"You had a textiles class today, right?" Cathy asked, before she shovelled in her first forkful of chow mein.

"Mhmm. I think I'm finally starting to get the hang of it. The designing part, that is; I still have to wrestle with the sewing machine every time I try and set it up," Sara replied, looking rather angry, as if glaring at an uncooperative

Singer. Her eyes widened suddenly. "Oh, that reminds me, and you have to say yes."

"Do I really?" That look of excitement ... she hadn't seen it many times, but it usually meant that something would bode well for Sara at the expense of everybody else.

"Yes. I need to use you as a model."

Cathy glared at her. "By which you mean ..."

Sara glared back. "I mean that I'll need to make all my designs to fit you."

"And?" Cathy was too hungry to keep glaring, so stabbed and twirled another forkful of chicken, bean sprouts, and noodles together. The food was starting to make her feel warm and relaxed; the greasy saltiness satisfying some need she hadn't noticed before. It appeared takeaway food was some kind of antidote for mildly-stressful, mildly-boring office jobs ... Hmmm, she'd have to be careful not to let it become a habit.

"And I'll need you to model said designs ... in a fashion show."

At least Sara had the decency to look contrite.

"No way!"

"Please, Cathy?"

"Why not someone else? Alison ... Gabrielle ... anyone!"

Sara put down her fork, leaning pleadingly towards her. "Gabrielle is too busy and Alison is more attention-averse than even you are. Plus, I see you the most, so it will be easier to make sure the clothes fit. Please, Cathy, it would really help me out."

It was a particularly difficult mouthful to swallow as she imagined a thousand eyes blinking up at her from the darkness surrounding an illuminated stage that she was stumbling down in some unflattering mess of fabric, surrounded by thinner, prettier women ...

"I'm not exactly size zero," she finally choked out.

"You don't need to be," Sara reassured. "No one should need to be, but that's a whole other discussion. Anyway, it's not Paris fashion week; it's a college fashion show. The models will all be family or friends of the students. And I will make sure you look gorgeous. Okay? Please? It will be fun!"

Sara and her hobbies ...

"It can be my birthday *and* Christmas present?"

Well, I had actually been struggling to think of anything ...

"Okay," Cathy tentatively agreed. "But you won't dress me in anything hideous?"

Sara shook her head while clenching her lips together to hide her gleeful smile.

"And nothing too revealing?"

The head shaking slowed until it stopped altogether and she shrugged her shoulders instead.

"*Sara* ..." Cathy warned.

"We can sort the details out later. Thank you! I promise it will all be fine." Victory achieved, Sara picked up her fork and started eating again. "Also, I'm going to a life-drawing class on Friday and I think you should come with me."

"I thought you always worked Fridays?"

"I do, but the class is at seven, so I have time. Will you come?"

Cathy held in her sigh. "You know I'm not at all artistic."

"You don't have to be. It's just something different; an experience."

There was something suspicious about that comment.

"You think I spend too much time inside," she pried.

"You do spend too much time inside, *alone*."

Oh ... the truth. It was actually kind of sad to hear it said out loud.

Cathy frowned. "You've been talking to Alison."

"Of course I have. It really worried her when she found you crying."

"I didn't mean to worry her. Things are getting better anyway ... I think I'll be much happier in this job." *If Sandra gets off my back that is ...* She pushed the half-formed image of Max to one side.

"Good. And I know I'm out a lot—"

"You're allowed to be," Cathy hastily reassured.

Sara smiled. "But it's not always with clients. It's the gym, art classes, seeing friends ... and you are always welcome to come with me, if you'd like a change of scene."

The sentiment left Cathy stunned. She'd been so fixated on the distance *not* living together had put between her and Alison, that she hadn't quite realised what she might have gained in living with Sara. She'd always felt slightly intimidated by her – by her skill, confidence, and sheer passion for life – her own wobbly self-esteem keeping Sara at arm's length, when maybe she was just the type of friend she needed right now. Someone who encouraged her to step outside, to try something new. Someone who was happy to hold her hand until she felt strong enough to stand alone. Alison had been the person she'd needed when she'd had to hide from the world. Maybe Sara was the person she needed to step back into it.

"So ..." Sara continued. "As part of my plan to get you living a little more, you'll come on Friday?"

"I'll give it a go. Though you are not allowed to judge the monstrosity I'll create."

"Of course I won't. How's the dating app going?"

"Slow. Wait, did you say life drawing? Isn't that when—"

Sara's gleeful smile was back. "Yes, it's when a model sits naked—"

"Sara!"

"What?" Her friend's smile curved playfully up at one side. "It's all done very tastefully. I thought it might be a good first step to help you get over your prudishness, you know, considering men might play a part in your life soon ..."

"Not with the lack of traffic my profile is getting," Cathy quietly joked, her mind preoccupied with the truth Sara had just spoken ... a truth that was suddenly more exciting than it was daunting.

*

With newfound confidence, she strolled into work beside Alison the following morning. The corporate building was no longer imposing. The maze of corridors and offices was no longer confusing. She smiled at the colleagues whose names she didn't know yet and felt like she had everything under control, until Alison turned off for her department and the colleagues she passed stopped smiling back.

"Morning," she said with diminishing brightness to the two women stood outside the staff lounge doorway.

Their conversation halted. Strained smiles pulled at their lips while intrigued eyes scanned her up and down. Once she was four feet away, their conversation started again, words hushed, eyes following her.

What is going on?

It became obvious when she neared her office door that Sandra was going on.

"She's just his type," Sandra muttered. "Young, pretty, curvy, *blonde*."

"But why give her a job?" Another voice said.

Cathy rested her shoulder against the wall, leaning in to hear better, even as her cheeks flushed a guilty pink.

"Because he can. God knows what they'll get up to in his office together. Anyway, I'm not going to entertain it. I'm not here to babysit his latest braindead tart so that he can have her nearby. And I certainly won't be forced into an early retirement so that he can replace me with her."

"What are you doing?" A voice suddenly whispered in Cathy's ear.

She jumped, barely managing to stifle her yelp of surprise, turning around to find Max leaning against the wall behind her. He was stood close, too close, as she inhaled a deep breath of his luxury aftershave; a cocktail of exotic spices and woods that not so much as coaxed but rather dragged her mind into thinking about masculinity and sex, in particular, the imaginary sex scene he'd unknowingly partaken in the previous night. She swallowed, her mouth suddenly dry as he stared at her. His eyes were bright, too bright for nine AM on a Tuesday morning, with a sense of humour she didn't quite understand. His smile deepened at her confused distress until she finally managed to tear her eyes away from his face, and summoned her voice.

New rule: don't include staggeringly handsome young bosses in erotic fantasies.

"Sorry," she mumbled, quickly moving to enter the office to get away from him before her body could betray her, if it hadn't already.

The second voice she'd heard was Louise's. She stood up slowly from where she perched on the edge of Sandra's desk, watching Cathy closely as she headed over to her corner. Cathy briskly sat down and turned on the desk fan to stem her sudden anxiety sweats.

"If you wouldn't mind giving these a once over before passing them on to be signed off, Sandra?" Louise said with deliberate coolness.

"Of course. I'd be happy to." Sandra cracked a bright red smile that swiftly died when she noticed Max watching their pantomime from the doorway. "Oh, good morning, Max. Everyone's confirmed for your meeting at half past. I'll just go set up—"

"It's quite all right," Max replied smoothly, holding up a hand to indicate she should stay seated. "I can see you have other ... *matters* to occupy you." He gave Louise a sidelong glance that seamlessly moved onto Cathy, as if she was in on his secret amusement, before resting firmly back on the now cowering Sandra. "While you check over Louise's work for her, Cathy can prepare for the meeting. If you'd please let her know what to do ..."

He left them in stunned silence. Blinking slowly, Louise finally decided to move, scurrying back to her office with her tail between her legs. Sandra woke up a second later, the embarrassed blush on her cheeks changing from chagrined pink to furious red as she glared at Cathy.

"Don't think I don't know what's going on here."

"I don't know what you mean," Cathy snapped back as she got to her feet. "So, what do I need to do?"

Five minutes later, following a very terse series of instructions, Cathy staggered into Max's office carrying a few hundred sheets of organised, and probably unnecessary, paper. Max nodded his head to her in acknowledgment before looking out of the window and carrying on with his phone call in a low voice. She turned her attention firmly to the table she had to prepare. A meeting for eight people ... eight glasses on the table, two water jugs, coffee machine turned on, handout A, handout B, handout C ...

As she walked around the table, she glanced over at Max, slightly surprised to find him watching her, not intently, but lazily, as one might watch people passing them in the street. Still, it made her stand up a little straighter, move with a little more purpose. She thought his stare hardened as she leaned over the table to neaten a stack of paper on the other side, a second later remembering the looseness of her blouse. Quickly straightening, she purposefully turned away. The last thing she needed was Max thinking she was coming on to him, especially with Sandra spreading rumours. Not that he'd be at all interested in her. He probably had a supermodel or an Olympian or a minor royal for a girlfriend ...

"Cathy?"

"Yes?" She jumped around, leaning against the table, legs suddenly unsteady as he approached.

"All sorted?" He asked, idly surveying the table.

"Erm ... I think so. It's a lot of paper."

"I know. I really need to work on Dad about the company going paperless," he said in an oddly serious way for him. "But, to add insult to injury, could you give these a read over?" He placed a new pile of paper in her unsuspecting hands. "I'll send you the files too. We've had to update some of our policies—"

"But I don't know any of the legalities," she blurted, despairing as a wave of tell-tale warmth washed over her. His eyes were too keen. His aftershave too delicious. His posture too relaxed yet somehow purposeful as he stood slightly too close beside her.

His smile was cruel. "But you can read?"

She stared at him, dumbfounded. "Yes."

His smile twisted into something else, something playful yet unnerving, as if she'd somehow impressed him by stupidly answering his rhetorical question. Before she could try to rectify her mistake, he spoke again.

"Good. So, please, put that English degree to good use."

She gripped her fingers around the paper and hurried away before she could make any more of a fool of herself. Sandra's eyes were on her and the classified documents she carried immediately.

"What's that you have?"

Every word Sandra said felt like an attack, full of spite and disapproval. It made Cathy's remaining meekness fade away.

"Just something Max asked me to read over," she replied tersely.

Sandra's frown soured further and Cathy was filled with the distinct feeling that she would have to watch her back or she'd quickly find a knife in it ... or a pair of health-and-safety-approved scissors.

Chapter Six

"You were right," Alison declared, looking slightly panicked as they sat down in the staff lounge for lunch. It already felt like *their* table, placed next to the wall of floor to ceiling windows, the neighbouring tables all just far enough away to allow for private conversations, whilst being only big enough for the two of them.

"About what?" Cathy forced herself to ask. She wasn't at all interested in being panicked just then, not after spending three hours in a particularly inimical atmosphere. All she wanted was a quiet hour where she wasn't glared at constantly. She turned her eyes to the window to watch the city streets below, scanning over the traffic and pedestrians to focus on the pigeons shuffling along the pavements or perching on ledges. She wished she could feed them, pet them. Pet something. Being around animals always made her feel better. Maybe she'd ask Sara about getting a cat ...

"Sandra," Alison continued. "She has it in for you."

"Hmm?"

"She thinks you got the job because you're sleeping with Max."

"I'm not sleeping with him," Cathy snapped back indignantly before realising her mistake. "Obviously." She laughed uncomfortably under Alison's discerning stare. "But I already knew she thought that."

"Yes, but did you know she's telling everyone?"

If the scandal had reached Alison's office, Sandra really hadn't wasted any time in tarnishing her name. Day two and she was already a shady harlot.

"I had a suspicion. A few funny looks from people and then overhearing her calling me 'his latest braindead tart'."

Alison pulled a face. "That's rather unflattering."

"And absolute nonsense!" Cathy sighed. "Has something like this happened before? Max hiring someone underhandedly ..." She didn't know how to finish the sentence without both greatly flattering and grossly insulting herself.

"I don't know; I really haven't been here that long."

"Oh well," Cathy said, forcibly bright. "So, an insecure middle-aged woman, who is yet to realise red really isn't her colour, doesn't like me. What's the worst that could happen?"

"You could lose the respect of all your colleagues and be stuck working in a toxic environment," Alison answered too quickly. She smiled to herself. "It is kind of funny that you, Miss-Virgin-Mary, are at the centre of a corporate sex scandal."

"I really don't know why you and Sara insist on painting that picture of me," Cathy muttered, fishing her Kindle from her bag. "Not everything I read is Jane Austen, you know."

"What are you reading right now?" Alison predictably challenged.

Cathy waited a breath, whilst glaring, unamused, over the top of her Kindle. Alison did not need to be privy to the title of the dark mafia romance she was currently sinfully reading, so she thought of a safe classic to offer up instead. "Tess of the d'Urbervilles."

"Oh, you're right, that's much saucier."

Cathy stuck her tongue out. Smiling, she turned back to her book and forgot about the rest of the world for half an hour.

*

It was a long four days of glares and whispers but, finally, five o'clock on Friday arrived. She'd survived her first week, albeit reputation barely intact, but survived nonetheless. Sandra left first, with a very curt "Enjoy your weekend" muttered over her shoulder as she passed through the doorway, Cathy's delayed and deflated response of "You too" almost certainly going unheard. With a sigh, she got to her feet.

"That good?" A voice asked from the doorway.

She almost dropped her bag with surprise, while her eyes greedily sought out the owner of the delicious voice, their tone already amused, *always* amused.

Seeing Max stood there, arms folded, one shoulder leaning against the doorframe in that casual way of his, she couldn't help thinking about the rumours. They should have made her want to run and hide, avoid him at all cost in case eyes saw them together and conjured up more licentious lies ... but they didn't. Reputation aside, they fuelled the lascivious stories her mind seemed inclined to create and fixate on; made her body lean towards his rather than away.

"Long week," she bashfully replied, hoping that was a tactful enough answer.

Max raised an eyebrow. "They usually are. How have you found it?"

A boss that actually cares?

"Fine – good, I mean. I think I've just about got the hang of everything now."

Whatever he had been about to say, whatever thought had made his smile curl to one side, was silenced as Alison appeared at his side, coat on, handbag cradled at her elbow.

"Hello, Max," she said briskly, seemingly immune to his authority and innate attractiveness, eyes lingering on him for barely a second when Cathy could quite happily stare at him all day. "Ready to go, Cathy?"

"Erm ... yes." Cathy realised how hot her cheeks were. "Unless there's anything else that needs doing, Max?" She almost choked on his name, as if saying it out loud with an audience would give away just how much he unsettled her.

"No, nothing that can't wait." He glanced between them as he turned away. "Have a good weekend."

"You too ..." Something heavy settled across her shoulders as he disappeared from view. It took her a second to recognise it as disappointment; the fleeting hope that he would look back at her unfulfilled.

Get a grip ...

"Everything okay?" Alison asked with seeming innocence.

Cathy slowly released a deep breath. "I just feel kind of awkward around him," she whispered, conscious that he could still be nearby.

"Because of the rumours?"

She nodded. *And my overactive imagination. And the fact he smells like sex on legs. And the fact no man has ever looked so good in a suit. And the—*

"They'll blow over," Alison reassured. "Anyway, it's the weekend."

"Thank God. Though I'm not sure how much I'll enjoy tonight."

"Me neither."

Cathy crossed the room and they started down the corridor towards the lift. She had to resist the urge to look over her shoulder to try and catch another glimpse of Max.

"You're coming to the class?"

"Sara wouldn't take no for an answer," Alison explained with a grimace. "So, at least we'll get to feel awkward together."

"I'm not sure I need to go anymore."

"How so?"

"Well ..." Cathy grimaced. "So far in the world of dating apps, I've had one half-decent conversation – until he just stopped replying – two offers of casual sex and, this afternoon; an unsolicited photo that is making me question if I want anything to do with men."

Alison shivered. "Eugh, why do they feel the need?"

Cathy shrugged. As unwanted and repulsive as it was, it had made her afternoon slightly more interesting. "In the words of Sara: a man's true love is his dick."

*

It was funny, considering how Sara and Alison insisted on labelling her as a prude or sinless virgin, that if someone had ranked the three of them by level of discomfort as the model stepped into the room in just a dressing gown, removing said gown as he took his place before the half-moon of easels, Alison most definitely would have won the gold.

Sara didn't bat an eyelid, so accustomed to naked men that one more had no impact.

Cathy, whilst as inexperienced as Sara was experienced, initially averted her eyes, curiosity soon got the better of her, and she assessed the undressed male form before her with interest.

And Alison, the only one of them in a long-term relationship with a man, could only bring herself to stare at his toes.

"You have seen Dylan naked before, right, Alison?" Sara asked, looking at Alison like she didn't know her.

"Yes," Alison muttered, putting her pencil to the paper clipped on the easel before her, and started drawing the model's toes.

"So why are you literally the palest I've ever seen you?"

"I don't know."

"Because it's literally just a penis."

Alison hushed her. “Stop. Nakedness just makes me uncomfortable. Is that okay?”

“It’s okay but—”

“I don’t want to talk about it,” Alison snapped, as much as Alison could snap, before turning all her concentration on her drawing.

Sara leaned back in her seat, widening her eyes at Cathy.

“Are you okay?”

Cathy shrugged. “Fine.”

“Our Cathy, all grown up ...”

She couldn’t resist. “If you saw my Kindle library, you’d know I’m already grown up.”

“My, my ...” With an impressed smile, Sara turned back to her canvas, leaving Cathy to stare undistracted at the model again.

The whole experience was much less awkward than she’d been expecting. The artists were all quiet and respectful; the model holding himself with a confidence she could only marvel at. He wasn’t what she’d been expecting: a rather average looking man, late forties or early fifties, probably a tradesman of some kind, liked watching the football on a Sunday, religiously played the lottery once a week, a regular at his local pub but still a family man at heart. The hair on his head was so short it was basically non-existent, whereas his chest was kept warm by a threadbare rug. His hands were large, plump fingers curled into loose fists. Even from where she sat, Cathy could see the grooves and coarseness of hands that worked hard for a living. Face impassive, arms at his sides, stomach protruding, legs slightly parted, flaccid penis resting innocuously between them; not so much Hercules made flesh but rather a homage to the modern man.

Why he would choose to stand naked before a group of strangers (aside from a little cash in hand) she would never know, but she admired him regardless. He was easy to look at and easy to draw, her untrained fingers settling for a rough, scribbly style rather than realism. If he had been a younger, fitter man, she imagined it wouldn't be quite so easy to concentrate.

Don't think about him.

Don't picture Max standing naked in front of you.

She glanced at her neighbours' drawings; Sara's a masterpiece, bold lines and careful shading capturing the model perfectly, while Alison's was an empty silhouette apart from his very detailed feet. Cathy couldn't help but snigger.

Alison looked morosely at her. "I'm never coming again."

"Probably for the best."

*

Their three drawings were proudly displayed on the fridge like the schoolwork of doted children; Alison's rather creased after being discarded in the bin and then stealthily retrieved by Sara. It really elevated the atmosphere in the kitchen.

While Sara was out working on Saturday night, Cathy baked two cakes, smiling to herself as she cradled the mixing bowl to her chest and stirred, three naked men watching her, though only two had eyes. One of the cakes was a thank you to Sara for making an effort with her; the other was a futile attempt to sweeten Sandra.

"I'm trying to watch my weight," Sandra muttered, mortally offended, as she glared at the slice Cathy handed to her on Monday morning. "But I'll go see if Max would like it."

"I—"

But Sandra was already through the door and letting herself into their boss's office, returning a minute later empty-handed, wearing the grin of someone who had successfully taken candy from a baby.

"Might as well put the rest in the kitchen," she said before picking up the cake tin and sashaying out of the room again.

Cathy didn't even try to stop her.

With a sigh, she sipped her tea and ate a large forkful of cake from the slice she'd fortunately taken for herself first, before the rest was stolen away and taken credit for. The fork was still between her lips when a message popped up on her screen.

Max Cannavale

In the six years I've worked with her, not once has Sandra brought in anything homemade. So, either she is a changed woman, or she has stayed very much the same ...

Max Cannavale

Thank you very much for the cake. Always welcome on a Monday morning.

Why was her face suddenly burning? Why didn't it matter if no one else thanked her as long as he did?

She slowly licked her fork clean before typing a cautious reply.

Cathy Watson

Thank you very much for noticing it was from me. I would have offered you a slice but I was beaten to it.

Max Cannavale

I'd recommend working on your baking skills and your punctuality in parallel.

Cathy Watson

Is this a professional objective?

Max Cannavale

Very much so. We'll assess your progress at your first probation review.

She sat for a good five minutes struggling to think of a witty reply, conscious of the fact that the longer she took, the more obvious it was that she was overthinking, the more obvious it was that she cared too much about what he thought of her, the more obvious it was that she had a pathetic schoolgirl crush on her boss.

He put her out of her misery.

Max Cannavale

Carrot cake is my favourite.

Cathy Watson

Duly noted.

She quickly closed the instant messenger so that she couldn't dwell on, what was probably totally innocent repartee, but that her mind was eager to consider as something much more significant.

Regardless, it was time to practice her carrot cake.

Chapter Seven

The fork-tongued whispers and vociferous glares continued. Sandra's passive-aggressive warpath continued.

Cathy could cope with it. She knew the rumours would blow over eventually and then people would stop looking at her and immediately see a scarlet A. And through the mere-exposure effect, Sandra's animosity towards her should eventually decline. Until such a time, she tried to keep her head down and, when that wasn't possible, her smile polite. Sometimes though, neither was possible, like on Thursday, when Caroline from accounts came over while she was atthe photocopier. Caroline had a reputation for being utterly unsubtle.

"So," she began in a hushed voice, wearing a smile that somehow showed both her scheme to appear a trustworthy confidant and her notorious avarice for gossip. "Is it a dating thing, or more of a trading benefits thing? You get a job, he gets—" Raised eyebrows filled in the blank before she barked out an ugly laugh. "You know what I mean. Or is he giving you a little extra on the side? I mean, he could have given you a better job—"

To save tearing the documents she'd just copied in half, Cathy bit her tongue and walked away.

Suddenly, she didn't *want* to cope with it.

She didn't want it to carry on any longer (*It's basically bullying, right?*), which meant either sending out a company memo explaining that *No, I am not his whore* or talking to the man himself. Both options were opposite sides of the same unlucky coin, but only one would most likely get her fired.

She'd just made it back to her desk when the phone rang.

Speak of the devil ...

"Hi, Max," she answered in her overtly cheerful telephone voice.

"Cathy, could you come through?"

"Sure."

She slammed the phone down a little too hard. After resolving to talk to him about it, suddenly faced with the opportunity; it felt impossible. She slowly approached his office.

How to phrase it? *Oh, hi Max, I know you're busy running a multimillion-pound international company, but you know how you hired me like really quickly and without your assistant's input? Well, that lovely assistant decided to tell the world that the only reason that would happen is because I'm your personal sex-slave and you wanted to keep me nearby so that we could have earth-shattering sex any time you fancy in your office.* That would probably do. And if he decided not to help her, that was when she'd have to escalate to HR.

She knocked once and let herself in, feet pausing as her eyes found Sandra sat beside him at the conference table.

What was the bitch up to now?

"Cathy," Max said, inviting her with a wave of his hand to take the seat opposite him. "Please take a seat."

His voice was utterly apathetic, giving her no clues as to where the situation was headed. Nevertheless, she did as she was told, lowering herself slowly onto the padded leather chair, returning the daggers Sandra glared at her with equal enthusiasm.

After glancing over the document in front of him, Max leaned back in his chair and raised his eyes to Cathy, mirth dancing in his eyes.

Well, at least one of us is finding whatever this is funny.

"Cathy," he began, his voice warm with humour. "Sandra has come to me with some concerns over your position here. I, myself, have seen no problems with your performance but I appreciate that you and Sandra work closely, so I want to resolve any issues quickly. Her main concern is regarding your suitability, so, if you wouldn't mind, she would like to go through our standard interview questions with you."

Cathy raised incredulous eyebrows at him but his gaze was unwavering.

"But I'm already employed," she stated, banally.

"You are, but since there were minimal notes from your original interview, there's a gap in your file. This will help complete the paper trail."

And give Sandra a chance to find fault and fire me whilst I'm still on probation. Easy in, easy out.

It was bizarre and totally unfair but, as Cathy fixed her eyes on Sandra, she realised she could play her at her own game. Something that Sandra didn't quite seem to understand was that Cathy wasn't undefended; she had armour. Even though she wasn't sleeping with him, even though there was no obvious reason for it (ignoring all the well-articulated reasons he had given her, since her chronically low self-esteem could not accept them); Max wanted her there. And based on his smirk, he thought the situation was ridiculous too, but was quite at his leisure to sanction and observe the incoming car crash. A bit of light entertainment. And he was going to enjoy every awkward minute, the privileged bastard.

Dance, peasants, dance.

"Okay," she smiled, and made herself comfortable.

"What made you apply for the role?" Sandra began, pen at the ready.

"My friend Alison, who works here in finance – young, pretty, slim, *black* hair, wears great glasses; you might know her – recommended the role and the company. I'd been working as a waitress since graduating. I wanted to find myself a full-time job and gain some office experience. This seemed perfect."

"So you have no previous administration experience?" She asked, giving Cathy a firm stare over the top of those ghastly, *not-great*, red glasses, as if the rogue question would be her downfall.

Cathy flashed her eyes to Max for a second, to confirm that he was thoroughly enjoying the show.

"Not in a previous job, no," she replied tightly. "But that's not to say I have no administrative experience. Through school and university, I developed most of the necessary skills, which I think is a fair assumption considering that, since starting here, nothing has been asked of me that I couldn't readily do."

Sandra pursed her lips. "What are your career goals?"

"At the moment, I don't really have a long-term goal, but I am certainly open to any opportunities that may come my way," Cathy replied coolly.

"Tell me about a time you worked as part of a team."

Despite her internal groan, Cathy smiled to herself. It was probably time to make the 'interview' into the farce it really was.

"Of course," she hastened to answer. "I think it was during my second year at university, my friend and her partner were looking for someone to experiment with. As the third party, I felt like it was my responsibility to ensure it all went smoothly; procuring supplies, planning logistics, and communicating effectively to ensure everyone was comfortable and satisfied with the service provided. I received outstanding feedback and became the top-rated third wheel at the university."

She'd heard Max snigger at the word 'logistics'. It had almost made her burst out laughing but she'd managed to remain composed as Sandra, very seriously, carried on with nothing more than a huff at her ridiculous answer. *Tough crowd.*

"Tell me about a time you had to prioritise your workload under pressure."

"Oh, well ..." A devilish idea came to mind. "After the threesome, my friend and I thought it would be a great idea to host a sex party—"

"I don't think you're taking this seriously," Sandra accused.

No shit, Sherlock.

"Actually, Sandra, it's you who hasn't taken *me* seriously since day one." Oh, it felt good to see the woman's surprise at discovering she did in fact have a voice, and teeth.

"I feel like I'm missing something here," Max said, looking between the two of them, intrigued rather than concerned. "Would someone care to explain?"

Cathy was only too happy to oblige.

"Sandra has been spreading unsavoury rumours about me around the office," she said quickly. "Which I find totally unprofessional."

"What kind of rumours?"

Sandra's eyes grew wide, and yet there was still something in her expression that doubted Cathy would tell the truth. On any other day, maybe she would have been right. Today, however, Cathy was beyond embarrassment and absolutely done with being ridiculed by anyone.

She turned her unflinching eyes on Max. "Sexual ones, involving you."

He raised an intrigued eyebrow. "Is that so?"

"She thinks I've been hired for the *wrong* reasons."

"Well, we can't be having that," he said in a low voice, holding her gaze for a lingering moment. Eventually, he turned his attention to the trembling Sandra. "I hadn't expected I'd need to explain my decision, but I hired Cathy because she is a promising graduate, who has the potential to go far in this company, and most certainly has all the competencies to perform well in her current role. Your planned attendance at the interviews was always a courtesy, never a requirement. Is that clear?"

Sandra, tight-lipped, eyes brimming with tears, mutely nodded.

"Good." He continued on, his voice suddenly harsh and inexorable, like an icy winter morning you had no choice but to step into. "And whilst there is no personal relationship between myself and Cathy, I'm sure you are aware that there is no company policy prohibiting such relationships between colleagues. It is therefore not a topic for gossip or ridicule. If you ever genuinely suspect there's an abuse of power in effect, there are discreet routes for you to report this to trigger an investigation – in these instances, spreading gossip is at the detriment of the victim and I'd consider such behaviour to be wilfully malicious.

"As such, I don't expect to hear of any more rumours of this nature, and any that currently exist, I expect to quickly disappear, otherwise we will begin formal disciplinary action. I will not tolerate bullying. Now, I hope this is the end of the matter, unless there's anything else I need to know about?"

The two women obediently shook their heads.

"Very well. Sandra, you're free to go."

There was an awkward moment while Sandra didn't respond, shock and indignation pinching her features. Eventually, the frost melted from her skin and she moved, slowly exiting the room, eyeing the two of them with reinforced distrust until the door clicked closed behind her.

Cathy forced her eyes to Max, all the energy and brashness that had loosened her lips earlier suddenly heavy in her stomach and tight in her throat. Maybe she shouldn't have been quite so brazen ...

Max relaxed into an arrogant half-smile as he read her mind.

"You're lucky I have a sense of humour."

His tone of voice, his intense stare, even his choice of words and the sexual content they referred to; if she hadn't known better, she would have thought he was flirting.

She kept her eyes on him.

"Am I? I'm certainly not very lucky that you have such a precious secretary." That comment earnt her a raised eyebrow. "I thought it was only fair to make her feel a fraction of the discomfort I've felt being here these past two weeks. I thought you wouldn't mind."

Where had this confidence come from? She was never this confident, never this vocal, especially when it came to authority figures and he most certainly was one. Why did talking to him in such a way feel acceptable? Not just acceptable but *right*. She wanted to push the boundaries, see that smirk, make that brow rise and fuel the amusement brightening those dark eyes. She wanted to impress him, beguile him with her previously non-existent wit and charm. Was it flirting? Or was it just a relaxed working relationship, made possible by his laidback attitude and the easy-going atmosphere that existed between them? She wasn't sure. She just knew she liked having his eyes on her, even if it did make her blush.

"I don't, but others probably would," Max replied slowly, as if he enjoyed saying every word. "So I wouldn't tell your stories about threesomes and sex parties to just anyone around here."

"But you'd like to hear those stories?" She boldly asked, changing the intonation of her tone to playful at the last second.

"They'd certainly be more entertaining than most things I'm told."

"Then I'm sorry to disappoint. I only said such things for dramatic effect."

His eyes narrowed slightly. "Shame. Looks like I still have no one to trade stories with."

Was it just her or was the room suddenly really warm?

"Anyway," he said, abruptly getting to his feet, "I do hope you and Sandra can get along now."

She mirrored his movements, standing and approaching the door.

"I will try to make an effort," she appeased.

"Thank you."

He opened the door and, with his hand lightly resting on the small of her back, manoeuvred her out of the office. The door clicked softly closed behind her and she all but sagged against the wall, suddenly exhausted, head light with heat. It wasn't the only part of her that felt warm. She realised with a start there was a slight dampness between her legs and a familiar tingling, itchy sensation her fingers were desperate to soothe.

Maybe she'd been too hasty in banning staggeringly handsome young bosses from her fantasies.

Composing herself, she stepped into the office, immediately seeing Sandra sat at her desk, straight-faced and typing furiously on the computer. As much as Cathy disliked the woman, she figured she'd try to make an effort, just this once.

"Sandra?"

"Yes?"

The woman didn't even take her eyes off the screen. It was almost enough to make Cathy change her mind.

"How about we go out for lunch together? I'm sure there's a nice café or something nearby."

That got Sandra's attention. The question *Why would I want to go to lunch with you?* hovered between her parted lips as her wide eyes tried to figure out the motivation behind such an offer, especially after that painfully awkward meeting.

Just accept the fucking peace offer, Cathy thought in her head as she waited for a response. She was about to give up when Sandra finally smiled.

"That would be lovely. I know just the place," she said, immediately turning back to her computer.

"Great."

Great... something to not look forward to. She deliberated for a moment, torn between sitting down at her desk and getting on with her work or heading to the bathroom to sort out her clit that was still itching for attention. Seeing that she was being the bigger person and would have to suffer

Sandra's company for a whole extra hour, she decided she deserved a treat. She turned on her heels and headed down the corridor.

Thank goodness for self-contained, gender-neutral toilets.

Chapter Eight

Lunch wasn't even that bad. Sure, Sandra spent most of the time talking about her children and how *incredibly well* they were doing for themselves, but when she paused and finally asked Cathy a question about her parents – to which Cathy replied she'd had a very fractured relationship with her mother for several years – Sandra softened, changing from wicked witch to supportive agony aunt in seconds.

When she continued to be amicable even as they walked back to the office, and then in the office, passing the colleagues she'd previously slandered Cathy to with a haughty smile, Cathy wondered if maybe the new mood between them was forecast to remain.

Max looked thoroughly confused when he passed by their open office door on his way to a meeting, and saw them sat side by side behind Sandra's desk.

"Everything all right?" He asked cautiously, looking from one to the other and then back again.

"Perfect," Sandra quickly asserted. "Cathy's just looking over the plans for the Christmas party."

"Is she?" Max's eyes widened with surprise at the news Sandra was sharing her baby with someone who, only hours ago, had been her nemesis.

Cathy nodded, unable to look directly at him after the unspeakable things she'd been imagining him do earlier to help her get off quickly.

"Amazing what one lunch can do ..." he said under his breath as he walked away.

Cathy had hoped to avoid him for the rest of the day, feeling awkward and guilty to her core over her indecent imagination. At the end of the working day, Sandra disappeared with a cheerful goodbye as she wandered off to find Louise, while Cathy grabbed her helmet and bag to head home alone for the first time. Stepping out into the car park, she paused and cursed the universe.

The rain was torrential. Sheets of grey water slicing through the air, ready to cut through her clothes and chill her blood as she had to helplessly moped home. Trust Alison to be away when the weather was bad.

Gritting her teeth, she ran out into the rain, quickly putting the key in the ignition to open the seat and grab the emergency waterproofs she kept there. Within seconds, she was drenched, coat completely saturated so the water started creeping through her shirt to stroke an icy hand over her skin. Cursing under her breath, she was about to throw her jacket on when she heard the creep of tires behind her.

"Cathy?" A voice called.

She glanced over her shoulder to find Max looking at her through the open window of his very expensive car. She didn't know anything about cars, but even she could tell a body that sleek, crowned with an unfamiliar emblem shaped like a trident, must have cost a small fortune. For a few seconds, she just stood there, tracing the smooth, attractive lines with her eyes as the rain continued to pour.

Suddenly, she understood how cars could be considered sexy.

"Cathy?" He asked again, brow creased with concern.

"Nice car," she shouted back.

"Thanks, but I didn't get your attention for your opinion on my car." That naturally charming smile returned. "Do you want a lift?"

"Really?"

"Yes."

"But I'm soaking wet. I wouldn't want to ruin your car."

"The upholstery can cope with a bit of water."

"You're sure?" She eyed the car again. Her instinct was to take several steps away, not get inside it. "I probably can't afford to pay for the damage."

"Fuck's sake, stop staring and get in."

At that command, she jumped to action, quickly stuffing the waterproofs back under the seat, locking the bike, and dashing over to the car. Max pushed the door open for her and she clambered inside, suddenly breathless.

"Thank you," she panted, peeling the coat off her arms as Max took the helmet and placed it on the backseat. Cathy glanced nervously at the pristine black interior and the droplets of water falling from her whenever she moved.

"Don't worry about it," he said, noticing her awkwardness. He carelessly chucked her coat on the backseat too, then stared at her for a good five seconds before sliding off his jacket and handing it to her. "Here."

"I couldn't."

"Yes, you can," he said firmly, while giving her a meaningful look.

She followed his eyes, almost gasping as she noticed her damp, translucent blouse clinging to her skin, perfectly outlining every swirl on her lacy bra and the peaks of her hardened nipples.

"Shit," she whispered, snatching the jacket off him to cover herself. "Thank you."

"No problem." He busied himself with tapping at the car interface. A second later, she felt the seat start to warm. "Where are we going?"

"Oh, you really don't have to. I've ridden in weather like this before. It's not pleasant but—"

"Cathy," he said with a sternness that cut right through her. "I'm driving you home."

That silenced her protests. At his indication, she entered her address into the satnav, slowly sitting back against the pleasantly warm seat, and tried not to feel too awkward about the fact Max had basically seen her tits.

"Thank you," she remembered to say.

"You're welcome." He put the car into drive and joined the traffic. "Why the moped anyway? Can't you drive?"

"I can; it's more about the expense." She felt particularly pathetic at that statement, considering she was currently sat in a car that probably cost the same as a modest family home. "Anyway, when Alison's here I get a lift with her. I just got unlucky with the weather today."

"Is she back tomorrow?"

Her shoulders sank, bringing her nose a little closer to the jacket that smelt so deliciously of him. She resisted taking a deep breath. "No, she's not. It's okay, I'll just get the bus."

"I'll pick you up."

"You really don't have to—"

He half-smiled as he watched the road. "I insist."

There was no point arguing with him. As the conversation ebbed, she looked out the window at the crawling traffic, flanked by morose pedestrians with umbrellas fighting against the wind and unrelenting downpour. She glanced around the car interior, seeing all the craftsmanship and luxury she couldn't put a price tag on, and finally onto the man beside her, who was as helpful as he was domineering. She assessed his posture, relaxed yet prepared, always prepared; one hand griping twelve o'clock on the steering wheel, the other resting in a loose fist on his thigh, as he calmly despaired at the rush-hour traffic. He oozed effortlessness and confidence, utterly unawkward in his skin, completely comfortable with his place in the world. Nothing could throw him off-balance, not even his slightly tragic assistant's assistant as she stepped into his car in a see-through blouse.

The itch was back. Something about him, something about his driving, so at ease handling that intimidating masterpiece of machinery, almost as if it was an extension of himself, that unconscious level of competency ... it was sexy. *He* was sexy.

And good God how she wanted to bury her nose in his jacket.

"How much does a car like this cost?" She asked just to say something.

"About two hundred," he replied, criminally blasé.

Thousand, she finished in her head.

"Bloody hell," she whispered. That would explain why she felt more valuable just by sitting on that (she presumed) hand-stitched Italian leather seat.

"All electric, seven hundred and sixty-one horsepower, max speed one hundred and eighty miles per hour, acceleration two point eight seconds. Convertible. She's a beauty to drive." And then he had to go and flash her the most gorgeous boyish smile.

Her answering smile was a weak, distracted thing.

"Now that you've seen the plan for the Christmas party," he continued, barely pulling her attention back to the mundane, away from sportscars, attractive millionaire bosses, and, if she was being honest, just straight up sex. "I expect to see you there."

"It's not a compulsory party, is it?" She teased, relieved his eyes were back on the road.

"No, but you'd better have a good reason for not attending. Partners are welcome to come along," he added.

Was he fishing for information about her relationship status? Or was he just being polite?

"That's very generous of the company," she replied coyly. "Will you be bringing anyone?"

"No one to bring."

Either he was being totally unsubtle or she was reading way too much into everything he said and did. *Your multimillionaire boss does not fancy you*, she told herself, and yet; she couldn't completely shake off that feeling of suspicion instilled in her every time they interacted, the possibility that maybe, just maybe, she intrigued him too.

"That surprises me."

"How so?" His quietly amused smile was back.

How to phrase it ...

"May I be crude?" She asked, remembering when he had so crudely explained his reasons for semi-underhandedly hiring her.

"I'd encourage it."

"Well, considering you're young, wealthy and ... not unattractive, I'd have thought you'd have your choice of partners."

His lips curled at *not unattractive*.

"You flatter me."

If you could hear the thoughts in my head; you'd realise just how much I could flatter you.

"That's not my intention," she replied coolly, though no part of her was cool anymore. "From a biological viewpoint, you're young and seemingly healthy. And socioeconomically, you have a stable job, sufficient finances—"

"Perhaps the issue isn't my appeal to potential partners, but rather my choosiness when it comes to mate selection," he smoothly interrupted, perfectly matching her academic tone. It was a surprisingly discreet way of saying *Yes, I know I am an absolute catch.*

"I've heard you only look for three things," she boldly declared, remembering one eavesdropped conversation she'd been unable to forget about.

That caught his interest.

"You'll have to enlighten me."

"Young, blonde, and curvy."

He turned to face her and she suddenly realised he wasn't driving anymore, the car stationary alongside the curb outside her block of flats, the electric engine silent once again. How long had they been there? How had she not noticed?

"Who told you this?" He seemed genuinely intrigued.

"That morning last week, with Sandra and Louise. Sandra was talking about why I was hired." *Yes, yes, I am well aware I'm insinuating that I'm your type, but Sandra said it first!*

He looked her over as if to confirm that she was, in fact, those three things.

She was desperately trying to think of a way to get his eyes off her before she either spontaneously combusted or threw herself at him, when he scoffed, shook his head and looked out of the windscreen.

"So, I take a date to one Christmas party and suddenly I have very particular tastes."

Something inside her sank.

"Sandra does have a habit of jumping to conclusions," she observed, trying to keep the disappointment out of her voice. She had no idea if she succeeded. "So, your blonde date isn't around anymore?"

He scoffed again. "She wasn't around for long. Taught me there are a few more characteristics I want in a partner."

"Such as?" She couldn't help but ask, that ever-vigilant, ever-defensive part of her brain hoping to hear something impossible, so that it could stop wasting its energy yearning after an unobtainable thing. And yet, when he looked at her, when he spoke, slowly, honestly; she couldn't stop her pathetic mind from thinking every single word was about her.

"Intelligence, for one thing. Integrity, authenticity. Someone who doesn't think the world should revolve around them."

"I don't," she whispered, before realising she said it out loud. She forced out a cough to try and hide it, but his slightly widened eyes told her he'd definitely heard. "Erm ... I'm sure she had some redeeming features."

"She was an ex-gymnast, which had its benefits."

"Oh ..." was all she managed to say, her mind reeling because she wasn't a gymnast and never would be.

"I'm joking," he clarified at her crestfallen expression. "A slightly crass and, apparently, poorly executed joke."

"Oh ..." Okay, seeing that she could only make noises, it was definitely time to leave. And yet, a part of her didn't want to step out into the rain, away from the man that seemed to mess with her psyche more than anyone else ever had. Just as well she'd always had more sense than sensibility or he'd have to drag her out of his car.

"I should head in. Thank you," she managed to say, about to pass back his jacket when she remembered the state of herself underneath. "Erm ..."

He left her in distress for a few seconds. "You can return it tomorrow."

"Thanks." She carefully slipped her arms through and wrapped it across her chest.

"I'll be outside at eight-fifteen tomorrow. Have a good evening."

"You too."

Her eyes lingered on his roguish half-smile before she jumped out of the car and ran through the rain to her building, the car's roar as it accelerated away making her spine tingle. She caught a glimpse of her reflection in the nearby window – clothes dishevelled; hair a damp, tangled mess – and thought to herself firmly *Nothing about this look was attractive to him. He was just being nice. He was just making conversation. Stop kidding yourself.*

Sara was waiting by the door when she entered the flat. "Cathy, did I just see you step out of a Maserati?"

"If that's what it was, then yes." She kicked off her shoes and started rolling her tights down her legs. Gods alive, she was suddenly freezing.

"Are you wearing a—" Sara checked under the collar. "A Prada jacket?"

"If that's what it says ..."

"Oh my God—"

"He just gave me a lift home," Cathy wearily explained. "Don't read into it. It was raining, and I looked like a pathetic mess about to moped home, so he offered me a lift."

"He let you keep his jacket—"

"Only so that I didn't have to show the rest of the world my bra!" She opened the jacket for a second to show Sara the state of her clothes underneath. "Anyway, I'm having a shower."

"You're allowed to like him, you know," her friend called after her. "I fancy him and I don't even know him."

"That's because you find money attractive!"

"Money is attractive! Power is attractive. Young hot men that drive sports cars are attractive!"

"I can't hear you anymore!" Cathy sang, turning the shower up.

She peeled off her clothes and stepped in. Sighing, she tipped her head under and let the water fall down her face and back, dragging all the tension out of her limbs as it slipped down her body. The tension returned as soon as she stepped out of the bathroom in her dressing gown to find Sara waiting for her again.

"I've made you a cup of tea," she quickly said. "Because I'm a good flatmate that you're not allowed to get mad at."

"I'm not mad at you," Cathy reassured, gratefully taking the mug and curling up on the sofa.

"Then be honest with me."

She sighed dramatically. "Okay, I fancy him. I fancy a completely unattainable man, who basically saw my boobs through my rain-soaked shirt earlier. Happy?"

"Ecstatic!"

"Why?" Cathy laughed, despite the embarrassment scorching her cheeks.

"Because he's *real*," Sara replied cheekily, taking the other side of the sofa. "And not completely unattainable."

"Hmm ..."

"I know, I know, you have this whole humble, quiet village-girl vibe, but that could be his thing. This could be your very own rags to riches story. Plenty of offensively-rich, ethically-challenged men fall for their secretaries or their maids or whatever."

"Are you sure that's not just in porn?"

That earnt her a withering look.

"At least be open to the opportunity."

"I am, but it feels more like a fantasy than my desire to be snubbed a dance by Mr Darcy."

"But it isn't. What?" Sara narrowed her eyes at Cathy's wounded expression.

"I really don't think I'm attractive enough—"

"Stop right there. You're a fucking goddess. You hear me? Besides, it's not for you to decide who should and should not find you attractive. So, there'll be no more self-deprecating talk like that. Okay?"

Cathy smiled shyly. *Sara, my eternal cheerleader.* "Okay."

"Is there something else?"

"Well ..." Cathy sipped her tea, wincing as she scalded the tip of her tongue. "I'm not sure I like who I become around him," she confessed. "I mean ... it's strange. I feel confident, like I want his attention, but normally I don't want any attention from anyone. And it sounds like everything I say comes out flirty and my mind interprets everything he says as flirty. It just doesn't feel like *me*. Like in the car, he asked if I was bringing a partner to the Christmas party—"

"So, you *can* bring partners?" Sara asked with deliberate, probing slowness as she leaned in closer.

"Yeah ... but I obviously don't have one. He was probably just being nice but my brain assumes he's fishing for information."

But Sara wasn't listening anymore. "I'll be your partner."

"I'm flattered but you're not my type," Cathy replied sardonically, finally managing to drink her tea without burning herself.

"And you're not my type," her friend confirmed. "But you can still bring me along."

"But it's partners only."

Sara gave her a perfected *you're-being-dense* look. "So? They don't know that we're not together."

"If I bring you, everyone will think that we're lesbians!"

"I can pretend to be a lesbian for an evening if it means I get to come along to your fancy work party. And I'd get to meet Max and steal him from you."

Cathy scowled. "How would you steal him if you're meant to be a lesbian?"

"Jesus, Cathy, lighten up. I don't actually plan on pursuing him. Off-limits, remember? I'll be there to help you ... and enjoy myself."

"So, making him think I'm gay will help?"

"Once we're in, we don't have to pretend we're a couple. I doubt they'd kick me out for only being your friend anyway."

That was a fair point.

"Please," Sara continued as Cathy paused for thought. "Don't deny me an amazing evening out with my two best friends."

"You forgot black-tie, live music, free bar, all expenses paid for, amazing evening."

Sara jumped to her feet and headed towards her bedroom.

"I'm coming with you whether you like it or not. In return, I'll make sure you look so gorgeous Max can't help but fall in love with you."

Cathy rested her arm on the back of the sofa, creating a cushion for her chin, while she watched Sara saunter away, and then listened to the sound of hangers chinking together as she hunted for a suitable dress that wouldn't be there and would, naturally, require a full girls' day out to acquire.

Despite knowing it was a foolhardy dream, Cathy smiled to herself.

"I guess it's worth a try."

Chapter Nine

"You should wear the jacket."

"I'm not going to wear his jacket!"

"It's a power move."

"It's brazen."

"He'll like it, trust me; men find it sexy when women show dominance. And it will make him think about you around his things, in his house, perhaps wearing one of his shirts after a wild night of incredible—"

"Fine," Cathy grabbed the jacket from Sara and slipped it over her arms. The jacket she *definitely* hadn't worn for a significant portion of the evening yesterday whilst alone in her room, the jacket whose lapels she *definitely* hadn't pressed her nose to every five minutes ... because only a weird, hopelessly infatuated girl would do that.

But damn, if there wasn't something incredibly sexy about wearing his clothes.

She suppressed her delighted shiver as the perfect weight of the fabric rested on her shoulders, and continued the conversation. "But if instead he thinks I'm incredibly rude and crossing a professional boundary and I get fired, then you owe me a new job."

Sara placed her hands on Cathy's suddenly expensive shoulders, spun her around and pushed her towards the door. "You're more likely to get fired for making him wait five minutes for us to have this argument."

"Maybe if you didn't always put up such a fight."

"Me? I'm the one that puts up a fight? I'm the one trying to help you appear a little less frigid."

Cathy frowned over her shoulder. "You did not just call me frigid."

But Sara just cackled with laughter. "At least today you look less like a virginal schoolgirl and more like a sexy secretary. You're welcome. Anyway, have fun, work hard, and don't forget to add me to the Christmas party guest list!"

With a final shove, Cathy was through the doorway and heading downstairs alone. The more stairs she walked down, the harder it was to maintain her smile. Her bright mood, nurtured by Sara's playfulness, dimmed at the thought of seeing Max again, this time wearing an outfit that was definitely pushing the limits of the company dress code, and was basically screaming *Eyes on me please*. At least for now the jacket helped to make the black bodycon dress, that barely reached halfway down her thighs and covered about seventy percent of her cleavage, a little more modest. She had explicitly told Sara she'd feel more awkward than sexy wearing the dress – which, she'd pointed out, would also look more suitable on Sara at a bar meeting one of her clients than on herself sat with a middle-aged woman in an office all day – but in typical Sara fashion, she was told to *Shut up and own it.*

The air was cool as she stepped outside, blanching her face and biting through her denier-insufficient tights – she had put her foot down when Sara had suggested *fishnets* (it was obvious her friend had never had a desk job). At the sight of Max's car waiting for her, she forgot all about the cold as a flush of desire warmed her blood. Remembering to stand up straight and tame her fearful expression, she tried her best to *saunter* over to the car.

"Morning," she said, letting herself into the passenger's side. She almost moaned aloud as her back rested against the preheated seat.

"Morning," he replied, not looking up from the phone he was texting on. She looked him over as she waited, trying to quell her imagination at his perfectly tousled hair and stubble-covered jaw she desperately wanted to drag her teeth over. "Latte?"

"Hmm?"

His eyes finally moved to her, widening slightly at her unexpected wardrobe choice. After a second of thorough inspection, he picked up the coffee cup from the centre console and passed it to her.

"I wasn't sure, so I had to guess. If you don't want it—"

She snapped back to her senses. "Oh, that's fine, thank you. I'm not much of a coffee drinker, usually just tea." Her words came to an abrupt stop as the voice in her head told her to *Stop babbling*. She cradled the cup between her hands, focusing on the warming of her fingertips rather than the warming of her loins at the mere sight of him. The frown he gave her, that inherently seductive frown, never failed to set her blood simmering.

"Is that my jacket?"

"I'd left my coat in your car," she offered by way of explanation and apology.

"I'd noticed," he replied coolly.

"So, rather than wear a different coat ... seeing as I had to return your jacket anyway ..." She crumbled under his relentless gaze. "I'm so sorry, I shouldn't have."

"It's all right." He suddenly smiled. "I think you almost wear it better than I do."

Her heart fluttered, actually fluttered.

"Only almost?"

He scoffed with amusement. "Especially based on your interpretation of 'dress down.'"

Her mouth opened in question but no words came out as she suddenly noticed his lack of tie. Rather than one of his usual designer suits, he wore a pine green jumper and a deliberately scruffy pair of dark blue jeans that snugly hugged his thighs. As he watched her panicked eyes scan over his attire, his smile slowly pulled to one side.

"Did I forget to tell you we have dress down day every payday? Sorry," he added, not at all contrite.

Bastard, she thought to herself, as a wave of embarrassment crashed over her.

"Does everyone participate?" She asked, hoping she wouldn't look completely out of place, though based on the fact her boobs were practically under her chin, she thought that would be the case regardless. *Mental note: don't let Sara dress you for work ever again.*

He shrugged. "Pretty much, unless there are external meetings."

"Oh ..."

"Do you want to get changed?"

"But we'll be late."

"I'm sure your boss won't mind if you're ten minutes late," he teased smugly. "Actually, I can guarantee he won't."

She bit her lip. "Are you sure? It would make you late too."

"I can check with my boss, if you insist. Though, since it's currently the middle of the night in New York, Dad might not be too pleased." He started getting out of the car. "Come on."

Oh God, Max planned on coming upstairs too. He was going to see her slightly shoddy flat. He was going to meet Sara ... Oh God, he was going to meet Sara!

It was a tense walk up the stairs, tension that solely radiated from her. Max, on the other hand, seemed completely at ease, walking like he knew exactly where he was going, holding himself like he owned the place. But that was just Max being Max.

"I can wait outside if you'd prefer?" He offered, ever the gentleman, ever the rogue, as he read the discomfort plain on her face and enjoyed it at his leisure.

She fumbled with her keys.

"No, it's fine," she lied.

With a deep breath, she pushed the door open and walked in.

She was nothing but fond of the flat, designed around her desire to be surrounded by comfort and beauty, whilst also indulging Sara's artistic flair. Over the months they'd been there, it had become rather bohemian: none of the furniture matched, the floor was covered in a patchwork of rugs, the chintz sofas lost under countless blankets and cushions. The walls were covered with feathery dreamcatchers, macrame wall hangings, and Sara's acrylic paintings. In the kitchen, no two plates were the same, since most of the crockery were trophies from Sara's pottery classes. It really was a wonderful amalgamation of their personalities. Normally, Cathy felt no unease inviting others inside the small, charming space. But Max wasn't their usual sort of guest. He was surely much more comfortable drinking from crystal wine glasses than wonky handmade mugs, and seeing rooms lit by chandeliers rather than fairy lights and scented candles.

Still, she'd rather he was distracted by the eccentric décor than Sara.

Maybe Sara won't even notice us, she thought wishfully. *Maybe she's gone back to bed ...* Her hopes were quickly dashed as she heard Sara shout from her bedroom.

"Cathy, is that you?"

"Yes!" She called back. "Don't worry; I just forgot something."

She hoped that would be enough to satisfy Sara's curiosity.

She was mistaken.

"I'll just be a minute," Cathy told Max, voice trailing away as she saw Sara emerge, wearing nothing but a matching bra and high-leg thong, topped with an open robe, whose sole purpose was to keep the chill off her shoulders, its silk tie hanging loosely at her sides. Cathy was used to seeing her friend in a state of undress, but she didn't appreciate Max being privy to such a sight, particularly since Sara was one of the most gorgeous women she'd ever seen.

"Oh ... You're not alone." Sara halted in the doorway, making no immediate attempt to cover herself, and stared at the surprise visitor.

"This is my boss, Max," Cathy said, suddenly deflated. "I'll just go get changed."

She moved away, watching Sara the whole time, seeing every calculated movement she made. The tweaking of a bra strap. The half-hearted tying of her robe to leave plenty of flawless skin on show. The slow, predatory walk across the room, hand outstretched in invitation. And when she spoke, every inflection of her voice was made to sound seductive and scandalous.

"It's a pleasure to meet you, Max." She purred, emphasising his name like it was delectably sinful thing, all the while giving him a very deliberate up-down; a connoisseur sizing up a new specimen.

"And you."

Cathy closed her door with a slight bang. She wallowed in despair for a moment – why did she have to have one of the most gorgeous, confident, talented women ever as her roommate, why couldn't she be like that too – before deciding it wasn't worth the effort or the energy. If Max fell for Sara, like most men did, and was willing to pay for her, then whatever; she'd just fall back in love with fictional heroes.

When she emerged from the bedroom, now dressed more sensibly in her favourite pair of jeans (even she admitted they worked wonders on her bum) and a grey Fair Isle jumper, Max and Sara were still deep in conversation ... Sara still had her bra completely on show.

"I'm ready," Cathy said, walking straight past them, pausing only to shove Max's jacket in his hand. "See you later, Sara."

"Bye, darling."

She didn't look back, uninterested in the smug look that would surely be on Sara's face. She was almost at the car by the time Max chose to catch her up.

"Your girlfriend seems nice," he said, unlocking the car with a click.

"She's not my girlfriend," she muttered back, retrieving her coat from the back seat. Rather than the sodden mess she'd half-expected to find, it had been ironed and pressed. *Probably by his servants*, she grumbled to herself.

"Fiancée? Wife?" He continued once they were both seated.

"We're not together. We just live together."

Oops, guess that's her invitation to the Christmas party gone. Sorry not sorry.

He restarted the engine and smoothly joined the traffic. "My mistake. Though it sounded like she thought you were a couple. Maybe you should have a conversation."

"She wanted us to pretend, so that she could be my plus one to the Christmas party," she replied dryly. Her phone buzzed.

SARA: He's gorgeous! I 100% approve. I think he's into you. He barely looked at my tits ... unless he's gay ... maybe try to find out if he's gay, otherwise you've got this! xx

Her heart sank; the mantra *I'm a terrible friend* repeating in her head three times before his next words raised her heart back into place.

"Bring her anyway."

"Really?"

"Of course. I don't see any reason why it's restricted to partners. Anyway, it's not really anyone's place to question it, though Sandra might."

"If it's just Sandra, then I can handle that," she smiled, feeling much lighter, until after a pause he carried on.

"Interesting artwork pinned to your fridge. A friend of yours?"

She spluttered out an awkward laugh. "They were our spoils from a life-drawing class. We thought they deserved pride of place on the fridge ... Only one of them definitely did."

"Not yours by the sound of it? The one with the feet?"

"No, no, that was Alison's. She's decided it's not for her."

"Is that why Sara was looking for a substitute?"

Cathy watched him out of the corner of her eye. "What do you mean?"

"She invited me to join you." He glanced at her, smiling cruelly. "Judging by your expression, it's just as well I said I was busy."

"Erm ..." Dear God, Sara's audacity knew no bounds. "I can't think of many things more disconcerting than drawing naked people whilst sitting next to your boss." *Your really hot boss.* "No offence."

"None taken," he replied flatly.

"It's much more Sara's thing anyway."

"I'm not surprised. She seems very artistic – and talented."

Oh ... maybe he has fallen for her. Another filthy rich client for her roster.

"Yeah, she's a creative all-rounder," Cathy grumbled, totally not jealous.

"Except writing. She said that you're the writer in the relationship."

She wilted. "I think calling me a writer is rather generous." *An outright lie, in fact.* "It's much more of a dream than a reality."

"Could it not be a reality?" He asked, seriously.

"I ... I seem to be very good at making excuses why I can't write. Too busy with school, too busy with university, too busy working. I feel like I need to be completely free mentally to make a proper start. But that's unrealistic, and I know it is, so I'll probably never make a start. Sorry, I'm rambling."

"It's fine. Starting anything often feels like the hardest part. My unsolicited advice is that you have two options. One: just start writing. Anything. Lower your standards, fuck having a plan, pick an idea and run with it, just to get some words down and prove you can do it. But, being academically minded, I imagine you thrive with a little more structure. So, two: set yourself a task, a deadline, hold yourself to it, and see what happens."

As they pulled into the carpark, she looked over at him. He had read her so easily. But what really unsettled her was seeing the strangely solemn expression he wore, completely void of the innate humour she'd come to associate with him.

"I wouldn't have thought you'd ever struggle to start anything."

He turned the car off and silence filled the space between them.

"Why would you say that?" He calmly challenged, dark eyes locked on her. In that moment, they appeared more green than brown, the colour brought out by his jumper and the muted morning light. Normally, eye contact made her want to hide, but there was something about his gaze, something reassuring, something honest, that held her steady instead.

"I guess because you seem to have enough confidence and drive to do anything you want to."

He didn't miss the slight edge to her tone. "You think my family's wealth has made my life piss-easy, don't you?"

Luckily, he was smiling, else she would have flung herself from the car wailing apologies as she ran up to the office and tried to hide from him for the rest of her career there. Instead, she firmly maintained eye contact.

"I think it gives you a substantial head start."

"I won't deny that."

"And I think it is easier to grow up confident and driven when you know you could genuinely do anything you want to, and daddy will help you get there."

"Touché." He looked away, his frown darkening. "Though, if you had a parent – or anyone, for that matter – who could give you a job that you would be good at, that you wanted to do, that you would get to on your own one day just after years of unnecessary grind, wouldn't you take it?"

"I've never had the luxury of that sort of choice."

"Well, if you ever do, you should. Life's too short not to take shortcuts when they're offered. You can always pay the world back in other ways for your good fortune," he said with an air of finality before getting out of the car.

She followed, walking quickly to catch up with him.

"And do you pay the world back?"

"I gave you a job, didn't I?" He said wryly.

They passed through reception to a chorus of "Good morning, Mr Cannavale," ogling eyes following them. Once they were in the lift, Cathy replied: "I hope you've done more than just that."

"Saving your soul wasn't enough?" He teased, grinning as her eyes widened. "I can assure you, I do my fair share, and I try my best to make this company do more too."

"Such as?"

The doors slid slowly closed and suddenly all the air disappeared. Something about the privacy, the intimacy of being alone in such a small space – standing rather than sat, no obstacles between them unlike in the car – made the sexual tension turn up a few degrees. Not that Max seemed to notice. While Cathy leaned back against the cool silver wall and felt her cheeks rush with blood, he carried on with nothing more than a sidelong glance in her direction.

"Well, this is a profitable business and I don't see why our success should only benefit shareholders. Since I've been here, we have become a Real Living Wage employer, improved maternity and paternity benefits, introduced mental health representatives in every office, bonus schemes for all our staff not just those office-based, green initiatives ... Not that I take full credit for any of it, but I have been a strong advocate for improving this company and had many late-night phone calls with my dad trying to persuade him of the benefits of having a happier workforce. Maybe you don't think that's enough, but I'd say I've done my bit." He flashed her an arrogant smile. "And I couldn't have done it all as a junior accountant."

It was hard to gather her voice when all she could think about was hitting the emergency stop button and having Max's firm body pressing against her.

"Is that supposed to impress me?" She quietly asked, barely snapping out of her fantasy.

The cocky smile she got in return served only to make her blood hotter. He could really smoulder when he wanted to. It was a smile that said *I know exactly what I'm doing to you and I'd like to do more.*

She wasn't prepared for his body to turn towards her, one hand holding the rail on the back wall, as he leaned into her space, leaving almost no air between them. She also wasn't prepared for his next words; words that cut her open in the worst, and best, possible way.

"I thought I already impressed you."

He held her gaze for a moment and she was sure that her expression gave everything away, but she was powerless to hide her blush or shake off the lust that made her eyes heavy and her lips part.

Suddenly, the lift came to a stop. One second Max was still looking at her, stealing her air. The next, he'd gone, striding out into the corridor. He turned back when he noticed she wasn't following.

"Everything all right?" He smirked, as if he knew just how damp her underwear was.

"Fine," she said, forcibly bright. "Probably not the best idea for Sandra to see us arrive late together. And after that speech you gave about office relationships, I think she'd jump to conclusions."

"Would that be such a bad thing?" He challenged.

Her mouth hung open as she searched her mind for an appropriate reply. He gave it a second before claiming his victory and disappearing down the corridor. She watched him until the doors closed and she was dragged back down through the heart of the building.

"No," she said to herself.

Chapter Ten

In the weeks leading up to the Christmas party, with Alison back in the office and the boss spending two weeks at the New York headquarters, there were no more rides in sports cars or suggestive conversations in lifts. Work was rather boring without all the drama Max brought to Cathy's life, real and imagined.

"I'll come pick you up in about an hour," Alison said as Cathy got out of the car post-work, pre-party.

"Thanks. See you then."

Cathy waved goodbye and headed for the flat. As expected, Sara was armed with hairbrush and makeup bag as soon as she stepped through the door, hair straighteners and curling wand already warming beside her dressing table.

"Ready for me to make you beautiful?"

"Can I at least have a cup of tea first?"

Sara marched over, grabbing her hand and pulling her further into the bedroom. "No time. I only have an hour to work my magic, on you *and* me."

"Is there really that much magic to be done?"

That earnt her an annoyed glare and the comment, "Such ignorance."

Cathy just smiled, perfectly happy not knowing what the hundred different products Sara had laid out before her did. She was also perfectly happy for Sara to dress her up every once in a while. While makeup and fashion were a chore to her, to Sara, they were forms of art, skin just another canvas.

"Just don't make me look too orange like last time."

"It's not my fault I didn't have anything matching your exact skin tone! Anyway, now I do, so you'll get to be your best self."

After half an hour of slightly frantic pampering, Cathy carefully pulled on the lacy black dress she'd bought for the occasion. With a tight bodice and a generous skirt that ruffled into a dip hem, it was playful and sexy. Sexy, not just because of the hint of thigh, but mostly due to the plunge neckline that revealed far more cleavage than she was used to or strictly comfortable with – it was just as well her new bra made her boobs into perfect full orbs, whilst holding them snugly in place. She would have chosen something more conservative but Sara had convinced her this event was the time to use her *assets* to her advantage and properly test the waters with her enigmatic boss.

While Sara put herself together, Cathy made a cup of tea, holding it between her hands as she watched the city from the tiny kitchen window, lamenting at the herbs struggling to grow on the sill and contemplating the strange sense of vertigo currently slicing through her body. It was just a party. There was no guarantee of anything dramatic happening. And yet, she was sure she stood right at the edge of a precipice, and tonight would push her over, for better or worse.

"How do I look?" Sara asked as she cat-walked through the open-plan living area towards Cathy, pausing hand on hip by the fridge.

It was a difficult mouthful of tea to swallow.

Sara looked gorgeous. Her dark-and-milk-chocolate hair was piled on top of her head, out of the way of the statement plum-purple backless maxi dress she wore. It was tied in a bow at the back of her neck and draped low between her breasts, hugging her waist to leave little to the imagination. Along with the thigh-high split in the skirt – revealing the black straps of her high heels where they twisted enticingly up her calves – she was showing just about as much skin as possible without being refused entry for indecency.

"Wow ..." Cathy breathed, trying to fathom how someone could look so effortlessly flawless.

Sara frowned at the slight despair she noticed in her friend's expression.

"Don't worry. Like I said before, I promise I'm not trying to steal him from you."

"Are you sure?" Cathy half-teased. "Because that dress says otherwise. Not that he's mine to steal ..." She muttered the last part under her breath.

"He wasn't interested in my tits before, so he won't be tonight either. I promise the only attention I'm seeking is from other potential clients. What are you drinking?"

"Tea."

"Just tea?"

Cathy nodded.

"Who drinks tea before a night out?"

Cathy shrugged. "Me."

That didn't stop Sara from grabbing the mug from her hands and placing it upside-down in the sink.

"Let me get you a proper drink."

There was time for one sambuca shot each – from a bottle that had been hibernating at the back of the food cupboard, behind rice and pasta bags, for God knows how long, but it tasted okay – before Alison rang to tell them to head down. Cathy carried her shoes to save her feet – to which Sara told her, quite bluntly, that she was pathetic and it wouldn't make any difference – all but running from the building to the car to escape the cold of the dark winter evening.

"Hi Alison. Hey Dylan," she said breathlessly, as she bundled herself into the car, closely followed by Sara.

"Hey," Dylan replied cheerfully, looking over his shoulder from where he sat in the front seat. "Looking good ladies."

"Of course we are," Sara laughed back. "You look rather suave."

"He's not too hard to tidy up," Alison teased, before she started the car and concentrated on driving.

"Is that eyeliner?"

"Yeah, do you like it?" Dylan asked, fluttering his eyelashes.

Sara considered it for a moment. "You actually pull it off really well."

Dylan was second-generation, British-born Chinese, with the looks of a K-Pop band member and the temperament of a life-affirmed grandparent. He had endless kindness and patience, which was probably why he loved his job as a nurse on the geriatric ward of the local hospital. No one would have put him and Alison together: her from a Catholic, middle-class background, with a driven and slightly stern personality, while he was non-judgemental, full of joy, and happy to wander through life at a leisurely stroll. But they worked. She'd given him enough direction to decide on a vocation, and he relaxed her enough to lose the previously permanent hunch to her shoulders.

"Cathy, how's that hunk of a boss of yours?" Dylan asked, fixing his gentle eyes on her.

"I haven't seen him for two weeks."

"But he will be there tonight?"

"Definitely."

"Good, because I can't wait to drool all over him."

"Am I the only one that doesn't fancy him?" Alison despaired.

"Babe, you know I only have eyes for you really," Dylan mollified, placing a loud, sloppy kiss on his fiancée's cheek.

"Doesn't always feel that way," she continued, souring slightly. Alison had found it particularly difficult to come to terms with Dylan's bisexuality – she'd almost ended their relationship over it more than once – until he'd finally managed to convince her that it didn't mean he loved her any less than if he'd been straight, and that she was, and always would be, enough for him.

"Don't worry, Alison. Max will be too busy fawning over Cathy, while all the other men will be looking at me," Sara reassured, quite serious.

Cathy felt her body start to warm. "I don't think Max is the kind of person to fawn over anyone."

Sara flashed her a mischievous smile. "We'll see. If he doesn't fall for you tonight while you look like a fucking goddess, then he's a lost cause and we'll get you back on that dating app."

"I feel like dating apps are Cathy's version of hell," Dylan said, looking over his shoulder to see Cathy silently agreeing.

They pulled into the hotel carpark. Sara and Dylan couldn't get out fast enough, while Cathy took a moment to calm her rapidly beating heart with a few slow breaths. She looked up to see Alison turned around, cheek squashed against the edge of her headrest.

"You're always a goddess, you know."

Cathy laughed nervously. "Thanks."

"And you're not here for a man. You're here to enjoy yourself, so let's go."

They walked arm in arm, taking their time to catch up with the other two. Cathy looked up at the sky, at the pearlescent moon surrounded by a swirling halo of clouds. The stars were mostly obscured by the city's light pollution, so she imagined them instead, to put the world and the evening into perspective. Her body calmed as they stepped up to the entrance, Alison and Sara seamlessly swapping places as the woman guarding the gilded doors smiled tightly at them.

"Names please," the woman requested.

"How convenient for the company to be able to throw a five-star Christmas party in a five-star hotel," Sara whispered to Cathy as they waited their turn.

Cathy eyed the impressive Georgian building before them, with its tall windows and stately, pillared entrance. "If I owned a luxury hotel nearby, it's where I would hold it."

"How many hotels did you say they own?"

"About a hundred and ninety, all around the world."

"Bloody hell," Sara breathed before slapping on her perfect smile.

"Names please?" The greeter addressed them.

"Cathy Watson and Sara Jefferies," Cathy replied, feeling a slight blush bloom in her cheeks as she handed over their tickets.

The woman took the tickets and checked her list. "That's perfect, thank you. Please head on through. Enjoy your evening."

Sara squeezed in tight against Cathy's side as they crossed the entrance hall. It was a blur of orange-hued lights and smartly dressed people. It left Cathy dizzy – too many eyes pairing her and Sara together, too many chandelier crystals firing sparks of blinding light across the room – and her feet a little unsteady in their heels as she let Sara lead her, hopefully to somewhere she would find an empty seat and a strong drink. She crashed back to reality at the sound of a voice she hadn't quite been ready to hear again.

"Cathy, I'm glad to see you made it," Max said warmly, looking absolutely delicious in his black tuxedo.

On impulse, she raised her hand to wave but Max brushed it aside and stepped in closer, his hand skimming her waist, neatly trimmed facial hair tickling her skin as he pressed a kiss to her cheek. She was still in shock as he shook Sara's hand and smiled affably at the two of them.

"And a pleasure to see you again, Sara. This time wearing slightly more clothes," he observed dryly.

Sara gave him her sexiest smirk. "It's a shame, I know, but Cathy insisted."

"Well, you make a very attractive couple. Enjoy the evening." His eyes lingered on Cathy for a second before moving away to greet the next guests.

"Did you hear that?" Sara whispered conspiratorially. "We make an attractive couple."

Cathy looked despairingly around the room, watching the colleagues she vaguely knew look them both up and down as they walked arm in arm. She saw Sandra's vermilion lips part with a bemused smile.

"Well, at least one person will like me more, now that I'm pretending to be a lesbian."

"Call it a phase," Sara teased before exclaiming, "Have you seen this room? It's incredible!"

"Drinks, ladies." Dylan smoothly interceded them, passing over glasses of complimentary champagne.

"Champagne, already? What are we celebrating?" Cathy said with half-hearted humour.

"Being young and beautiful!" Sara merrily suggested.

"More like my one alcoholic drink for the evening," Alison countered, taking a sip. "Someone has to look after you guys."

*

It really was an evening of luxury. A Michelin-starred four-course meal with vintage wines or expensive liquors, live music, casino tables, and a silent auction, all under a beautifully frescoed ceiling and glittering chandeliers.

While Alison and Dylan slow danced before the band, and Sara turned her perfected smile on any man she deemed of moderate wealth and loose morals, Cathy leaned against the bar, contemplating her next drink. So far, the evening had been enjoyable; it was just her and her closest friends having an all-expenses-paid-for night out, drinking, dancing, and judging the questionable outfits her colleagues had chosen to wear. She was staring at a particularly flamboyant ballgown, when she felt someone move beside her.

"I hope you're on something stronger than raspberry lemonade tonight."

She'd had enough alcohol by then to feel nothing more than a tickle of nerves across her skin and a swirl of anticipation unsettle her stomach. With deliberate disinterest, she turned and raised her heavy eyes to Max.

"I have been, but I think just water will do for a bit. I don't particularly enjoy being drunk. Tipsy is fine. Not enough to feel ill, just enough to—"

"Dull your inhibitions?" He finished with a sultry smile before getting the attention of the bartender with little more than a flick of his hand. "Some still water, please, and I'll have another whisky."

"Thank you," she said, and turned her attention to the room, leaning back on her elbows against the bar. A moment later, he handed her a glass of chilled water, and watched the room with her, slowly sipping at the golden liquid in his tumbler.

"How was New York?" She asked, when it became apparent he was staying in her company.

"It always manages to be both tediously boring and unduly stressful. How has it been in the office?"

She shrugged. "Unduly boring and tediously stressful."

"Naturally." She could just see his smile out of the corner of her eye. "It looks like your girlfriend is enjoying herself," he observed, noticing Sara sat on a stool at one of the card tables, legs out, cleavage pushed up as she leaned back and enraptured two men with her conversation and enticing smile.

"I told you; she's not my girlfriend."

"Do you want her to be?"

She looked at him sharply, about to express her indignation, before biting her tongue at the sight of his playful smile. His eyes were on her, mostly on her face, occasionally on the half-moons of white flesh sitting between the generous neckline of her dress. She realised then that, like Sara, her posture was accentuating her *assets* rather obviously. She didn't move.

"She's not my type."

"You prefer blondes too?"

"Not usually. It's more the fact I'm not gay," she finally admitted.

"I'm glad to hear it." He took a slow swig of his drink. She watched the movement of his throat as he swallowed, her mouth becoming dry.

"That sounded rather homophobic," she challenged, knowing exactly where the conversation was going, yet doubting every second of it. She'd never really considered herself desirable, and certainly no one had ever made her feel that way ... but the way he looked at her was almost convincing.

"Not at all. In fact, my brother is happily married, living with his husband in Australia." He downed the rest of his drink, placing the empty tumbler on the bar top with a quiet crack. Moving in closer, he placed his lips against her ear and continued, every word tickling her spine, while she held her breath. "But it would put me at a disadvantage with you. I'm in the executive suite, top floor, if you'd like to join me. You look stunning in that dress, by the way."

She sat frozen as he walked away, out of the function room and into the foyer. The way he moved was effortless. The way he smiled and acknowledged the people he passed was effortless. Most of all, the way he'd invited her to his room was effortless.

This was it; this was the precipice.

Not the proposal she'd been expecting or hoping for – no dating, no relationship, just sex. To step forward into that unknown darkness, she'd quickly have to refresh her opinion of herself; she'd have to quickly become someone open to casual sex, rather than dreaming of all-in romance.

It didn't feel real. Her fast heartbeat, her hitched breathing, her suddenly sensitive skin; none of it could convince her it was true. It was a fiction made flesh. The wave of disappointment ebbed away quickly as she accepted the new fantasy. It wasn't nothing, it wasn't everything, but it was something. She could accept something. She wanted something, *anything*. If her undeniably attractive boss wanted to have sex with her – because she certainly wanted to get her hands on the boss – well; it was about time she found out if all those erotic novels had been at all truthful.

Alison noticed her approach, meeting her halfway, leaving Dylan to dance enthusiastically on his own.

"Cathy?"

"I might be gone for a while."

"Where are you going?"

"Max invited me upstairs." It felt like the smuttiest thing she'd ever said – it probably was. "And I'm going to join him."

"What? Really? Cathy, are you sure?" She frowned with distress, her questions like bullets. "You didn't wait this long to have a one-night stand."

"I wasn't waiting for anything really; it just never happened." She smiled with relief at the absolute clarity of the decision. "But now it could and I want it to, honestly. I just thought someone should know where I am because he may be the CFO of a multimillion-pound company but that doesn't mean he isn't a murderer." She laughed quietly, relieved to see some of the tension leave Alison's face. "But please don't tell Sara," she pleaded, wincing.

"Why not?"

"She thinks I'm far more delicate than I actually am. That, and she'd never stop going on about it."

Alison nodded in reluctant agreement, before grimacing apologetically. "I do have to point out that he's your boss. It could make things difficult."

Cathy shrugged. That was problem a for future Cathy; current Cathy was far too distracted by the thought of finally getting laid to worry about mundane things like office awkwardness.

"I think it will be okay. I really don't interact with him much day to day. And if it's not, then I can get another job. But I won't get this opportunity again."

"There are other men, Cathy."

None like him.

"I promise I want to do this. Don't worry about me." She was just starting to regret telling her about the whole thing, when Alison bit back any further concerns and nodded in surrender.

"Text me if you decide to stay the night. Otherwise, I'll call the police in about two hours."

"Thank you." She pulled her friend into a hug.

"Stay safe, have fun. Oh, and don't forget to pee afterwards."

"Yes, Mum."

"My girl, all grown up."

Smiling, Cathy let go and walked away, feeling her back straighten with purpose as she crossed the room, then the foyer, and headed into the lift, punching the highest button. As the lift glided up, the brief weightlessness leaving her stomach queasy, she took a few deep breaths and tried to gather her thoughts. Of some things she was certain:

1. She was ready to lose her virginity
2. Max would make for a good first partner
3. It probably wasn't the best idea to sleep with the boss
4. But it was too good an opportunity to pass up

And maybe he wouldn't just be her boss forever ... She snuffed that spark of hope quickly. It was just one time. Beyond that, she forced herself to have no expectations.

The lift opened silently to a small vestibule with two dark-wood doors labelled with gold plaques: one for staff only, one for the executive suite.

She stepped up to the suite, knocked quietly on the door, and waited. It opened ten heartbeats later.

"Cathy," Max purred. He no longer wore his jacket and his tie hung loosely around his neck, collar undone. "Please, come in."

She brushed past him as he held the door open, her heels making a satisfying tap on the lacquered floor as she approached the centre of the spacious room. Her eyes couldn't open wide enough to take in the luxury she found herself surrounded by. The style was modern and minimalist, which the interior designers had somehow managed to integrate seamlessly with the original architecture. White drapes, heavy grey curtains, a black baby grand piano in the far corner, a sleek white marble kitchen in another ... Everything was just shapes and colours as she struggled to piece the room together, like some taxing geometric puzzle.

"Would you like a drink?" Max asked, his voice grounding her a little.

"No, thank you," she whispered, eyes still darting around. A drink certainly would have made it easier to tame her anxiety, but she wanted to be present for this.

A moment later, she felt him approach, felt a hand rest on the small of her back. Even that slightest touch felt *right.* She turned to him, and smiled.

"It's quite a room."

"It is." He sipped his drink, his eyes already undressing her.

"And it's a very good party. I'm surprised you wanted to leave it early."

"Are you? I thought I'd been rather obvious."

She felt her knees go weak at the sight of his roguish half-smile. She wanted to ask *Why me? Why, out of everyone, would you want me?* But she didn't, knowing it was definitely not the time to indulge in low self-esteem. Not when he moved with such confidence, such ease.

He finished his drink, placing it down on a nearby table.

"A few ground rules though," he began, holding her gaze. "This is a one-time thing: it's not the start of anything;

it's not the end of anything. Second, this does not impact our relationship at work—"

"So you're still going to look at me like you want to fuck me every time I step into your office?"

Luckily, he laughed.

"Probably," he confirmed with a sly twist to his mouth. "And of course, nothing has to happen at all. You're free to leave right now."

"I don't want to."

He smiled darkly.

"Good."

Chapter Eleven

He grabbed her chin and pulled her in for a short, fierce kiss.

"Shall we?" He asked, releasing her and leading the way towards a half-open door on the far side of the room.

Like the lamb she'd become, she followed him in, hearing the door click quietly closed behind her, as her eyes fell on the super king bed with its crisp white sheets and thick feathered pillows that smelt of fresh laundry.

A body pressed in behind her, hands on her waist, lips against her neck.

"How do you like it?" He asked softly, kissing her again.

Holy hell ... She indulged in the sensation for a moment, closing her eyes and sighing internally, feeling lightheaded at those merest of intimate touches, until she realised she'd have to answer.

"I thought we were here for you."

"I enjoy it more if my partner is also enjoying herself," he explained, as she heard the rumble of a zip and felt her dress go slack. "So, any preferences?"

She was a fawn that had just learnt how to stand. Suddenly, she was being asked to run. There was no point pretending; he'd quickly discover her knees were too weak to keep up.

She pulled away, turning around to face him while hugging the loose dress to her chest.

"I don't really know what I like. I haven't done anything before."

She dared him with her eyes to mock her, but he just frowned.

"Nothing?"

She shook her head.

"May I ask why?"

This really was laying herself bare.

"The opportunity never arose," she said.

"I doubt it," he quickly countered.

"Why?"

That got a smile out of him.

He approached her slowly, stopping barely an inch away to look directly down at her. "There's nothing about you that would make no one in the world want to fuck you. So, if the opportunity never arose, it's because you weren't looking for it. Why?"

She shrugged.

"Why?" He demanded.

Because no one has ever made me want to have sex, before you.

"I suppose I wasn't ready," she offered instead.

"And now you are?"

"Yes."

"Prove it," he ordered.

She blinked up at him, feeling the embarrassed flush in her cheeks start to spread to the rest of her body.

"How?"

"Have you at least masturbated before?"

He didn't even flinch. She felt like melting.

"Yes ..."

He smiled again. "Prove it."

She steeled herself enough to reply tartly, "I didn't come here to pleasure myself."

"You won't have to for long, just long enough to convince me you're ready for this."

"Why do you care?"

"Because you don't get many pretty, twenty-something virgins for no reason. And if it's not for a god or a lack of interest, on your part or others, then it probably means you were waiting for the right person." His voice became low and dark, a rumble that cut right through her. "I can promise you that I'm not the right person. I am not *the one*. I'm not your knight in shining armour. I'm just a man who wants to fuck you. I don't want you to develop any feelings for me beyond awe at how well I can make you come. So, take off this pretty dress, lie on the bed, and show me you're ready."

Well, if that didn't set the dynamic ...

She stared at him defiantly for a moment. While her underwear was already soaked with arousal at the dominant vibes he was giving, a part of her still didn't like being told what to do.

"Well?" He prompted.

It didn't matter. None of it mattered. He'd made a bold claim, and she was going to find out if it was true.

She stepped out of her heels, quickly removing her tights before shimmying the dress over her hips. It dropped to the floor with a sigh. While his eyes appreciated the sight of her in a different outfit of black lace – a black and nude plunge bra paired with a delicate Brazilian – she slowly approached the bed, moving in such a way that his eyes were always drawn to one of her curves. Following his previous instruction, she lay down on the bed, propped up by the comfiest pillows she'd ever had the pleasure of lying on. Bending her knees slightly, she slowly opened her legs.

Max stood at the end of the bed, barely moving as he watched her hand stroke over the top of her breasts, from one side to the other and back again, before following the curve down to the centre of the bra. Lazy fingers glided over the dip of her waist and the slight rise of her stomach, pausing as they reached the silk bow on her underwear.

He inched forward in expectation, and she smiled.

"Surely this is proof enough?"

"Definitely not," he vetoed, eyelids heavy, lips staying parted.

After a deep breath, her hand explored lower.

She closed her eyes and tried to pretend she was alone in her room, indulging in her usual self-care. She checkedthe dampness of her opening, stroking up to lubricate her engorged clit. Barely touching it, she felt it pulse, so aroused by the erotic scene she was playing out. It didn't matter if her eyes were closed; she knew Max was watching every move she made. The thought of someone watching her, becoming aroused by her, made every inch of her skin feel warm and desperate to be touched. She touched the part that mattered most at that moment, softly rubbing the pad of her middle finger over the small, blooming bud.

A quiet moan escaped her. It had never felt so good before, or so easy. She knew that if she increased the pressure just right, rubbed a little harder, in seconds she could have her release. But she wasn't there for that.

"How long? Because I'm close," she said, opening her eyes.

In response, Max pulled the tie from around his neck, carelessly dropping it on the floor. He started unbuttoning his shirt as he paced slowly around the bed. By the time he reached the side nearest to her, his shirt was open, revealing a toned chest with a dusting of hairs; though her eyes were more interested in the shallow outline of a six-pack with its trail of darker hairs that disappeared below the waistband of his trousers – trousers that were suddenly looking a little tight.

"Ahh ..." she gasped, back arching as she stepped too close to the edge.

But she didn't fall, as Max grabbed her hand and pulled her back.

"Not yet," he murmured, sitting down beside her and pulling their bodies together.

As their lips locked, she felt his heat and size wrap around her. His skin felt gorgeous; firm and warm and smooth. His kisses were fierce and fast, like he was fighting with her, like he couldn't get enough. When his tongue demanded entry, she readily opened up to him. It was a novel sensation, but one her body instantly recognised as right, wanted, and good. It was amazing. Even with her lack of skill – her intuition struggling to keep up with someone who knew exactly what they were doing, someone who seemed so *hungry* for her – any anxiety at her performance was crushed under the chase for pleasure.

So focused on following the dance of lips and tongues, she hadn't even noticed he'd unclasped her bra until the straps slipped off her shoulders. She discarded it herself, desperate to have more of their skin touching, but he retreated.

Sitting back, she breathlessly watched as his fingers explored her uncovered skin. His fingers stroked with deliberate slowness from waist to ribs to breasts. He cupped one, as if testing its weight; squeezed softly as if testing its firmness. A thumb brushed her dark pink nipple. Her gasp brought a smile to his lips.

"Do that again," he ordered.

"Do what?" She gasped again as his other hand abruptly slid beneath her lace underwear, a finger immediately finding its way inside her.

"That was easy," he grinned, hiding his face against her neck to tickle her there, kissing, sucking, grazing her with his teeth, while a second finger joined the first.

"How does that feel?" He asked as his fingers slowly moved inside her, only shallowly, a knuckle deep if that, to a steady rhythm her hips were desperate to follow.

"Amazing," she sighed before gasping again as his thumb found its way to her clit, rubbing slowly in circles as he'd watched her do. Her body started to hum with pleasure. A pressure she knew well, and yet didn't know at all, started to build, coiling tightly underneath where his hands worked her.

"It feels so much better than touching myself," she confessed, murmuring happily as he increased the speed.

"So you have fingered yourself before?" He asked, biting at her earlobe.

"A little."

"Only a little?"

"I mostly ..." She paused to breathe. "Just use a vibrator on my clit."

"So nothing bigger than my fingers has been inside you before?"

She bit her lip and shook her head, the pressure building, almost too high.

He watched her, saw her flushed cheeks and parted lips; eyes closed to lose herself in the sensation of his fingers expertly working her. He felt her hips try to move with him, felt her fingers dig gradually deeper into his arms as she started to slip away. As soon as her frown appeared – a frown of concentration, of determination to achieve orgasm – he removed his fingers.

Livid eyes snapped open.

"Not yet," he denied her again. "Not until I'm inside you."

She'd never been so wholly aroused. She'd never been so desperate to finish.

"Get inside me then."

His expression changed in an instant. Amusement replaced with sternness as he simultaneously shoved his fingers back inside her and gripped her chin. Her distressed moan brought a wicked smile to his lips.

"I don't normally like being told what to do," he growled. "But I'll let you off this time." He kissed her cherry lips and got to his feet. "Take those off."

There was no hesitation. She slipped the damp lace down her legs and lay back against the pillows again, this time without armour.

He was still for a moment, allowing his eyes to greedily devour every inch of her. A part of her wanted to curl up and hide, escape the relentless attention. Instead, she rolled onto her side and propped her head up on her hand.

"Your turn."

He scoffed, and pushed the shirt from his shoulders. Next was the belt, followed by trousers and socks, until he wore only a pair of black Calvin Klein's. It had been obvious, even when wearing a suit, that he had a gorgeous figure, one he'd earnt and worked to maintain. It was even better not covered with fabric; the powerful thighs, strong arms, trim waist, golden skin ... He tugged down one corner of his hipsters and then the other.

She'd seen penises before. She'd seen erections before. But it was very different seeing them in the flesh, seeing them hard, and knowing in a matter of seconds all those inches would be inside her.

"How ..." But she couldn't finish the stupid question. She knew how the biology worked; she just couldn't quite believe it.

His smile wasn't kind. "Don't worry, you'll stretch too."

She swallowed her apprehension as he climbed onto the bed. At his silent request, she turned onto her back, spreading her legs wider as he nudged her thighs apart. She froze as she felt his weight lower onto her, her lungs suddenly paralysed with the undeniable truth that it really was about to happen.

"I suppose, since you're a virgin, you're not on any birth control?" He asked, utterly pragmatic, while her mind was consumed with the slightly daunting erection aimed at her vagina.

"No, I'm not," she breathed.

"Shame. To be expected, but still a shame," he smiled wryly, leaning over to the bedside table.

"You were prepared," she observed as he sat back, stroked his cock, and tore the condom wrapper open with his teeth.

"I had a hunch this was going to happen tonight."

"Why?"

He chuckled to himself while lowering the head of his now covered erection to her opening. "I've never seen someone more obviously into me, without trying to tell me they're into me." The look he gave her then would have gotten her straight into bed with him, if she hadn't already been lying naked and ready. "One last chance, are you sure you want to do this?"

Words of a gentleman; eyes of a rogue.

"I wouldn't have taken all my clothes off if I wasn't sure."

He huffed at her sarcasm.

"This will probably hurt a little," he warned, and pressed forward.

Suddenly, at the mention of pain, she wasn't ready. It was definitely something she should have contemplated earlier, instead of choking on panic while the thick head of his cock pushed against her slit, demanding entry.

"Wait!" She placed a hand flat to his chest. He immediately stilled, barely inside her, but enough for her mind to stagger at the sensation, the delicious *rightness* of it. "How much will it hurt? Do you know what you're doing?"

He released a slow breath. "I can't say how much, but it won't be for long. And yes, I know what I'm fucking doing."

It was sexy when he swore; a promise rather than a threat.

"You don't mind that I'm a virgin?"

What she really craved was some indication that it was a good thing. While she hadn't been saving it for any real reason, it still felt like something that needed to be acknowledged, appreciated in some way, and he'd brushed past it like it was nothing.

"It doesn't bother me. It's a nuisance if anything."

He was still resting at her opening, tempting, infuriating, but those words felt like a slap across the cheek, so she pulled back, removing him from her whilst keeping her hand on his chest. She matched his frown with one of her own.

"It's a privilege," she told him. "If you don't want it, don't take it," she challenged, hoping he wouldn't call her bluff.

"If you want it to mean something, don't give it to me," he growled back, his fingers finding their way back inside her as if to remind her of what she'd be giving up. "Yes, it's a privilege that my cock will be the first one inside you, but right now, your virginity is getting in the way of me fucking you senseless." He smiled darkly, feeling her unwittingly ride his fingers. "So, shall we continue? Or is fucking my hand enough for you?"

Shame burned hot on her cheeks.

How mortifying. She hadn't even realised she'd been moving. She felt her body tense, preparing to bolt, but then she froze as he leaned forward, covering her body with his chest, his weight a comfort not a cage. As his forehead pressed against hers, she felt a new rush of heat in her cheeks for a whole other reason.

"Don't fight it. Don't hide it," he told her, the rawness in his eyes stripping her bare. "It's hot as hell to feel how much you want it. But, if this is enough, then this is as far as we go—"

"It's not." Her embarrassment, like her resistance, was short lived. Even if it hurt, even if it was only the once; she was not going to lose her chance with him, the man that had finally unleashed the libertine in her. Time to wake up and sully the sheets.

She fell back onto the pillow in submission, letting herself drown in his dark stare.

"Fuck me, Max."

Something in his expression sharpened, attention honing in on her, and she knew he liked her words. But he didn't need to hear them twice. She felt his hand move between them, bringing their bodies back in line. He stayed above her, his face close. She wondered for a moment why his eyes were still locked with hers and not watching their sex like the lens of a porn camera. But then he was pushing against her entrance again, and all conscious thought vanished.

He lowered himself down, delectable pressure building until he pushed past her body's natural resistance, and slid in slowly, inch by inch, filling her. The tightness, the sudden tearing pain, made her writhe, made tears spring behind her eyelids, but he didn't stop, didn't even flinch, moving with one slow, smooth thrust until he was nestled deep inside her. Then, he paused.

"*Fuck*." He released a jagged breath before brushing his nose against hers, placing a kiss on her unresponsive lips. "Are you okay?" He asked. She felt the shift of his weight onto one arm, and then fingers were stroking the dampness from her cheeks. For all his talk, he was surprisingly – thankfully – gentle.

She hissed, wincing, and fought to open her eyes; the sight of him above her enough to coax back the eroticism even with the presence of pain.

"It hurts," she whined, tense with the feeling of something about to snap inside her.

"Let me help," he whispered. "Try to relax."

Her eyes fluttered closed a moment later as more kisses brushed over her lips, cheeks, and neck. His hand roamed down from her face to her breasts, squeezing caresses warming her skin, gentle pinches warming her core. She gasped at the pleasure blooming in her tormented nipple, his tongue slipping between her parted lips. She drank his kisses, arched into his hand, returning to a world of heat and pleasure. It wasn't until he pushed his cock back into her that she realised he'd started moving again. It didn't hurt so much the second time. By the third, his presence was a purely welcome thing.

"Better?" He asked against her lips She didn't have to open her eyes to know he was smirking.

She could only nod in response, feeling him move inside her, the tightness suddenly delicious, the fullness better than anything she'd felt before.

"You feel amazing." He murmured what she'd been thinking, grazing her neck with his teeth, and hooking her leg around his waist to allow him to penetrate deeper.

"Oh God ..." she groaned.

"Don't hold back," he ordered, whispering in her ear as he noticed her biting her lip. "I want to hear you."

He thrust deep into her as he said it, and she couldn't help but moan.

"Like that?" He pulled out and thrust into her again, as far as possible, awakening that fabled spot of pleasure deep inside her. At her breathless sigh, he laughed. "I'm going to make you come."

It didn't take her long. After being denied twice, her body was quick to climb and even quicker to collapse over the other side.

After a few more thrusts, she suddenly felt it; a knot of heat right where his cock was hitting. Every nudge made it grow hotter and hotter until it burst, and the blissful heat seeped out in waves. She moved with them, surging and ebbing, savouring every second until there was nothing left, just peaceful fatigue and lingering delight that made every inch of her feel soft and warm. Content just to lay there and bask in her body's success, she almost forgot about Max above her, chasing his own release. Seconds later, he shuddered and moaned and finally stilled.

She blinked heavy eyes open to see him knelt between her thighs, chin on chest as he breathed deeply through his nose. A moment later, he shook the hair from his eyes, leaned down to kiss her once, before wordlessly removing himself and getting to his feet. He kept his back to her as he removed the bloodied condom, tied it in a knot and discarded it on the bedside table.

"Tissues are there. Clean yourself up," he said with disinterest, and headed over to the bathroom.

Something heavy dropped in her chest and started slowly sinking. She watched him walk away, eyes drawn to his perfect figure and toned ass. The weight dropped to her stomach and she sat up.

"Max?" She checked the panic in her voice as he paused and turned, one unfeeling eyebrow raised in question. "Erm ... aren't you going back down ... to the party?"

"No," he said blandly and carried on walking. "I'll see you Monday."

And he disappeared into the bathroom. She heard the shower turn on a second later.

Guess that's my ten-minute warning to get out, she thought to herself, the heaviness turning to nausea in her stomach. The corners of her eyes stung. *At least he was upfront about it ... It's just the serotonin making me feel all romantic ... It really was just a one-off fuck ...*

The nausea turned to hollowness as she waited a moment, dressed once again, staring at the bathroom door and imagining Max in the shower. She could picture with absolute clarity the water dripping over that gorgeous body, hugging every dip and curve of his muscles, hands lathering soap over that flawless skin. What would he do if she joined him? What would he do if she waited for him? It probably wasn't worth finding out. He'd already told her exactly where she stood.

"See you Monday," she muttered, before showing herself out.

Chapter Twelve

During her slow descent back down to the ground floor, Cathy used the time to wade through the fog of thoughts in her mind, unchecked emotions sporadically exploding in plumes of colour behind the haze. She decided to reevaluate her 'truths' from barely an hour earlier:

1. *She was ready to lose her virginity* – Check. She'd seen the bloody tissues as proof. Goodbye and good riddance really.
2. *Max would make for a good first partner* – CHECK! Hot guy, good sex. No complaints.
3. *It probably wasn't the best idea to sleep with the boss* – Check ... Alison had been right; work was going to be weird. How were you meant to carry on like you hadn't rubbed naked bodies together? Like you hadn't seen each other at your most raw? How did that kind of intimacy just disappear? Coldness might be the answer. Max got a full ten points for the sex, but only a one for aftercare (and that was purely for the mere presence of tissues). The man had been Baltic. She was under no illusion that he'd want to repeat the experience. Shit. Had she been bad?

4. *But it was too good an opportunity to pass up* – Check. She stood by her decision. No regrets. Heck, she'd do it again right now.

She reached the ballroom, the twinkling lights making her feel like she was stepping from one dream into another. Thankfully, there was no immediate sign of Sara; she was in no state for an inquisition. While Sara probably hadn't noticed her absence, Alison's eyes may have never left the doorway. Cathy found her standing in the exact same spot where she'd left her, eyes wide like a meerkat on sentry duty. At Cathy's reappearance, Alison jumped awake and scurried over.

Be gentle with me, Cathy silently begged even though she knew Alison couldn't be anything else.

"How did it go?" Alison asked, slightly frantic eyes assessing her as if for injuries. "Are you okay?"

Cathy offered her a tired smile, pushing thoughts of that disappointing ending out of her head.

"It was great." It wasn't a lie. It had been a near-perfect first time, his touch and kisses intoxicating things; and yet the words felt fuzzy on her tongue. "And definitely a one-off," she continued at Alison's unspoken question, taming her expression and tone before her next words. "He was very transparent about that."

"Did he say why?" Alison cautiously pried.

"No, and I didn't ask," Cathy shrugged. "Maybe he already has a girlfriend. Maybe I'm not girlfriend material. Whatever. I don't really care," she muttered in a way that revealed she did care quite a lot. Having tasted the forbidden fruit, she knew there was no going back, and if Max didn't want to taste her twice, maybe she'd have to bite the bullet and sample someone else. At the very least, it might lessen his potency over her, stop him from living rent free in her head. No point staying obsessed over a man who didn't want her.

"I'm glad I did it though," she admitted out loud.

"That's good. Fingers crossed work won't be too awkward."

A hollow smile curved Cathy's lip. "I don't think he knows how to be awkward." The genuine, heartfelt concern in Alison's blueberry eyes was almost worse than an inquisition. Cathy forced herself to brighten. "You know, I think I should try the dating app again. Give it a serious go. Unless you suddenly know of any nice, eligible guys?"

Alison pondered. "David in legal is nice—"

"No one from work," Cathy quickly clarified. She didn't need things to get even messier in the office.

Her friend grimaced in sympathy. "I'll ask Dylan if he knows anyone."

"Thanks." Cathy glanced around the room, shifting the attention away from her. "Looks like the party is winding down."

"Yeah, I'm about ready to go. Not sure about Sara ..." Alison nodded her head towards the bar where Sara had just ordered another drink. "Or Dylan ..." And then to the dancefloor where her betrothed was showing off with some questionable moves. "He's bit much sometimes ..."

"You get yours; I'll get mine," Cathy ordered affectionately. "Meet you outside."

*

It was a weekend of trying to distract her mind from imagining Monday morning, and all the ways Max could simultaneously impress and disappoint her. Between keeping a hungover Sara company – and acting equally surprised that *nothing* had happened with Max at the party – finding some new spicy novels to read, googling *How to be better at sex*, and browsing through potential suitors on the dating app she'd reluctantly re-joined, she was kept fairly well distracted, even if when she lay down and pleasured herself on an evening, it was Max she pictured above her.

Rather than seething rage or wretched despair, it was with stubborn apathy that she stepped into work Monday morning, waving goodbye to Alison as they parted ways in the corridor. She went to her office, Sandra watching the doorway as if she'd been waiting for her.

"Morning, Cathy," she said brightly, jumping to her feet.

"Morning, Sandra ..." Cathy headed over to her desk in the corner, vainly hoping to avoid dealing with her colleague's strange mood.

"Wasn't the Christmas party a success?" Sandra beamed, following Cathy over and perching on the edge of her desk, while Cathy sat down and tried not to sigh.

"Yeah, it was really good."

"And your girlfriend is absolutely stunning!"

Cathy felt her insides twist. "Yeah, she is."

While it had been easy enough – since apparently losing one's virginity was a purely internal change, even if it felt like she had a neon sign flashing 'open for business' above her head – it hadn't felt good keeping such a big thing from Sara. There had been multiple moments over the weekend where the truth had slipped to the tip of her tongue, only for her to swallow it back down again. A part of her wanted to dissect it with Sara, ask for advice even, but another, stronger part of her, wanted it for herself, the memory left pure, untouched by any opinion but her own. So, Sara remained oblivious, and with each day that Cathy hugged the secret closer; the less likely she was to ever share it.

"She really is quite beautiful," a new voice said from the doorway.

Speaking of secrets ...

The two women turned their eyes on Max; Sandra brightening; Cathy unable to prevent her scowl.

"How long have you been together?" He asked, as if being polite, as if his singular intention wasn't to push the limits of her patience.

She gave him a withering look that told him exactly how unimpressed she was. And after his post-sex coldness, she was not in the mood for any of his teasing. Not in the mood for him full stop.

"Erm ... not long, only a few months."

"Did you always know you were into women?"

She very much wanted to tell him to fuck off, would have done if not for Sandra sat there.

"No, actually. I'd never fancied girls before I started living with Sara and accidentally saw her naked once. And, well, things changed," she replied, her tone bright for Sandra, her smile scathing for Max.

"How extraordinary ..." he said, words heavily laced with sarcasm, amusement dancing in his eyes. "Well, I just wanted to thank you both for your hard work organising the party. I look forward to the next." His gaze switched between the two of them, lingering on Cathy. He made to leave, turning around at the last second as if only just remembering he had something else to say, though Cathy knew everything he did was purposeful and premeditated. "I'm in meetings most of the day but, Cathy, I would like to see you at half-four to discuss the monthly reports."

"Of course," she said, giving him a questioning look he didn't care to answer, as he turned away and disappeared into his office.

"Well," Sandra carried on as if she hadn't noticed the drop and rise in temperature coinciding with Max's presence in the room. "If I'd known you had a partner, I never would have suggested anything between you and Max. I really do apologise for the whole misunderstanding. It was very unprofessional of me."

Cathy tried to smile. "Honestly, it's fine."

"Good. Well, let's get to it then." Sandra wandered over to her desk and back again, returning with a ream of paper. "Lisa's team has been down two people for a week, so they're running a little behind with data entry. I offered our help." She dropped the stack in front of Cathy with a deliberate thump, flashed a mischievous smile, and headed back to her paperless desk.

"Wonderful," Cathy muttered under her breath, and she grabbed the first sheet.

*

At four thirty-five, she knocked on Max's door and entered. She didn't give him the satisfaction of her attention as she crossed the room and sat down, looking out the window at the early winter night while he finished his phone call. She knew he watched her, saw every movement her body made, noticed every subtle change to her bored expression. Before, she'd liked having his eyes on her, but that casual fuck had demonstrated exactly how special she was: remarkable enough to fuck once but not remarkable enough to fuck again. She wouldn't let it damage her ego – what was one man's opinion after all? *He's not just any man*, her psyche started to argue – but she'd decided, over the course of a particularly dreary day, that there would be no more teasing, no more smart comments, no more pushing of professional boundaries. He'd told her what he thought of her, so now she would be what he deemed her: unremarkable.

Still, it was rather hard to forget the fact they'd seen each other naked.

She heard him set the phone down and lean back in his chair, the padded leather sighing quietly at his movement.

She felt his eyes on her, felt him waiting, eager for her attention. He quickly grew impatient.

"Cathy," he ordered, so she slowly turned her eyes on him. He rested a thoughtful hand under his chin as he held her empty gaze. "Is everything all right?"

"Everything is fine, thank you," she replied coolly. "You wanted to discuss the monthly reports?"

He frowned. "I told you it wasn't the start of anything."

"Are there new reports or changes to existing ones you'd like me to make?"

"And I'm pretty sure you understood that, so what have I done to offend you?"

She didn't answer.

"Well?" He prompted.

"We're not here to talk about the reports at all, are we?"

"No, we're not."

She folded her arms and crossed her legs, noticing his eyes flicker to where her skirt rode up her thigh. "So, what then?"

"First, tell me why you're sulking."

"I'm not sulking," she almost snapped. "I just thought that since it was a one-off, we should be professional with one another."

"And you call this professional?"

She shrugged.

"Well, I'm going to put professionalism to one side for a moment," he calmly informed her. "Because what I wanted to talk about is not to do with work, but rather the 'one-off' that has clearly left a sour taste in your mouth."

"Exactly. It was a 'one-off'. Just enough to satisfy your curiosity—"

"Trust me, I'm not satisfied in the slightest." His heated smirk did nothing to soften the blow of his words.

She straightened indignantly in her seat. "Thanks for the feedback; sorry for the disappointment. It was my first time, I'll get better," she grumbled, reddening as his eyebrows rose in surprise.

"Cathy, you already have the two main things down."

"Really?" Gosh, why did him just saying her name turn her on?

"Enthusiasm, and a willingness to communicate." His expression darkened, a playful smile teasing her for a moment before his words overtly flirted with her. "Everything else is just a matter of practice, and we have plenty of time for that."

"We have plenty of time for what?" She dumbly asked, her mind becoming as flustered as her body.

"I have a proposition for you." His mouth flattened as her eyes narrowed with intrigue. "It might not be appealing to you, given your current state of mind, but I'll offer anyway. If you refuse, then no harm done, and we can revert to being wholly *professional* with one another." He paused to assess her, eyes lingering on her lips and where her shirt pulled snugly across her breasts. "I'm keen to make the 'one-off' a regular occurrence. In exchange for your company and fidelity, I will pay you generously. I promise it would be very worth your while."

At some point her mouth had dropped open. It had to be a joke, a trick of some sort, but she had never known him to be malicious – a little cruel, yes, but never genuinely mean. Mockery wasn't his style. So, it had to be a genuine offer ...

"You just said I was disappointing!" Was the first thing her frazzled mind decided to fixate on.

"No, you inferred that," he replied with frustrating calmness. "I said I wasn't satisfied because there are so many more things I'd like to do to you."

She flushed. *Oh, well that's much better than being actively bad in bed.* So that left the money curveball to hit back at him.

"Even so, I'm definitely not good enough at sex to charge for it," she said, trying to keep her voice steady. She'd never expected to be offered money for sex ... She wasn't attractive enough, not inherently sexual enough. It didn't make sense, no matter how her brain tried to spin it. "If you genuinely *want* to pay for sex, I can give you Sara's number," she offered.

"I don't want Sara."

"Escorting is what she does, and I gather she's rather good at it. Anyway, you said it yourself, she's beautiful."

He leaned forward, face devoid of humour as he repeated, "I don't want Sara."

"But she's sexy and gorgeous and pretty much better than me in every single way!"

"And yet," he purred, "It's not the thought of her that makes me hard."

Well, if she hadn't been turned on before, she was now.

"I don't understand ..." she started, pausing as she watched him get to his feet and walk to the door to lock it. Something made her stand up as he slowly walked back. "If you like me, why not just date me?"

"I don't do relationships," he replied blandly, as if there was nothing untoward about such a statement.

What kind of man, especially a man as rich and attractive as him, would choose to pay for sex over being in a relationship? The world was tilting again, shifting into something new. She'd transmuted from wanting romance to accepting casual sex – for him – but now there was sex work on the horizon. That had to be a step too far, right?

"Why?" She asked, as if a decent enough answer could persuade her.

"I just don't."

Hmm, not convinced.

"But—"

He grasped her face in his hands, large palms covering her cheeks, and pulled her into a kiss. Despite her better judgement, she kissed him back. His kisses were filled with fire, just like his words, just like every single look he gave her. She breathed in his heat and felt her body set alight.

Her thighs touched the edge of the desk. He continued to drink kisses from her, pushing her further back until she had to put her hands behind her on the solid wood. Fingers unbuttoned the top of her blouse and lips placed kisses over the swell of her breasts.

"It would be good for you too," he whispered between kisses. "I'm not selfish when it comes to sex, since I get off on seeing my partner come."

"I know," she breathed, she blushed, as all rationality seeped from her mind.

"And I promise I'm not Christian Grey—"

"You're not rich enough."

He laughed; a low rumble deep in his throat. "True. But I also don't want to hurt you. Pain isn't really my thing. But I do like to be in charge."

As if to prove his point, his hand buried under the waistband of her skirt, pushed aside the tuck-in blouse, undeterred even by the presence of tights. He found his way under all the layers to reach her underwear, fingers delving inside to hold her burning sex without missing a beat. A small part of her brain wondered if she should be letting him come on so strongly, taking what he wanted as if he had permission; the larger part of it didn't care, especially at his next words, whispered in her ear: "And I want to make you feel good."

She wanted to feel good too.

He made true to his words a second later, one finger testing her wetness before stroking her clit. She sagged against the desk, barely managing to keep her elbows locked and her body upright as he continued to touch her.

"This is why I wanted to watch you," he explained, his voice low, velvety. "I wanted to learn how you like it, so that I could make you feel good. Fuck ... You look so sexy when you're aroused. These flushed cheeks and parted lips." He stroked a thumb over her bottom-lip. “You can barely keep your eyes open.”

Her eyes fluttered open and closed as she drowned under the sensation of her clit being rubbed. The heat started to build in little crests of pleasure that drew sighs from her lips.

There was a knock at the door.

Panic made her push him back but he held his ground, his finger keeping their rhythm.

“Forget it,” he ordered. “I want to see you come.”

“But—”

He silenced her with a kiss. His touch became firmer, the sparks of pleasure suddenly sharp, almost painful.

There was another knock at the door.

She winced as she concentrated, the sudden urgency making her desperate for it to be over.

“Come for me,” he whispered in her ear.

She focused on her clit, felt its heat and impatience, and willed it to concede.

Her body gave in. As she started to moan, savouring each pulse of the orgasm, his lips locked with hers to soften her sounds. When it started to fade away, she noticed how heavy her breathing was, how weak her limbs were. She looked up at Max’s smug face and read the unspoken question in his smirk.

Can you really resist me?

Just as abruptly as the first time, he removed himself and walked away. Too flustered to quickly neaten her appearance, she collapsed onto the chair and hoped the visitor wouldn't notice her. After a mumbled conversation by the door, Max returned, leaning back on the desk in front of her, his crotch level with her eyes. She had no doubt it was intentional.

"So," he began, still wearing the same arrogant smile, as if one orgasm was all she'd needed to convince her. "How about my offer?"

"I still don't see why you'd rather pay than date me," she muttered back, holding herself steady when all her body wanted to do was fall into his arms. "It's not exactly complimentary."

"I mean no offence by it. And it doesn't have to make sense. Just consider my offer as it stands."

"I don't want to sell my body."

"Then don't," he said levelly. "But at least think about it. You could quit this job, or go part time and focus on your writing, or just enjoy the extra income. Like I said, I'd make it worth your time."

"How much?"

"It's negotiable."

She could tell he wasn't going to say any more about it until he had her approval. It was objectively a good offer. She would get to have sex with a guy she was slowly becoming crazy about *and* get paid for it. And yet, by paying her, it meant he'd probably never be crazy about her back.

After making him patiently wait for her opinion, she got to her feet, and finally shared it.

"I'm not interested. If you want to fuck me, you can date me."

"You want me to fuck you, so why not get some money out of it too?"

"I ..."

"Just think about it. You might change your mind when you realise it's a beneficial arrangement for both of us," he added with a smile before dismissing her. "Enjoy your evening."

Chapter Thirteen

You might change your mind ...

He could change his fucking mind more like.

But after a week of swanning around him in short skirts and tight blouses; nothing changed. So, she decided to end the matter and try to find a guy that would actually commit to her.

"Any plans for the weekend?" Sandra asked her on Friday, as they both waited for five o'clock to arrive.

Cathy was about to reply with her usual *No, not really*, and then spend the next twenty minutes half-listening to Sandra ramble on about her *extraordinarily interesting* plans, but Max stepped into the office, so she decided to share a little.

"Yes, actually. I've got a date tomorrow night," she said, deliberately not paying Max any attention.

"What about Sara?"

Oh shit, Sara, my imaginary girlfriend.

"Oh, yeah, I meant a double date." *Nice save*. "A friend of ours is meeting a guy for the first time, and she thought it would be more fun with us there."

"How did she get to know him?" Max asked from where he stood, leaning against the doorframe, piercing eyes on her.

"Through a dating app."

"You do have to be so careful meeting people like that," Sandra muttered. "It's no wonder she wants you two along."

"Yeah, well, he sounds nice, and they've been chatting for a week, so I'm hopeful they'll get along. It's about time she found someone steady." She turned feisty eyes on Max, disappointed to find him looking rather uninterested.

"Are you going anywhere nice?"

"Erm ..." Cathy turned her attention back to Sandra. "A little Italian restaurant called Sorelle, if you know it. It's my favourite."

"And your friend's too, I suppose?" Max asked slyly before slinking from the room.

Cathy's eyes watched the doorway long after he'd gone, feeling an uncomfortable sense of humbleness washing over her. Of course he didn't care. Why would he? She'd said no and he'd moved on. Shame on her for assuming she'd hold his attention for longer than a week. Maybe she should have accepted ...

"Well, I hope your friend enjoys herself," Sandra concluded.

"Me too." She shook herself back to the present. "What about you? Any plans?"

"Yes, we're super busy. Martin is visiting ..."

Cathy's attention wavered but she remembered to intermittently smile and nod for the next half an hour, like a good little assistant's assistant.

*

"How do I look?"

"Like you put in minimal effort," Sara replied, scowling at Cathy's half-hearted attempt at getting dressed up. "Are you not even going to wear heels?"

Cathy glanced down at the black ankle boots she was wearing. "I really don't enjoy wearing them, so no. Anyway, he might as well get to know the real me, which, when it comes to my appearance, minimal effort is an accurate description."

"I'd say," Sara confirmed, looking in the mirror to check her makeup. "It's not often we're both out on a Saturday evening."

"By which you mean, it's strange for *me* to be out."

"Just a shame it's not with Max. I really thought he was into you."

"Yeah, well ..." Cathy checked the time, feeling the secret inside her growing bigger. "Sara, your lipstick is fine. I really need to go."

"Calm your tits. I'm ready."

They shared a taxi to the city centre, stepping out under a canopy of almost tasteful Christmas lights. After a few words of encouragement, Sara strutted away, disappearing into the crowd of late-night Christmas shoppers and early partygoers, heading to whichever VIP bar she was meeting her client at. Cathy blew her cheeks out against the cold, acknowledging the waves of dread and anxiety that washed over her, before firmly pushing them aside. Her phone buzzed.

SARA: You're going to be fine! If he turns out to be a creep or boring as fuck, just say "sorry, got to go, crimson wave" and leg it. At least you won't have to pay.

CATHY: Have you used that line before?

SARA: Only twice! But really, good luck.

SARA: And give me a heads up if he ends up back at the flat with you ;)

CATHY: Won't happen but okay.

SARA: Love you xx

CATHY: Love you xx

Feeling a little lighter, Cathy followed the crowds down the street until she arrived at the tiny Italian restaurant she'd visited countless times before. Its familiarity calmed her further as she stepped inside, remembering immediately why she loved the place, with its quaint little tables, overfilled flower vases, and excessive candlelight. She gave her name to the manager and was shown to her table by the window, her date already sat there waiting.

Mark got to his feet as she approached, leaning in to kiss her cheek.

"Cathy, nice to meet you."

"Yes, you too."

They sat down, eyes subtly comparing the person before them with the photos they'd seen online. Mark had a pleasant but rather unremarkable face, a good head of short sandy-brown hair, clean-shaven jaw, slightly angular nose, and ears that may have been a tiny bit too small for his head. Wonderfully average. His smile was kind, if a little unsure of itself, his eyes shy, eye-contact seemingly a plight they had in common. Yet it only took about ten minutes for her to find talking to a man who wasn't overflowing with confidence to be, not only refreshing, but also a bit like pulling teeth.

"So, you're a scientist?" She boldly paved the way towards some wholesome conversation once they'd placed their order. "That's a bit vague," she gently teased.

"Um, yes. I work in a lab testing pharmaceutical drugs before they're used in trials."

"Oh, that must be interesting."

"Not really. It's very repetitive," he said shortly.

"Right ... Well, I can't say my job is interesting either but, you know, it pays the bills and could lead somewhere one day. The company is very supportive if people want to do qualifications or training ..." She paused to let him ask her a question, but she was met with silence. So, she searched her brain for a new topic, grateful for their drinks arriving so that she could take a sip and stall a little longer. "Sorry if I'm being a little awkward, but this is the first date I've ever been on. Have you dated much?"

"No, not really," he replied nonchalantly.

"Okay ... I also recently started going to life drawing classes. It was my friend's idea ..." She fell silent at the look of horror on his face.

It took until after the starters for Mark to warm up a little. Cathy put it down to nerves, but even after he realised he would actually have to participate to make any semblance of conversation happen, it was often halting and stagnant. She sighed with genuine relief when he excused himself to use the bathroom after he'd finished his main course. At least it was just dessert to go ...

"That bad?" A voice asked.

Her eyes snapped open, but rather than a cheeky waiter or sympathetic diner she'd expected to see, it was Max taking the temporarily vacant seat across from her. *What the fuck ...*

"Max! What are you doing here? Are you like, stalking me?" She babbled.

The only response she got was a dark smile and a question. "Are you trying to make me jealous?"

That calmed her suddenly malfunctioning brain. *Maybe he is still into me?*

She decided to join in with his game.

"Is it working?"

"I wouldn't be here if it wasn't," he admitted, while blatantly undressing her with his eyes. "Are you going to sleep with him?"

"I don't see how, as my employer, that is of any relevance to you."

His smile pulled to one side. His lips parted to say some scandalous retort, but he was beaten to it.

"Um, excuse me. That's my seat," Mark announced, standing next to the table.

Max leaned back and slowly turned his eyes on him. "You don't need it anymore," he said coldly.

"Excuse me?"

"Trust me, you're not her type."

Mark took a step back in offence. "What makes you say that?"

"You're not me," Max explained, wearing the cockiest smile she'd ever seen anyone wear *ever*.

Mark's mouth opened to retort but no words came out. His eyes sought Cathy, expecting her to jump to his defence, but she was stunned, mortified on his behalf whilst simultaneously never being more attracted to Max. She was appalled at herself. And yet, as callous as the whole situation was, there was no iteration in the whole damn multiverse where she'd even contemplated choosing Mark over Max.

Only a deep-rooted sense of politeness made her raise her eyes to him.

"Sorry," she winced, before shamefully lowering her gaze.

"Here," Max said, everything about him still ridiculously laidback, as if he started pissing contests and won every night. He took Mark's jacket from the back of the chair and passed it to him. "The evening isn't a complete loss. At least you got a free meal out of it." He then turned his attention firmly back to Cathy.

It took a painfully long time for the cuckolded Mark to finally leave. Cathy couldn't look at him or Max while he was still stood over her, worried how much her face would give away. While her heart ached with sympathy for him, the longer he stood there, the more desperate she was for him to leave, the less charitable her opinion of him became. *If you hadn't been so painfully awkward. If you had been so utterly uninspiring ...*

She stared at the peonies in the middle of the table, until there was movement in her periphery, a shadow wordlessly leaving.

Thank God, she thought one moment.

I'm a terrible person, she thought the next.

She raised moody eyes to Max. He was sat comfortably in his seat, arms folded across his chest, patiently waiting for her attention, never doubting she would give it to him. She just knew he hadn't given Mark a second glance.

"That was probably one of the rudest things I've ever seen," she chided him, indignation rushing through her once again. It was easier to direct it at him rather than herself. No one, especially not quiet, unassuming people, deserved that kind of treatment, and especially not from the likes of Max: alpha vs beta was an unfair fight, almost no fight at all. "It's not okay to be so arrogant."

Max leaned forward, drawing her eyes to his chest shifting beneath his white work shirt, and then onto that wicked mouth as it whispered, "But it turned you on, right?" It caught her off-guard, her widening eyes all the confirmation he needed. "So it was worth it."

It was clear that Mark meant nothing to him. But what about her?

"Was it worth ruining my date for? *My* evening?" She snapped, feeling the indignation turn to fury inside her.

At least it made his smile dim a little.

"That date wasn't going anywhere," he told her, his voice low and steady as if to convince her the games were over. "You don't want him, or anyone else—"

"Because I only want you?" She finished, words laced with contempt.

He didn't flinch. "At the moment, yes."

"But you don't want to be with me, so it doesn't matter."

"I do want you."

"But you don't want to *be* with me."

"No—" Max was cut off as a waitress approached with two desserts. He waited impatiently while she set them down and scurried out of earshot. "No," he repeated. "I don't want to be with you romantically."

"But why?" She whined.

His jaw locked. "I don't want to be with anyone. I have no interest in maintaining a relationship," he muttered tightly, before his words came a little easier. "But I want you. I want you quite badly. And I appreciate that you do want to settle down one day, but that doesn't mean an arrangement between us wouldn't work in the meantime. If you meet someone you like, we can stop. If you ever just don't want to fuck around with me anymore, then we can stop."

Goddamnit, he was almost convincing.

"Then why pay me?" She asked in a small voice.

"To set and maintain the boundary. It's a transaction, nothing more. Even if I buy you things, or take you places, or hold you while you fall asleep; it will always be me paying you for the privilege. And when the money stops; we stop."

"Do you have an idea how long you'd want it to last?"

"For me; indefinitely. So, it will probably be you who calls it off," he admitted.

Her mind was reeling. That was it then, his offer laid out on the table. No relationship, not even fuckbuddies; sex work or nothing. She sat with that truth for a moment, really contemplated it, whispered the word *escort* to herself. The word didn't suit her, didn't *fit* her, but if that was the only way, if that was what she had to become ... Was he worth the price on her psyche? This man who didn't compromise. This man who took what he wanted. At least he was being transparent, seemingly sincere. As bizarre and unnecessary such an arrangement seemed to her, it obviously made sense to him, worked for him...

"Have you done this before?" She asked, nausea stirring in her stomach at the slight discomfort that briefly crossed his face.

"Yes, a few times."

Well, that put it into perspective. She really wouldn'tbe anything special, just his latest personal whore. Her eyes widened at a sickening thought.

"Was Sandra right? You hire girls just to make them your next ..." But she didn't know the correct term. She almost said victim.

"Fuck no." His abhorrence at the accusation was palpable; immediate and genuine. The following sigh was as annoyed as it was disgusted, his composure slipping as he sat back in his chair and ran a hand through his hair. "I can see how it looks bad, but I've never had an arrangement with anyone at work before. You're an exception. And I couldn't exactly fire you just because I wanted to fuck you."

I'm an exception? Flatter me some more, Max.

"So, this wasn't your plan when you hired me?"

His stare hardened. "No. I hired you because I enjoyed your honesty, and I like the way you think. Turns out I like it a bit too much, along with the rest of you."

She flushed at the compliment, felt the tingle of a high at the confession that he liked her, that she was more than just a sex object. But that still didn't quite banish her suspicion. "So why did the last one end?"

"She became too attached, so I called it off. It wasn't pleasant," he elaborated, at Cathy's morbid frown. "But it wasn't fair on her to let it continue. I would end *this* if I had to."

This. Us.

So, this was the way he did it. No relationships, just sex. She wondered for a moment why that was the case – he wasn't fooling anyone; there had to be more to it than just disinterest in maintaining a relationship and apathy towards romance – but her thoughts quickly moved on to the more pressing matter of what she should do. She decided to ask herself some simple, mostly non-loaded, questions:

1. *Would I like to sleep with him again? Yes.*
2. *Would I like to earn some extra money? Suppose so.*
3. *If I did fall madly in love with him, could I cope with it not being reciprocated? Probably. People get heart-broken all the time. People get over it. So would I.*

It made sense. If she thought about it objectively, she would gain so much from the arrangement. It was a good deal. And yet, a whisper at the back of her mind told her she was only thinking that because she hoped he'd fall for her anyway, despite the past, despite himself.

"Okay," she said, carrying on quickly at the beginnings of a victorious smile on his face. "But how much?"

"How much do you want?"

"I have no idea how much these things cost ... sell for."

"How does five hundred sound?"

"A month?"

"A night," he clarified, his smug smile returning in full force. "I said I'd make it worth your while."

"But that's insane! How often?"

"It's flexible, but at least once a week. So, do you accept?" He encouraged, looking to close. "Five hundred for every night you spend with me and your fidelity while the arrangement stands?"

Oh, go on then.

"I do, but I have a condition of my own."

The words surprised her: an intrusive thought transforming into intrusive speech before her mind had even noticed the security breach. But she couldn't unsay them, so she had to get the rest out.

Her mouth was suddenly dry, her tongue heavy. A flash flood of sweat wrecked her body, as she tried to get out the words she shouldn't say.

"Go on," he ordered calmly, though with a slight edge to his tone, a stiffness to his shoulders. He clearly wasn't used to his business partners making demands of their own.

She took a deep, bracing breath. "My one condition is that we don't use protection."

His scowl was immediate. It darkened at the sight of the waitress approaching.

"Can I get you ..." She looked at their untouched desserts, half-full wine glasses, Max's unforgiving expression, and froze.

"We're fine, thank you," Max told her, not moving his eyes from Cathy.

As the waitress walked away, Cathy felt her heartbeat quicken in anticipation of his next words. She hadn't expected him to take the request well, but he looked like he was about to snap the table in half.

"Are you infertile?" He asked, his voice coiled tight, just like his fists where they rested on the table.

"I think you mean sterile. It's a common misconception, but infertile "

"Cathy." He growled in such a way that made her spine tingle. "Now is not the time to get clever with me."

Ah.

"Not that I know of," she admitted quietly.

"Then what possible reason could you have for wanting to risk getting pregnant?" He suddenly wore a particularly malicious smirk. "It didn't seem like the money was that important to you, but getting pregnant; I can't help but think it's a scheme to get child support payments from me for the next eighteen years. Though why you wouldn't have just lied about going on the pill, I'm not sure ..."

She leaned back, affronted. "I'm not scheming."

"Then what is this?"

"If I did get pregnant, I wouldn't expect any money, or anything else, from you towards the child. I'll even sign something to that effect if it would put your mind at rest."

"So, you want to live on benefits?"

"I have the means to provide for a child without the support of the father or society," she snapped.

"Regardless, I'm struggling to think of a plausible reason as to why a twenty-three-year-old graduate, who could do whatever she wanted, would *choose* to become a single parent," he said, his tone bitingly cold.

But she wasn't to be deterred by his derision. She could change parts of herself for him, give him pieces to hold and never return, but this was addressing the part of her that couldn't be altered; permanent, fundamental. The part that made her, *her*.

"I've never had the ambition to become anything, apart from a half-serious pipedream at being a writer. But I do know I want to be a mother," she said tightly, trying to justify herself, even though she knew he wouldn't agree. He was an achiever, a somebody, but that wasn't her and it never would be. "You've made it quite clear that, in you, I'm not going to find a long-term partner, and there's no saying I will in anyone else. So, I might as well take this opportunity. If it happens, it happens. If not, then whatever. I'm not going to be tracking my ovulation or suggesting weird sex positions, if that's what you're worried about. But without any concerns about me, or being financially ensnared for the next eighteen years, I can still appreciate why you wouldn't want to father a child you'd have nothing to do with."

For a relationship that was built purely on sexual attraction, it was getting a bit serious. She was almost surprised he was still talking to her, hadn't just called her unhinged and left to prepare her termination letter.

"That doesn't really bother me," he said blandly.

"Really?"

"With straight sex, there's always a risk of pregnancy. This really isn't that different, but at least I know you're a decent human being who would probably make a decent parent. And assuming you do somehow have the means to be financially secure, I know their quality of life won't be compromised." He tapped his fingers on the table as he looked down, a frown pulling his brows together. "Anyway, conceiving a child doesn't make you a father; raising one does. I'd consider myself little more than a sperm donor in this case ..."

"Max?" She asked as his voice trailed off.

He raised his eyes to her, the seriousness of his expression leaving her raw.

"Fine, no contraception. And if you get pregnant; it's over."

"Okay," she answered weakly.

"I hope you know what you're doing."

I hope so too.

"I do," she said, with more confidence than she felt.

"Good." He smiled, but the harshness remained in his eyes. "We can start tomorrow, if you're free?"

She nodded.

"I'll text you my address." He got out his wallet, casually dropping five twenties onto the table. "Send me your bank details."

"Wait!" She exclaimed as he got up and started to walk away. "What do I tell my friends when I disappear for hours, or *nights*?"

He shrugged. "Whatever you want. If the truth is too unsavoury, tell them we're dating. I don't care."

Maybe he noticed her dejection. Maybe he wanted to dispel the solemn mood that had settled between them. Whatever it was, something made him turn back, place a hand under her chin, and lean down until his face was an inch away. He smelt of expensive aftershave that tricked her mind into imagining him naked. He looked as gorgeous as always, his frown as sexy as his smile, but she was glad to see kindness in his eyes after all the tension. She liked the reassuring hand on her chin, forcing her to see him and only him, a gentle reminder that he was and always would be in control.

"I look forward to tomorrow," he said, closing the distance to steal a deep kiss from her; lips lingering, tongues entwining. She forgot all about the public setting they were in as the kiss passed right through her, bringing her body back to life and convincing her mind that she had absolutely made the right choice. She would take as much of him as she could get; as much as he was willing to give.

He pulled back and turned away, his half-smile bolstering her confidence. She watched him until he disappeared from the restaurant, the warmth the kiss had filled her with lingering.

"Tomorrow," she whispered, before turning her attention to the two desserts that still needed eating, almost breaking into a fit of giggles as she wondered what the other patrons must have thought of her, starting the evening with one man, ending it by kissing another. Their thoughts might have been right on the money.

She was officially a scandalous woman after all.

Chapter Fourteen

Cathy paid the bill with Max's generous hundred pounds, leaving the remainder as a tip to compensate for being such dramatic diners, and texted Sara as she headed towards the main road to meet her Uber.

CATHY: Meal finished, about to head home (alone).

SARA: I'm all done here too!

SARA: Pick me up on the way? I'm at The Royal.

CATHY: Sure. I'll be there in a few minutes.

SARA: Thank you!

It was only a short wait for the Uber and an even shorter drive through the empty streets to the hotel. Sara was waiting outside, looking like a lost Hollywood starlet with her bold makeup and the collar of her faux-fur-lined coat clutched between leather-gloved hands under her chin. As Cathy waved through the window, Sara ran over with perfect balance despite the four-inch stiletto heels she wore. She bundled herself into the car and immediately showed Cathy her widest smile.

"How did it go?"

But Cathy was more concerned with her friend's unusually early finish.

"Is everything all right? With your client?"

"Oh, yeah, fine. He just needed me gone because his wife decided to fly over. So I got full pay for half the time! Anyway, Mark?"

Cathy tried for a demure smile to hide her lies. "Yeah, he was nice, actually."

"Just nice?"

"Sometimes nice is good enough! At least good enough for a second date. I'm seeing him again tomorrow, at his place."

"Oh, wow, Cathy," her friend cheered. "This is so good! Maybe he's the one ..."

"Maybe." Cathy's smile wilted, one lie spinning into another before she'd even had the time to think it through. It was too late. She couldn't bring Max into it now, especially not after she had agreed to whore herself out to him. Despite Sara's occupation, she knew the truth would go down like scalding hot black coffee. It would cause drama no one needed. Better to lie. Keep calm and lie and lie and lie.

Right?

Once they'd returned home, Cathy followed Sara into her room and belly-flopped onto the bed. She watched as her friend stepped out of her heels and sat down at the dressing table to slowly remove the layers of makeup she hid herself behind. Cathy knew the real Sara; a Sara that rolled out of bed on a morning to spend all day painting or crocheting, never changing out of her pyjamas, the thought of putting on makeup or styling her hair not once crossing her mind. She was two people: the wholesome artist and the glamour model, or whatever the man paying her wanted her to be. And yet the whole selling-her-body thing, it didn't seem to weigh her down or diminish her at all.

"Sara," Cathy started hesitantly, waiting for her friend to meet her eyes in the mirror. "How do you do it? The whole escorting thing, I mean."

It was a risk bringing it up, but she wanted to know how mixing business with pleasure worked, what the price on her identity would be, what becoming a *whore* would do to her.

"It's really not that difficult. A bit of style, a bit of confidence ... Oh, you mean, like emotionally?" Sara asked, scrunching her nose up at Cathy's bad-smell of an expression. "Do you have a problem with me doing it?"

"Not at all," she quickly reassured, internalising the panic that had leaked onto her face. "You have the right to do whatever you want with your body ..."

Her thoughts became scattered for a moment, as she mentally berated herself. She would never call Sara a whore, had never looked down on her for her choices – she'd been in awe of them if anything, that fearless ownership over her own existence – so why didn't she extend the same kindness to herself?

She shook her head clear. "But, if I ever try to picture myself doing it, it feels so wrong, like I'd be selling a piece of myself, like it's degrading in some way ... I know it isn't."

Sara smiled, utterly unoffended, mildly perplexed. "Well, then it isn't for you."

That was a kick in the chest. It took everything to keep her expression smooth.

"But for me," Sara continued, "Sex has never been a sacred thing. I'm not losing anything because I'm not giving anything away. And there is nothing degrading about being in charge of your own choices. Honestly, I would find it more degrading to sit at a desk all day, making rich men richer," she said, her voice a knife that wasn't quite sharp enough to draw blood. "No offence."

Okay, I deserved that one.

"I don't know how you do it," Sara added, her smile a little warmer, her stare pointed.

"Do what?"

"Have someone put a price on your time, tell you when to work, what to do and how to do it. The sheer lack of autonomy."

Cathy shrugged. "I quite like letting someone else decide those things."

Sara sniggered.

"What?" She asked, not completely sure she wanted to know the answer.

"Spoken like a good little submissive. Let's hope Mark is a dom."

Cathy's face burned, right up to her ears. A self-conscious laugh spluttered out of her at Sara's scandalous smile.

"Please don't," she begged, hiding her face behind her hands. "I have no idea what I am."

"*Yet.*" Sara left a pause. It grew heavy with mounting suspicions. "Is this about your date? If Mark—"

Cathy tore her hands away. "*No.* No. I was honestly just curious, since your night ended early ..."

"Ah. I'm probably going to sound like a bitch," Sara said, crossing her long legs as she peeled off her fake eyelashes. It was a weirdly gruesome sight, the viscous glue clinging, lifting her eyelid away from her eyeball. "But if there is any dishonesty, any cheating, that's on the client, not me. Most of the time, I wouldn't know anyway."

"Makes sense."

"My work isn't emotionless, but it's safer to not get *emotional* about it." Off came the earrings, necklaces, and bracelets. Then she started rubbing away the paint on her nails. "Anyway, ultimately, I couldn't do a desk job. I value my independence too much. I pick my clients, I pick my hours, and I make good money, all for me. Luckily, I had a pretty easy time getting into it. I've always known the male gaze loves me," she explained, nothing boastful in her tone; it was just a fact. "And it helps that I have a wide appeal; white enough for some, 'exotic' to others." She laughed as Cathy screwed her nose up. "I know, but I am absolutely going to capitalise on their racial biases."

"Oh, for sure." Cathy agreed, before giving in to her curiosity. "Do you actually enjoy it?"

"Hmm, some of it." Sara leaned back, running the silver chain of her necklace through her fingers. "Some of my clients are into some weird shit. I have my limits but, generally, I'm happy to give them what they want, be what they want, even if it's not my thing. What I do enjoy is how it makes me feel. Not the sex specifically," she rolled her eyes at Cathy's questioning frown. "I mean, sometimes it is enjoyable, sometimes there isn't even sex, but what I enjoy is the feeling of ... power, I suppose."

"Power?"

"So, my clients, right? They're all wealthy guys, hugely successful in their careers, disgustingly privileged, making obscene amounts of money. They're at the top of their game. But when they're with me, they're the vulnerable one, laying out their needs, trusting me to fulfil them. Usually sex. But sometimes they just need physical contact, or a sympathetic ear, someone to listen all the things they couldn't tell anyone else – because it's lonely at the top, or whatever. When we're together, in that luxury hotel room *they're* paying for, I am the most important person in the world ... until his wife rings saying she'll be there in half an hour," she added dryly. "And I'm not going to look this good forever, so I might as well make the most of it."

"I like that," Cathy said. "Balancing the power dynamic. But ... doesn't the money get in the way of that?"

Sara tapped a nude finger against her temple. "It's like most things in life: it's all about perspective. And people often forget that they're in control of how they perceive things, for the most part. Yes, I'm effectively 'selling' my body, but I don't think that's much different to how everyone else sells their time. At least I always have ownership over myself. With a client, if I don't want to do something, I won't. And if they're not happy about that, then there are plenty of other women out there who might. Paid or unpaid, sex is a choice. My choice. That's the most important thing. Anyway, I would like to take off this horrendously uncomfortable bra—"

"I'll leave you to it," Cathy smiled, suddenly feeling tired, but calmer, reassured. She had made a choice. The arrangement wasn't inherently right or wrong. It was just what two informed adults had agreed to, and it was okay for her to make the most of it. It didn't have to make her feel small or unclean. She should probably stop calling *herself* derogatory slurs, even if they felt valid. And no more doubt. That one was easy, any reservations immediately vanishing at the thought of him, the man she would be anything for, morals and dreams be damned.

Sara had spoken so levelly, so honestly. Maybe she could have handled the truth ...

"Are you okay though?" Sara asked, her tone full of kind concern. "I know dating can be scary. If you're worried about anything, even sex, I'm here, you know. Nothing is too much for me; I'll talk about anything."

Cathy paused, the secret jumping halfway up her throat before slipping back down again at the sight of Sara's tired but untroubled eyes, her statement from earlier echoing in her ears.

Then it isn't for you.

It *had* to be for her.

"Oh, I know you like things juicy." She forced a grin. "I'm fine, really. Curious – excited – to see where it will take me. I just want to make sure you're happy."

"Honest to God, I'm living my best life."

"Good. Love you," she whispered as she slowly shut the door.

"Love you too, darling."

Chapter Fifteen

Rather than try to navigate unknown streets on her little moped, she took a taxi to Max's address the following evening. She'd been sent off with a symphony of good wishes and unnecessary advice from Sara, that made it blatantly obvious how much she cared and progressively harder for Cathy to maintain her deceptive smile. As she sat in the back of the car, she unleashed her frown and let herself wallow in the icky feeling being a liar stirred in her. The taxi driver, noticing her bleak expression, decided it was best not to ask. Her mood nosedived a second time as she remembered she still hadn't gotten around to lying to her other friend.

Something crinkled against her phone as she retrieved it from her coat pocket. She peered down at the metallic blue square, throwing it into the footwell a second later when she realised what it was, glancing nervously around afterwards. The driver was staring at the road, unaware of the contraband she'd smuggled onboard. *A condom, really, Sara?* She loved the woman, but she could really do with a couple more boundaries.

She pushed the inherently mortifying item under the front seat with her foot and tried to forget all about it, while switching her attention to her phone.

ALISON: How did last night go?

She'd received the text at lunchtime. It was now seven. Hesitant thumbs punched out a response.

CATHY: Hey, sorry for not replying sooner. It went really well, so well that I'm seeing him again tonight! Assume I won't need a ride to work tomorrow ...

Only a minute later, she got a response.

ALISON: That's awesome! I'm really pleased for you. You deserve to be with someone serious. I got the feeling one-night stands weren't really for you.

CATHY: Yeah, probably. I knew what I was doing though.

ALISON: I know but it's still nice to like someone and have them like you back. At least the second time isn't so scary. Have a good evening xx

CATHY: You too. See you tomorrow xx

Phew. At least that was the lying over and done with for now.

Deciding she'd wallowed for long enough, she turned her mind to what the evening had in store for her ... what Max had in store for her.

So absorbed in imagining all manner of sultry potentials, she forgot to watch outside the window. It took the car coming to a stop and the driver ten seconds later declaring "We're here, love" for her to snap back to reality and look outside at the three-story Edwardian townhouse they'd paused in front of, one familiar Maserati parked on the drive before it. In a daze, she paid her fare and thanked the driver, stepping out into pale orange lamplight, eyes still locked on the gorgeous building before her. It wasn't the kind of property she'd been expecting. *Don't young millionaires usually pick flashy penthouse apartments, or have I been reading too many cliché romance novels?* Regardless, it was better than an apartment, and a compliment to the man who managed to keep surprising her.

After quickly checking herself over – no gunk in eyes, no food in teeth, no fly hanging open – she skipped up the short path to the front door, ringing the bell before nerves could get the better of her. As she waited, she turned her attention to the small front garden. It was a mix of low-maintenance woody green shrubbery and flowerless bushes, arranged to appear pleasingly wild, and yet not a single twig crept onto the flagstone path. The door opened behind her.

"Cathy," Max greeted warmly.

She slowly turned her eyes on him, a cautious smile on her face, wondering how on Earth she'd gone from looking for average to having the most remarkable man she'd ever met at her fingertips. *But,* she reminded herself firmly, *this isn't a date; it isn't even a hookup: it's work.*

Though nothing about Max had ever felt like work.

"Max."

"Please, come in," he stepped back, holding the door open for her to pass through into the entrance hall. She heard the door close, and then felt hands on her shoulders in a quiet instruction to remove her coat. "How did you get here?"

"Taxi." She set her bag down and let him slide the coat off her shoulders.

"Good."

She almost laughed at the amount of derision he could put into a single word. "You hate my moped that much?"

"I hate the idea of *you* on a moped, especially in winter. I'm half-tempted to buy you a car."

"Don't you dare," she snapped playfully as he ushered her through into the living room, feeling light with relief that the storm clouds from the previous day had not persisted.

It was a beautiful space, straight out of an interior design catalogue for bachelor millionaires, with a preference for dark woods and colours towards the blue end of the spectrum. Oversized fabric sofas and leather recliners faced a huge TV with all the latest consoles neatly arranged on an oriental table beneath it. Bright, abstract artwork tastefully filled the gaps on the walls; flashes of red and swirls of orange to break up the blues and greys. She didn't even have to go up to them to know they were originals and probably worth more than she'd earn in a year. Before the bay window, almost filling the alcove, was a huge plant in a white pot, long thick stems and wide leaves brushed with an almost iridescent sheen. Above the authentic Edwardian fireplace was a metallic centrepiece, as much clock as art as sculpture, which looked vaguely like a sunflower. Altogether, it was an impressive room, beautifully mixing modern and traditional, with a flair of luxury only excessive wealth could buy. She had no doubt the rest of the house would be just the same.

"Mopeds are objectively less safe," he commented, placing a hand on the small of her back to lead her through into the kitchen.

"And yet there are more car crashes than moped crashes."

"Well, statistically, there are significantly fewer mopeds to have crashes."

Yep, the kitchen was gorgeous, all sleek marble and polished metal, and *vast*. It was a kitchen, dining room, and sunroom all in one.

"Moped riders are also more cautious because we know we don't have a metal box to protect us ... well, the sensible ones," she replied, distracted by the wealth and luxury that surrounded her. Everything was beautiful and militantly neat, almost intimidatingly so, and clean. There wasn't a book or cup out of place, not a mark on the floor or a crumb on the counter. An unnerving lack of dust made the house feel unlived in, staged almost. Or maybe that was just because she never dusted and barely cleaned. The abundance of plants helped a little – leafy monsters in pots on the floor, bright flowers and gnarled succulents on windowsills – because someone had to look after them. Though she couldn't imagine Max doing the rounds with a watering can.

She leaned against the kitchen island as Max retrieved a bottle of white wine from the integrated wine cooler (*obviously, because where else would wine live?*), and started to pour it into two oversized wine glasses (*imagine owning wineglasses – he really has his shit together)*. They easily held half a bottle each.

"And yet, I would much rather my investment was surrounded by a metal box than not."

"Oh, I'm an investment now?" She muttered a little testily, accepting the glass he handed to her. "Be careful you don't start referring to me as property."

"Of course not," he charmed. "Though don't forget that whilst you're here, you're mine."

To business then. She sipped the wine, feeling its crisp coolness spread right through her, soothing the nerves she seemed unable to fully master whenever she was around him. Sips turned into gulps; her glass half-empty by the time she set it down.

"Okay," she started a little breathlessly, as the alcohol brought a flush to her cheeks. "Where do you want me?"

That sparked his amusement.

"This arrangement isn't so that I can bend you over the dining table for a five-minute fuck and send you on your way," he explained wryly. "There's no rush. I'm paying for the night."

"So, I *am* staying over?"

He shrugged. "If you want to. You can go home once we're done if you'd prefer."

"I would like to stay ... I mean, I kind of told Alison I wouldn't need a lift to work ... and I told Sara I'd be gone for the night. I know I should have checked with you first—"

He moved in closer, a hand sliding around her waist as he silenced her with a kiss.

"It's fine. You can come in with me in the morning. Have you had anything to eat?"

She bit her lip, savouring the lingering pressure from the kiss. "I was too nervous to eat anything."

His smile became kind, or as kind as he could manage whilst seeming to find everything she said or did inherently titillating. “There’s nothing to be nervous about.”

“You do remember that I’ve only had sex once? And all I had to do was lie there? I might be terrible—"

He kissed her again, this time deeper, tasting the wine on her tongue, and longer, until the tension left her shoulders. His hands skimmed over the soft wool of her jumper and the worn denim of her favourite jeans to cup her ass, bringing her body in closer. She was about ready to undress herself by the time he stopped.

“You’re not going to be terrible,” he reassured.

“Will you dock my pay if I am?”

That earnt her a rumble of laughter. “No. Now go entertain yourself for ten minutes while I make you some food.”

The fog of lust that had made her eyes heavy suddenly cleared.

“You can’t make me food!”

“Yes, I can. I actually consider myself a fairly competent cook.”

That earnt him an eye roll. “I didn’t mean it like that. *You* are paying *me*. I should be doing things for you, not the other way around!”

“Cathy,” he purred her name. “Forget about the money.”

“I thought the point of the money is that I wouldn’t forget about it?”

"Fine, remember the money, but stop telling me what I should and shouldn't do. And stop making assumptions about what you should be doing. All I want is your company. If I want you to do something, I'll tell you. All right? Otherwise, just be yourself."

She nodded cautiously. "Are you lonely? Is that why you do this?"

"And don't psychoanalyse me," he said half-seriously. "Now, I'm going to make you something to eat, and you're going to let me."

"Yes, sir," she replied saucily as she started to walk away.

"Any dietary requirements? And don't call me sir."

"Master?"

"Max will do just fine."

"How unimaginative ..." She tutted. "But no, except fish is gross and I'm a wimp when it comes to heat."

"Noted," was his deliberately non-judgemental response.

As she heard cupboards open and close, followed by the clank of a pan being set down, she lazily started exploring the open-plan kitchen-diner, her feet quickly finding their way to the glossy black Steinway piano in the far corner.

"I hope you play," she called, raising her voice above the hiss of the frying pan.

"Not as much as I should."

His reply filled her with relief; there was something inherently sad about instruments – especially the best in their class kind – that became nothing more than glorified ornaments.

"Do you?" He asked.

"Only if you count Twinkle Twinkle Little Star and Chopsticks."

"They are essentials in every pianist's repertoire."

With that in mind, she took centre stage and gave him her best rendition of Chopsticks ... on repeat.

"How good are you?" She shouted above the noise, smirking to herself at how bad she was, her finger slipping onto the wrong key yet again, the discordant sound making her grimace.

He finally looked over at her, his smile a playful thing. "Better than you."

"Ouch!" She laughed, pressing firmly on the keys to make her poor playing even more obnoxious. "You'll have to show off for me sometime." But the teasing in her tone faded away at the thought of him sat at the piano, fingers dancing skilfully over the keys, playing for her. Maybe she would sit beside him and rest her head on his shoulder, or stand behind him, her hands skimming over his chest, while he filled the room with beautiful music by his adroit hands ...

His answering smirk was a heated thing. "Gladly."

She had to look away. Lowering her eyes to the keys, she tried to focus on improving her performance. She was on her third attempt when she felt her phone vibrate in her back pocket. The name *Sara* appeared on the screen once she'd retrieved it.

"Hi, Sara. I can confirm I haven't been murdered yet," she said, keeping her voice low.

"You can't be too careful!" Her friend replied passionately.

"Shall I ask him if he plans on murdering me?"

"Cathy, it's not a joke," Sara snapped, uncharacteristically serious. "It happens! Which is why it's so important to take precautions. Take it from someone whose job is being alone with unknown men. Always make sure someone knows where you are, always—"

"I know, I know," she conceded, but her smile held; Sara's fussiness was just a demonstration of her affection. "I do appreciate you checking up on me but, honestly; he's good."

"That's what they all think before they're strangled, chopped up, and stuffed in a suitcase!" There was a moment of silence while Sara realised it wasn't quite the right time to be thinking about violent homicides. After she cleared the morbidity from her throat, her tone was suddenly much brighter. "Anyway, how's it going? Apart from the not being murdered thing, which is a big plus!"

Cathy swivelled on the piano stool to watch Max putting her impromptu meal together. His attention was firmly on his task, as if to give her some privacy.

"Good," she smiled stupidly, avidly watching every movement he made, assessing every tiny change to his impassive expression. "He's cooking for me."

"A man that cooks; definitely a keeper," Sara said. "Oh, what's his house like? Is it nice? Does he live alone?"

There was a quiet tap as crockery touched marble. Max finally looked at her, inviting her back over.

"Sorry, Sara, food's ready. I have to go."

"Okay, fine, but you are telling me everything, and I mean *everything*, tomorrow. Love you!"

"Love you too," Cathy ended the call a little wearily.

But she was soon tingling with excited nerves as she wandered across the kitchen, feeling Max's eyes on her the whole way. It wasn't until she stepped up onto one of the bar stools at the breakfast counter that she returned his gaze.

"Everything all right?" He asked, sounding vaguely uninterested. He stayed where he was, standing on the other side of the counter, leaning forward on his elbows as he slowly drank his wine. *No private piano concert just yet then.* Probably just as well; watching him play would make her hands, mouth, and mind, much more interested in *him* than the food.

"Yeah, just Sara checking I'm still alive."

"Sensible. Though, if I were to murder someone, I'd like to think I'd be a little smarter than murdering an employee in my own home, whilst her friends knew where she was and who she was with."

Cathy was suddenly very done with the whole murder talk. The last thing she wanted right now was a lecture from him for doing the exact opposite of that: lying to her friends about where she was (a random address) and who she was with (semi-imaginary boyfriend Mark).

"Well, that's certainly reassured me," she replied wryly, before turning her attention firmly to the spaghetti carbonara sat patiently waiting in front of her. "Wow, thank you, it looks amazing." She wasted no more time in picking up her fork and getting to work.

"Easiest thing to throw together."

"Nothing about this says *thrown together* or *easy*," she retorted, pausing to sip her wine, feeling delightfully sophisticated doing so. The food was delicious, the fresh pasta al dente, egg sauce creamy and smooth, pancetta perfectly crispy; the man certainly could cook. "I bet you individually placed every parmesan flake."

"Not quite, but there's no harm putting a little effort into presentation. We eat with our eyes, after all."

She wondered if that comment extended to her, sat in his lavish home, eating restaurant quality food and drinking fine wine her unrefined palate couldn't properly appreciate, all the while sat in slightly scruffy jeans without any makeup on and her hair pulled up in a messy bun.

"Are they words you would like me to live by?" She asked sincerely, twirling more pasta around her fork.

"What do you mean?"

She waved her hands at herself. "I don't exactly make much effort with my appearance. But if you'd rather I did, I can do."

He half-smiled with amusement. "You're fine as you are."

"Okay ... What about body hair? Do you want me to get rid of anything or ..."

"I don't give a shit about your body hair."

Her stomach gave a funny little clench. It was so sexy when he swore.

"Okay. Well, just so you know, I normally shave my legs and my armpits because that hair annoys me. But down there I just tend to keep neat."

He scoffed. "'Down there'. Is that really what you call it?"

She blushed. "I don't really call it anything. I've never had to."

"I prefer the word cunt, unless that bothers you?"

Her insides clenched again.

She shook her head and watched as he downed the remainder of his wine. Once he'd placed the glass to the side, he leaned in closer, his face barely a breath away. "I don't care how you dress or what makeup you do or do not put on your face," he began, his voice low and decidedly sensual. "I don't care what the hair on your cunt or anywhere else on your body looks like. All I want is you, exactly as you want to be. And before we get upstairs and you let me do things to you you'd rather I didn't, because you've got it into your head that I've bought you; don't. If you don't want to do something, tell me and we won't. You're not a fucking sex slave. You're a consenting adult with a gorgeous body and a smart mouth, and that's why I find you so fucking irresistible."

Holy hell ...

She could only watch him, mind stunned into silence. In that moment, she would have been anything he wanted her to be, anything to keep those magnetic eyes looking at her with such raw desire and something close to reverence. A fleeting thought wondered at how he couldn't love her when he seemed to like everything about her so much. But it wasn't the time to dwell on what he'd promised was an impossibility. It was time to do what she was being paid for.

She might not have been a slave, expected to meekly service his every whim, but she still fully intended to be a good little escort and leave him thoroughly *pleased*.

Setting down her fork, she took a long, final drag from the wineglass before carefully placing it down too. She slowly licked her lips and watched his eyes intently follow the movement. She smiled.

"I think I'm done."

"Good."

He grabbed her hand and led her upstairs.

Chapter Sixteen

The room he took her to clearly wasn't his. Every surface was bare, aside from the table lamps and vases filled with bouquets of fresh flowers. It was a hotel room set out in expectation of a new guest, the décor classy but minimal, the walls and soft furnishings all crisp white with polished oak frames. It was a comfortable but soulless room.

"Are there chocolates on the pillows?"

It took Max a second to understand her taunt.

"I'll admit, it lacks personality," he muttered in response.

"Lacks personality? It's utilitarian!"

"It's a guest room," he explained, voice warm with humour. "And yours for the duration of our time together. If there's anything you want to make it more homely, then I'll get it for you, or you're welcome to bring your own things."

She started walking around the room, assessing every blank space and filling them with colour. "The bed could definitely use a blanket. Over here," she gestured towards the empty wall, "Really needs something, some artwork or a mirror maybe. And this shelf has *nothing* on it! That's like, illegal. At least put some books on it. Maybe a few ornaments. Oh, those little glass figurines, you know the ones—" Her voice died as she finally looked back at him, eyebrows high on his forehead in disbelief. "I mean, it's lovely, really lovely. Thank you."

"And I thought you'd be happy with just the flowers. How myopic of me," he teased. "Anyway, we can make some changes. In the meantime, I would like you to get changed into something a little less restrictive."

"I only brought some clothes for work tomorrow—"

"Look in the wardrobe."

With a final mischievous smile, he left the room.

On tentative feet, she approached the wardrobe and gripped the brass handles. The doors swung smoothly open to reveal a rainbow of lingerie. Hanging from the rail were lacy babydolls and silk chemises with matching wraps, while below lay a menagerie of bras in every style imaginable. She picked up the closest, a lacy pale-pink balconette, the kind seen in French-themed perfume adverts, barely catching the accompanying thong that had been tucked underneath it. She turned the bra over, checked the label, and felt her body still.

"You can have this," Max said, suddenly reappearing in the doorway, carrying a rich orange blanket that shimmered like liquid gold under the muted light. "An unnecessary gift from my mother I don't use. Cathy?"

"How the fuck do you know my bra size?" She shouted, voice acidic with accusation as she turned towards him, designer lingerie still clutched in her hands.

His mild shock at her outburst was smoothly hidden behind that darkly charming smile she knew so well.

"You have taken your bra off in front of me, remember?"

"You don't honestly think I'd believe—"

"That I saw the label when you dropped it on the floor?" He said a little testily. "Is it more plausible that I snuck into your flat to rummage through your clothes? I'm not a fucking stalker, Cathy."

"No ... I suppose not." She'd almost forgotten he seemed to have a convincing argument for everything. "You do have a few stalker qualities though," she countered, impulsive ire almost burnt out while her cheeks remained a pinched pink of indignation.

He laughed breathily. "I promise I'm not. If you wanted to leave right now, I wouldn't follow you."

"So, crashing my date?" She challenged him.

"That was to get your attention."

"And my first interview?"

"*That* was strictly professional," he scowled, prowling closer. He carelessly dropped the blanket on the bed, and towered over her. "At the time, I had no idea and no intention for it to lead here, otherwise I never would have hired you. So, can we carry on with our evening, or do you have more red flags you'd like to wave at me?"

She bit her lip and shook her head.

"Good. Now, pick something to wear and join me across the hall," he ordered as he started to walk away. "And here I was thinking clothes and flowers were what women wanted."

She held the bra up. "These clothes are definitely more for you than me."

"Perhaps," he agreed, glancing over his shoulder.

Oh, how he made her blood boil ... She supposed it was only fair to do the same to him.

Channelling what meagre sex appeal she believed she had, she pulled her jumper over her head and slowly started unbuttoning her shirt, watching as his smile changed to a smoulder, eyes narrowing with lust. He paused in the doorway, waiting for the final button to be undone, but she took her time, hands deliberately wandering to stroke the curve of her breasts and graze her stomach. Once finished, she left the shirt hanging on her shoulders, hands moving down to her jeans. She paused.

"I didn't realise you wanted me to put on a show," she said tartly.

His only response was a hungry smile, before he finally left.

She couldn't take her clothes off fast enough. Grabbing whichever costume her hand naturally gravitated towards, she quickly put it on, along with the matching thong. The mirror inside the wardrobe confirmed that she could actually pull off lingerie rather well; her breasts enticingly full, luxuriously half-encased in white satin that was almost entirely covered in pastel appliqué butterflies, a few fluttering down the gossamer white lace of the 'dress' that skimmed from waist to hips, concealing nothing. Thongs weren't her usual choice, but she had to admit, her bum did look pretty good. In fact, all of her looked pretty good, sexy even. Taking a moment to appreciate her reflection, she started to consider that maybe it wasn't quite so ludicrous that Max wanted her after all.

You're gorgeous, she told herself, though it was Sara's voice she heard in her head. *Go get him.* Forcing her mind to empty of any thoughts outside of the here and now, her and Max, she left the room.

Directly across the landing, she saw a doorway left open in invitation. She tiptoed into the new bedroom, where Max was sat on the end of the bed wearing just a pair of soft grey joggers, his broad, golden chest on show. She glanced briefly around the room but couldn't keep her eyes off him for long, not when his attention was so adamantly on her, tracing every line of uncovered or half-hidden flesh. She rested her shoulder against the doorjamb, waiting for him to say something. After a solid minute, it became apparent he was perfectly content to simply admire her, eyes particularly fond of the sweetheart curve of her breasts.

"So, you have a hotel room too?" She observed.

He was too distracted to smile. "I apologise for my minimalist taste."

She brought her hands to her neck, stroking down over her breasts, the butterflies' wings fluttering under her fingertips, and further, to the smooth satin thong. "I wouldn't say all your tastes are minimalistic."

That got a smile out of him. "Do you like the clothes now?"

"This one's pretty. Though I don't suppose I'll be wearing it for long."

She closed the space between them, treading silently over the thick carpet (*What are rich people's carpets made out of? Fucking clouds?)* with an exaggerated sway of her hips. His eyes were firmly on her and she loved it. She loved being able to demand and hold his attention, this man who could have his pick of women, a man who had already professed he liked to be the one in charge. A fleeting concern that maybe she shouldn't be so bold crossed her mind, but when she stopped before him and his hands instantly moved to touch her – fingertips brushing over her thighs, head leaned back, waiting to see what she would do next – she was reassured that, maybe, he liked to be seduced every once in a while.

The bed barely moved as she placed her knees either side of his legs and lowered herself down. Eager hands embraced her as soon as she stilled, moving from thighs to waist to ass, as if he couldn't quite decide where he wanted to touch her the most. Just as eager lips claimed her mouth, each kiss merging seamlessly into the next.

"Fuck, you're gorgeous," he mumbled, breaking away to trail kisses down her neck to the soft half-moons of her breasts. "I had planned on a little foreplay, but I'm feeling impatient. Fuck."

The expletive was in response to her hand slipping under his waistband to grip his cock. It was hot and smooth against her skin, with a texture she couldn't quite compare to anything else. As she gave it a light squeeze, she realised how hard he was. She toyed with him for a while, sliding her hand up and down his shaft, revealing and hiding the engorged pink head over and over. It was a pleasure to touch and a thrill to see just how aroused she made him – eyes hooded, lips parted, breathing shallow, cock somehow growing harder still. Suddenly, she understood what Sara had meant about feeling powerful when it came to her clients. There was something rather affirming about holding another person's gratification in your hands and seeing the most private side of them, a side the rest of the world didn't get to see.

Was he lonely at the top, too?

"Stop," he suddenly ordered, briskly removing her hands from him.

She raised contrite eyes to his. "Sorry, did I do something wrong?"

"Wrong?" He quietly laughed, a rumble at the back of his throat that stirred the heat in her blood. "I was about to come in your hands. Take these off," he said, hands tugging at the strap of fabric around her hips.

"But I just put them on," she teased, leaning back to invite him to admire her again.

In response, his hands went to her back, unfastening the babydoll before unceremoniously dragging it over her head. He tossed it aside, hands and eyes quickly gravitating towards her uncovered skin, shortly followed by his mouth. She watched him lower his head, gasping as she felt his lips enclose around one tight nipple. Sucking gently, tongue softly licking, she stiffened at the almost unbearable pleasure, feeling the sensation mirrored at her clit. She couldn't help but writhe, a part of her fighting against the building sensitivity, another wanting to give up and be overwhelmed by it. His lips moved across to her other nipple, giving her a moment of respite before his blissful touch came back again. She sighed and moaned, excitement building as she felt his hand stroke over her stomach and under her thong.

"Feels like you're ready too," he commented, releasing her from his mouth so that he could whisper in her ear. "Take these off so you can fuck me."

She didn't need telling twice. After scrambling to her feet and removing the (rather damp) thong, she walked around the bed to where he now lay, head in the pillows and gloriously naked. Unguarded, he watched her, absentmindedly stroking his proud cock. The movements he made were deliberate, with a uniformity and precision that showed the action was second nature, so ingrained he barely had to pay attention to get himself off. She noted what she could – the firmness of his grip, the slight twisting of the hand as he reached halfway down before going back up again, pulling the skin over the head before uncovering it again, over and over, the pace slow but consistent – learning how he touched himself, just as he had learned the same about her.

"So it's all about the head," she said, climbing onto the bed and straddling his thighs. "You don't move your hand all the way down."

"It's the most sensitive part," he confirmed, this time sliding his hand all the way down to the base and stopping, grip tightening to hold his cock up straight. "Whenever you're ready."

Oh, she was definitely ready, though she had an urge to lean down and kiss the top of that engorged head, maybe run her lips and tongue over it to see just how sensitive it really was ... But she could see the impatience in his stare, and she knew that, right then, he just wanted to be inside her, feel her properly without the barrier of a condom (*Sorry, Sara*). There would be time for testing her oral skills later, though she couldn't prevent her mischievous smile at how unsuspecting he probably was of her, just like everyone else who only saw her as an oblivious, unskilled virgin. Unskilled, but not clueless; she planned on sucking an orgasm from him faster than he had made her come from just his fingers in his office. And she had a pretty good idea how to. She wasn't *well-read* for nothing.

She resisted giving him a taster. Instead, she raised herself up, shuffling forward to sit directly above his cock, before lowering slightly. He placed himself against her opening, that merest contact of soft against hard enough to make her want to sit straight down and take all of him. A gentle squeeze on her thigh warned her not to.

"Steady," he ordered, wearing a smile that said he knew just how aroused she was. "It could still hurt a bit this time."

What did a little bit of pain matter now? But she did as she was told, slowly lowering herself down inch by inch, Max's hands on her hips forcing a careful pace. Even so, there was some pain, or rather, an uncomfortable tightness, enough to make her wince. She held it in as much as possible, closing her eyes to pretend she was frowning with pleasure instead. The hands that gripped her ass, forcing her to still and wait, told her she wasn't at all convincing.

"Slowly," he commanded, his hold loosening a second later.

She moved down another inch and another, until her ass was flat against his thighs and she had all of him inside her, filling her completely, almost too much. It was so *deep* like this. Confidence vanishing, she froze; the tightness stretched to its limit, one wrong move away from snapping back and breaking her.

"Come here."

She opened her eyes to find Max watching her, not with concern, but quiet authority.

"Cathy, kiss me," he continued, voice hardening as she silently refused to move. "Or I'll kiss you."

To prove he wasn't bluffing, he started to sit up, nudging his cock inside her, taking her control away. Panicked, she leaned forward to meet him, her mouth colliding with his. She focused on their dancing lips, the velvet softness, the delicious warmth, and his hands caressing her naked curves. Soon she forgot all about the tightness, fear fading away until her body felt flushed all over, starting with her skin and moving inwards. Kisses became passionate, touches became greedy; her body started to move. Some instinct made her bounce up and down, sliding over his erection, finding a rhythm that nurtured the heat inside her. Her confidence returned, so she boldly lifted herself off him as far as possible, before sliding all the way back down, his cock touching deliciously deep inside her, and laughed a little wildly at the moans he made.

She was moving too much to kiss him anymore, too breathless to speak.

"Fuck, you feel good. Slow down unless you're close," he said.

But she didn't want to slow down. She didn't know how close she was, and she didn't really care. She wasn't chasing an orgasm, just enjoying the sensation as it was. Enjoying him.

"Cathy—" Max started, but his warning went unspoken as she felt his body tense beneath her, eyes snapping closed as he climaxed. She kept moving, matching her rhythm to the waves of his orgasm, watching with awe and intrigue at his captivated, almost pained frown. After a moment, he stilled, breathed deeply, and sat up, arms wrapping around her waist to pull their chests together.

"You didn't come, did you?" He stroked the hair back from her face, continuing to run it through his fingers even after it was out of the way.

"No," she breathed, still struggling for breath, still amazed at their intimacy. The way he stroked her hair; it was such a gentle, affectionate action ...

"Let's finish you off then." He kissed her softly, hands massaging down her back.

She moaned in disagreement, not wanting to speak and break the kiss. She wanted to drown in that kiss.

But he broke away, waiting for a proper answer.

"No," she sighed.

"No?"

"I'm fine. I don't need to."

His eyes narrowed. "No one *needs* to, but why don't you want to? I'm normally very good at making sure my partner finishes first, but ..." He cupped her chin, dragging a thumb over her parted lips. "I'm still getting used to you. Seeing you lose yourself in the moment ... I could get hard again just thinking about it."

"Don't," she laughed, trying to lighten the atmosphere. "Honestly, I'm fine. I'm actually feeling pretty tired."

He looked like he was about to push the subject but, after a second, he smiled and kissed her again. "Fine. But I'm making it up to you next time."

That compromise worked for her. He lay back down and she rolled off him, attention immediately drawn to the excessive dampness pooling between her thighs.

"You're not going to lie back with your legs in the air, are you?" He teased, half-concerned she might actually say yes.

"Don't worry, I'm not trying to make it happen," she mumbled, gratefully accepting the tissues he passed her.

"Good, because I'd hate to knock you up first try and have to end this prematurely."

"Would you miss me?" She matched his playful tone, while her insides squirmed excitedly at the sentiment that he wanted to keep her around.

He flashed her that signature roguish smile. "Of course; you're a pretty good fuck."

"Better than you were expecting?"

He scoffed with amusement but didn't grace her with an answer. Getting to his feet, he headed towards a closed door she assumed led to an ensuite.

"Do I have to go back to my room now?" She asked.

He paused, turning back to look at where she lay, still naked, half tangled in the bedsheets, hair a wild mess, fear of rejection plain on her face. He gave it a moment's consideration before turning away again.

"No. You can stay."

Chapter Seventeen

Max didn't kiss her goodnight or hold her while she slept, but she considered sharing his bed for the night a win in itself. Whether it was the sex or just the emotional drain of a day's worth of anticipation, she was exhausted and quickly fell asleep, wondering vaguely how it would feel to have his arms around her.

She woke to a dark room and an empty bed. After using the bathroom in 'her' room, she checked the time, noting it was too early for Max to have reasonably gotten up to get ready for work. Too hungry to go back to sleep – her stomach cramping almost painfully – she put on one of the deliberately short nightdresses and matching robes from the wardrobe, and headed downstairs.

The ground floor was dark and silent, except for the faint thump-thump of a strong bassline. After wandering through the lounge, kitchen, sun room, and lounge 2.0 (fancy sofas and coffee tables at one end, full-size wooden pool table at the other), she found herself back at the foot of the stairs in the entrance hall. The sound was loudest there, so she turned on the ostentatious chandelier and quickly noticed a door leading under the staircase. She opened it, loud dance music welcoming her in and leading her down a small flight of stairs, to what appeared to be a sleek basement gym.

Max was on a treadmill, looking up at the news playing with subtitles on the flatscreen TV on the wall in front of him. He was jogging at a steady pace – steady, but he was still moving faster than she probably could at a full sprint, his stride long, his form, perfect. Blood warmed his cheeks a fetching pink, while the sheen of sweat coating his bare arms made them shine spectacularly, highlighting every curve and undulation of hard-working muscle. He wore a pair of high-tech running trainers, black shorts, and a loose, white (now near transparent), tank top that left little to the imagination, draping across his chest and shoulders just right. She would have been quite happy to take a seat and watch him flex, but she wouldn't want him to think she was creepy or, heaven forbid, falling for him. It was still three minutes after her arrival that she made her presence known though.

"You picked a gym over a sex dungeon? I'm disappointed," she shouted, staying back to not startle him.

She wasn't sure he could be startled. He just glanced over as if he'd expected her to be there all along, before tapping at the fancy watch on his wrist, never breaking his stride, the music quieting a second later.

"It seemed like the better choice at the time," he replied, pressing a button so that the treadmill started to slow to a brisk walk. He laced his fingers behind his head and she felt her mouth go dry. "You're welcome to use it too."

She almost hadn't heard him. "Exercise isn't really my thing," she answered, scrunching up her nose.

"Exercise should be everyone's thing," he chastised.

"I suppose ..."

"You could work out with me."

She glanced around the room at all the intimidating equipment. Some items she recognised – treadmill, rowing machine, bike, racks of dumbbells – but others looked more likely to be used for torture than exercise; fittingly, since love was to hate as exercise was to torture in her limited experience. She felt her mind retreat as brief, horrible memories of P.E. lessons at school flashed behind her eyes and made her skin crawl.

"I wouldn't be able to keep up," she said quietly, feeling her arms wrap around herself, the echoes of teenage laughter taunting her when she fell, when she missed, when she came in last.

"You've kept up so far." His dark smile told her he was no longer strictly speaking about exercise. The brightness in his eyes dimmed a moment later as he recognised her discomfort. "Bad experience?"

She shrugged. "Just school. I wasn't athletic enough for the teachers to care, and girls can be cruel." She waved a hand at the room. "And I wouldn't even know where to start with all this."

"I could show you."

She got the feeling he quite liked showing her things.

"Maybe," she appeased, though the idea of was quickly growing on her anyway. If anyone could make it worthwhile getting hot and sweaty; it was Max. "Do you use all of it?" She eyed some of the bigger weights with equal parts wariness and suspicion.

"Not really. Generally, I run, with a little weight training on the side. But friends come here too sometimes."

"Do you enjoy it?"

Suddenly, he was stepping off the treadmill and coming towards her. "I do. It clears my head."

Before she could ask what he needed clearing from his head, he made her an offer she couldn't refuse. "I'm going to shower. You're welcome to join me." That dark smile was back, informing her the invite wasn't at all innocent.

All she needed was one deep breath of his musky, sweat-enhanced, masculine scent as he walked past, to not feel quite so innocent either.

She followed him upstairs to his ensuite. It was about the same size as her bedroom back home, but it had to be for the generous double sink, round spa bath, and walk-in waterfall shower big enough for six let alone two people. True to Max's minimalist taste, everything was white marble and grey stone with silver accessories; spotless, expensive, and a pleasure to exist beside.

"How do you keep this place so clean?" She asked, searching desperately for a stray hair or speck of limescale, when it finally clicked. "You don't clean this yourself, do you?"

Max pulled his top over his head, leaving his hair sticking up at odd angles and those sculpted abs on show. "No," he replied blandly.

"Too proud to clean your own toilet?"

"Not too proud; just rich enough that I don't have to. Sally does a much better job of it than I ever would anyway," he said, as if in his defence, while turning the shower on and discarding the rest of his gym kit.

Cathy didn't even pretend not to look at his semi-erect penis. It was only fair since he was always so flagrant in his ogling of her.

"Does Sally wipe your arse for you too?"

That finally got his attention.

He prowled over, hands teasing the hem of her negligee as he stared balefully down at her.

"No," he began. "She cleans the house, tends the garden, and buys in food because I am uninterested in doing those things myself. It's honest work and I pay her generously. She's competent, discreet, and loyal, and I'm lucky to have her."

"She sounds like the perfect woman," Cathy goaded him.

"The perfect *housekeeper*," he corrected.

"So, what is the perfect woman?"

"Besides being non-existent," he began, hands adventuring under the fabric to follow the directions of his next words. "She has a tight little ass ... a willing cunt ... smooth hips ... big tits ... and a smart mouth." He ended with a kiss on her smart mouth, before removing his hands and stepping into the shower. "So, take off your clothes and join me."

She did as she was told, stepping out of silk and into titillating hot water.

There was something wonderfully intimate about sharing a shower, the mandatory nakedness a practical, relaxed thing. If she hadn't felt so comfortable around him, she would have shied away at having her body so exposed. But there was no awkwardness as she stepped in close to share the water, as their limbs brushed past one another. His eyes on her had never been anything but appreciative, and it seemed he enjoyed this aspect of her – wet hair dark, skin covered with droplets – just as much as any other. That unrelenting desire prevented her from feeling anything but utterly at ease ... and constantly, mildly, turned on.

Max had already lathered himself up, replacing musky sweat with spices, woods, leather, and whatever else perfumers had declared men should artificially smell of. And yet, whatever it was, it worked; he smelt of raw sex appeal.

She wasted no time slipping her hands under his arms, stroking the bubbles over his chest, then lower to his now unapologetically large erection. Carefully cleaning it, she continued until all the body wash had gone and its large pink head curved enticingly up to meet her.

"So, you like my smart mouth?" She asked, gathering her courage.

"You know I do."

She smiled. "I want you to like it more."

Without waiting for a response or permission, she lowered herself to her knees. Luckily, he blocked most of the water from falling on her face, so she was free to concentrate on the task she'd set herself. She worked his cock a few more times with her hands, barely noticing Max say her name questioningly, before steeling her resolve and pressing her lips to it with a kiss. Her tongue came next, tracing the curve of the head and running along its split, feeling it twitch as she stroked over the thick vein there. She did the same again, enjoying the little jolt of excitement it coaxed from him, the slight hitching of his breath. As fun as it would have been to continue teasing him, she hadn't given up on wanting him to come fast, as if speed somehow proved her worth. She kissed the tip again, before parting her lips and taking him into her mouth.

She could only take half of him easily and, with no intention of fighting her gag reflex, left her hand to do the rest. At first, she just gripped the lower half of his cock, keeping it still as she worked him up and down with her mouth, pausing occasionally to tickle the head with her tongue, before slowly sliding her mouth down its length again. When she felt a hand touch her cheek, she decided he was enamoured enough with her to pick up the pace and start using her hands as well.

One hand cupped his balls, softly massaging them, while the other stroked up his cock and back down again, her lips following.

"Fuck..." He said breathlessly above her, his entire body tensing. She did the same again, slowly bringing mouth and hand up and down again, smiling to herself when it brought another curse to his lips.

She was just about to pick up the pace when his hands stopped her, one claiming back his body, the other holding her head still. Slowly releasing him from her mouth, she raised her eyes to his.

"Was I doing something wrong?" She asked, watching his stare harden as she defiantly kissed his cock again.

A second later he was kneeling in front of her, the next; he'd dragged her up and pushed her back against the wall, hot water raining onto her face for a moment, while the steam and sudden movement made her head light.

"No," he said, face an inch away from hers, body pressed in close, shielding her from the water. "But I'd told you, next time was your turn." He kissed her firmly, all passion, no affection, and stroked a hand down her body, pinching a nipple as he went to cup her cunt. "You're already wet. Did you enjoy sucking me off?"

"You stopped me before I could," she retorted, relishing in the malevolent amusement that narrowed his eyes. She also enjoyed it as he placed his cock against her opening and started working her clit with his finger. She moaned as he touched her exactly right.

"You're too good at that," she mumbled, unable to finish her sentence as the pleasure grew. Too good at it for how long they'd been together ... for how few times they'd been together. She wasn't going to last long as those skilled fingers rubbed her in precise circles, applying the perfect amount of pressure.

"Practice," he replied with a smile, tickling her neck with kisses before bringing his lips to her ear. "Tell me when you're getting close because I want to be inside you when you come. I want to feel your tight little cunt gripping my cock—"

"I'm close," she interrupted as the itch grew hot and needy.

"Good." His teeth grazed her earlobe as his hands moved to cup her ass, lifting her off her feet and onto his cock, suspended between his body and the wall.

"Fuck." It was her turn to curse as he shoved himself in deep. There was no pain this time, just the perfect feel of him inside her. She wrapped her legs around his hips, feeling him slide in fully, exquisitely, and back out again, somehow holding her steady. "Oh, God ..." she murmured as he roughly pounded into her again.

"Not quite," he teased, giving her ass a squeeze. "It's not God making you feel this good."

"Max ..." she sighed, quickly losing her senses, surrounded by heat – the steam, his body, the knot of pleasure expanding inside her – and ready to drown in it.

"Come for me," he ordered as he started to fuck her faster.

Oh ... She reached for his face to pull their lips together, stealing hungry kisses to keep from crying out, to stop moaning his name like he wanted her to. Like she wanted to. She wanted to moan for him, come for him, let him own every second of her pleasure because he was so fucking good. She wanted to be enough for him, wanted him to be as enamoured with her as she already was with him ...

"Max ..." she sighed his name as her pleasure peaked and spiralled out of control.

She lost herself in it, barely noticing as he tensed and groaned and shared her orgasm. She gasped for breath, finding only airless steam to fill her lungs, which only added to the overwhelming warmth coating her skin, *beneath* her skin, centred around where he thrusted inside her. Waves of bliss made her body tense and relax, made her cunt massage him as he filled her with his fluid and whispered lustful curses in her ear.

Climax ebbing away, she calmed, basking in dreamy post-coital contentment, happily waiting for Max to finish taking his pleasure from her, until they both stilled. He rested his head on her shoulder, face against her neck, while she clung to him as if her arms alone were enough to keep him close. Thumping hearts started to slow. Once he'd recovered, he unhooked her legs from around his waist, and lowered her carefully to the tiled floor. Suddenly faint, she let go, hands reluctantly trailing over his broad shoulders and strong arms, to rest against the wall behind her. She closed her eyes to find her balance – physical, emotional – focusing on the sensation of the water running over her, waiting until she had to wash him from her skin.

His voice roused her, words brutally yanking her away from her meditative state and back to reality.

"Are you ... meant to start your period soon?" He asked, keeping his tone decidedly neutral.

Her eyes snapped open to catch a glimpse of his slightly bloodied cock, before he turned towards the shower stream to clean himself.

Oh. Shit.

"I'm so sorry! I didn't think ..."

"It's okay," he quickly reassured.

"No, it's not. I should have remembered. I should have told you! I'm so sorry ..." Her stomach clenched with embarrassment as she remembered the earlier cramps – the typical first warning sign of the red tsunami – that she'd mistaken for hunger pangs, while her mind struggled to think of a way to make it better.

"Honestly, it's fine. It's just blood." He rubbed himself down one last time, before stepping out of the shower and wrapping a towel around his waist. As unaffected as he sounded, she couldn't quite believe him.

"Really?"

"Really." He offered her a reassuring smile, albeit a slightly cocky one. "I still would have fucked you if I'd known, but a little warning would be appreciated. How long does it usually last?"

At least he was being nice about it, but why, after everything, did that question feel so personal? So invasive? Forget masturbation techniques and sexual preferences, her menstrual cycle was the thing that felt the most taboo to talk about; sharing secrets about her body that belonged only to her, medical professionals, and her hypothetical lifelong companion.

And him too, apparently.

"Three days usually, four if I'm unlucky," she said, feeling utterly laid bare.

"Done for next weekend then," he concluded slyly, turning to leave.

"Max!"

He looked back at her, some genuine concern creeping over his expression at the panic in her voice.

"I didn't ... *bring* anything with me," she confessed awkwardly, biting her lip. "I normally do in my work bag, but I brought a different one because I was coming here ..."

Her heart sank as he turned around and wordlessly left.

Oh God ... She tried to calm herself. It wasn't that bad. He clearly wasn't bothered by it, outwardly at least. Maybe there was time for them to stop at a shop on the way to work? Maybe Alison would have emergency supplies? Worst case, she'd have to stuff her knickers with toilet paper and change it every half an hour. That would be a lot of trips to the toilet. Sandra would definitely say something ...

While she thought it over and tried not to panic – or die from sheer mortification at the situation she'd negligently gotten herself into – she washed the lingering residue of their copulation from her body. She was just deliberating whether it was better to steal some of Max's shower gel and smell like a man for the rest of the day, or use nothing at all, when he reappeared.

"Hopefully these will do," he said, placing her bag on the floor, and a box of tampons and another of maxi pads by the sink, before sliding the shower door open to hand her a bottle of pastel-pretty, feminine body wash.

"Why do you have all this?" She asked, listlessly taking the bottle from him, eyes still locked on the life-saving sanitary products, thinking of his past whores and what traces they'd left behind.

His reply swiftly dismissed the jealousy that had started to rise in her.

"I told you Sally is the perfect housekeeper."

"She deserves a raise. Or at least a generous Christmas bonus," she said, giddy with relief, besotted with just how amazing he was. Nothing she did or said had ever thrown him. He was always, *always*, exactly how she needed him to be.

"I'll tell her you said that," he replied, a little laughter in his voice. "We need to leave in about twenty minutes. We'll grab breakfast on the way."

"Thank you, Max. Really." She turned off the shower and stepped out, smiling as she wrapped a warmed towel around her body.

"You're welcome." He turned to leave. "I'll transfer your money now."

"Okay ... thanks."

For a moment, she'd almost forgotten he was paying her, that last night and this morning were all just an emotionless arrangement for his amusement. That his kindness, while genuine, and their relationship, while blossoming, extended no further than casual sex and witty repartee.

As amazing as she found him, she was just a wh— *sex companion* to him. Just another woman to fuck for a while before disappearing from his life without leaving a trace, reset the bedroom, restock the wardrobe ...

Don't forget it, she told herself firmly. *Don't ever fucking forget it.*

Chapter Eighteen

Two thousand pounds. He had sent her two thousand pounds.

"Cathy? You okay?" Alison asked, fork full of heavily-dressed salad paused halfway to her mouth.

Cathy dropped her phone and forced a smile, suddenly remembering that she was sat in the staff lounge with Alison on their lunch break, and therefore not free to gawp at her magically healthy bank balance.

"Yeah, fine. Sorry. I completely zoned out."

"I thought maybe Mark had messaged you or something," Alison suggested innocently.

"Oh, yeah, he has. Just seeing how I am."

"How was last night?"

"Amazing," Cathy replied, before remembering it was her fictitious relationship she was talking about. "He's so ... considerate and ... really makes me feel at ease, you know. He's lovely."

"Aww. Well, if he's here to stay, we'll have to meet him. We could have a dinner party."

"Yeah, definitely," she agreed, panic clawing at her brain. "I think he's away for Christmas and New Year though, so maybe after."

Stalling, solid strategy.

"That's a shame. But Christmas is still a week and a half away, so maybe we could organise something before then?"

Alison pushed, trying to be a lovely, if inconveniently, supportive friend.

"Erm ... yeah, I'll ask him if he's free."

Shit, Cathy thought. *Making up a boyfriend was definitely the worst idea I've ever had.*

She picked up her phone again to send a text to her not-imaginary, not-boyfriend.

CATHY: Got the money, thanks. I don't remember increasing my rates ...

Max replied a second later.

MAX: I decided to go by fuck rather than by night. The rest is for the previous occasions.

CATHY: But they were before the arrangement ...

MAX: Yes but I still wanted to pay for them.

MAX: What's with the passive-aggressive ellipses?

MAX: ...

CATHY: I just don't understand why you're changing the rules.

MAX: It's in your favour, in case you hadn't noticed ...

CATHY: Don't you start getting passive-aggressive with me.

CATHY: But okay, I just wanted to know.

MAX: Are you actually pissed off or am I reading this wrong?

CATHY: No, sorry. Something just came up and I'm not sure how to fix it but it's not your problem. But thanks, for the money.

She sighed as she turned her phone face down on the table. So even that initial encounter had been paid for now.

She'd literally *sold* her virginity ... Was nothing about their relationship allowed to be genuine?

At that thought, she picked her phone back up.

CATHY: Actually, it's not okay. I didn't consent to selling my virginity. It wasn't for sale so you don't get to buy it.

The delay in his reply almost worried her, but she knew she had to hold her own against him, that he would want her to – probably. Her phone screen brightened.

MAX: Well, shit. I hadn't thought of it like that. I'm sorry.

MAX: Send the money back.

Her already inflated opinion of him rose a few points. A man that could readily admit he was wrong was a beautiful, reassuring thing.

CATHY: Thanks for understanding.

MAX: Your body your choice, baby.

She bit her lip to keep from grinning, distracting herself by opening her banking app to return the immoral five hundred pounds.

"Not good?" Alison asked, mistaking the lip bite as a negative thing.

Wait, what had we been talking about? Oh yeah, Mark.

"Yeah ... erm ..." God, she was terrible at this whole lying business. "He's busy this week, and apparently he already has a surprise planned for us this weekend."

"Shame. Wait, I completely forgot. It's Sara's birthday on Saturday!" Alison exclaimed, glasses slipping down her nose. "She'll want to do something. You can't miss it. Maybe Mark can cancel whatever his plans for you are and join in?"

Oh no ... Max had already booked her in for Saturday night *and* she somehow had to make up a convincing excuse as to why her imaginary boyfriend couldn't meet her friends when she'd just lied that he was only busy because of her. *Double shit.* Maybe she should just kill him off, figuratively speaking, and pretend to get a zero-hour night-shift job to account for her randomly disappearing to be with Max ...

Because that would be *totally* believable.

Alison was watching her, waiting for an answer, unflinching gaze making her sweat.

"Yeah, of course I'll be there," she said brightly. "I'll organise it with Mark ... I'm sure it will be fine. What does Sara plan on doing?"

"I'll ask."

While Alison texted Sara, Cathy tried to figure out the best way to ask her boss for a night off, when it was only her second official night on the job. She started to type out a message, quickly deleting it at Alison's next words.

"Okay, so a wild night out on Friday – her words – and then a civilised night in on Saturday, since Jacob is visiting."

"Oh, great. By wild I assume you mean—"

"Bars first before—"

"Clubs," they sighed in unison.

"I might try to find an excuse to leave before that," Alison said ruefully.

"I might join you."

Great, so that only leaves Sunday night free.

CATHY: Hey, sorry, another thing. I completely forgot it's Sara's birthday this weekend and her plans take up both Friday and Saturday, so is it okay if we rearrange for Sunday? I'm sorry, I know it's not ideal with work the next day ... (Apologetic and awkward rather than passive aggressive ellipses this time.)

She put her head in her hands and waited.

MAX: Come talk to me in my office.

"Shit."

"Is Mark mad?" Alison asked, worriedly.

"What? No, no ... I just forgot I was meant to do a thing before lunch ... I should get back upstairs."

Discarding the half-eaten sandwich she suddenly had zero appetite for, she slowly headed back up to the office, feet heavy with dread. Was he going to tell her off? Was he going to stop the arrangement because she was unreliable? Was he going to lock the door, bend her over his desk and angrily fuck her to remind her who was in charge? She didn't have a clue.

After a deep breath, she knocked on the door and let herself in, body tense, guard up, as prepared as she could be for whatever he had in store for her.

"Max?" She asked, seeing him sat, elbows on desk, head in hands. "I'm so sorry. I'd completely forgotten about Sara's birthday. Please don't be mad ..."

Weary eyes looked over at her, while a frown pulled his eyebrows together.

"I'm not mad with you," he said, though his expression was anything but reassuring.

"Really? You look ... fed up?"

"Because of work. I'm trying to get on top of everything before next week." His frown finally dissipated. "You thought I was mad about you changing nights?"

"I mean, your text sounded pretty mad."

He smiled tiredly as he got to his feet. "Pay back for your passive-aggressiveness, I suppose."

Rather than approaching her, he headed to the window to look out at the panoramic view, the Minster a humbling monolith against the grey, overcast sky; the world below moving like clockwork. He ran a hand through his hair, his shoulders relaxing a moment later. It was so easy to forget he had a serious job, responsible in part for the finances of a multimillion-pound company. He seemed too young, his personality too innately laid-back for him to have such a job, and yet, she couldn't imagine him doing anything else. Wearing expensive clothes and making money suited him.

Eventually, he looked over his shoulder, silently inviting her to join him.

"You are allowed to have a life," he said levelly. "I don't expect you to drop everything to suit me. Yes, I expect to take a certain level of priority, but if plans change; they change. As such, Sunday will be fine."

"Thank you." She stood at his side, her body turned towards his to try and read his expression. "So, why did your text sound so serious?"

"Because you're still misinterpreting what this arrangement is. Not that I blame you; it takes time to figure each other out, to find a kind of balance. But, to help with that, I will be honest with you."

"I'm disappointing in bed, aren't I?" She teased, cheeks flushing with pride when he laughed in response, before giving her a sly, sidelong glance.

"Is your self-esteem really so low, or are you fishing for compliments?" Her lips parted with an embarrassed denial, but he continued before she could formulate the words. "I'd fuck you right here and now if I didn't have so much work to do. No," he turned his attention back to the window, "You just need to stop thinking that because I'm paying you, I own you."

"But you do a little bit," she countered.

"I own time with you," he said firmly. "You're selling me permission to enjoy your company and your body, nothing more. Try to get that into your head."

"Yes, sir." She playfully saluted him, feeling the atmosphere shift at her sardonic tone.

"There was another thing," he continued, taming his smile. "I'm on leave from Monday until after New Year. Two weeks. It's an annual family thing, and I was wondering if you'd accompany me. I appreciate you'd have to use leave too, so—"

"You'll make it worth my while?"

"Yes." He flashed her an amused scowl. "Five hundred a day in addition to any *bonuses*. You probably already have plans, but I'd enjoy it more if you were there."

"I don't," she said too quickly, earning herself a questioning look. "I mean, nothing that I don't mind missing."

"If you're sure ..." He left a space for her to change her mind and magic together a fully-functioning nuclear family, high on Christmas cheer. His narrowed eyes softened slightly at her nod of agreement, hardening a second later as he moved the conversation away from the private and back to their usual teasing. "In that case, I suggest you submit your holiday request for the next two weeks, apologising profusely for the short notice, of course. Though, I have no doubt your manager will be obliging ..."

He purred the last part in that wildly seductive way of his. That, along with his dark smile, were enough to make her want to say *Forget your workload and fuck me instead.* However, the stomach cramps and intermittent nausea she always got on day one of her cycle were convincing enough deterrents. She also imagined period sex was probably a bit messy for the office, maybe a bit too messy and intimate full stop for her liking ...

"He usually is," she replied, flashing a saucy smile of her own. "Do I get any heads up about what to expect? Like, where are we going? Who else will be there? Do I have to buy them presents? Or will I just be hiding in your room as your secret sex slave?"

She loved the half-amused, half-exasperated smile that got from him.

"Anything else?" He taunted.

"I just want to be prepared. It's not like you've left me much time at all to buy things—"

"You will always have everything you need. But, to answer your questions, we will be going to Australia to visit my brother and his husband. My parents and eldest brother will also be there. You don't need to buy anyone presents. You won't be hidden away."

The cramps transformed into butterflies. "You're actually going to introduce me to your family?"

"It would be easier than trying to hide you the entire time," he replied, utterly deadpan, before heading back over to the desk. Rather than reclaiming his seat, he placed a fist on the wood, leaning onto it slightly, almost as if he needed to touch something solid. "To keep things simpler, I'd prefer to introduce you as my girlfriend, if you're happy to play along."

"Are you ashamed to have me as your whore?" She tested, following him across the room to perch playfully on his desk, swinging her feet slowly back and forth, while looking wide-eyed up at him. Her hand was an inch away from his, splayed fingers wondering what it would feel like to stroke over the back of his hand.

"That's not the word I'd use. But no, not ashamed, just ... private," he replied coolly. "My family don't need to know the details of my personal life. It would also save both of us from being asked too many questions. Unless you'd like to explain to them why you agreed to my terms, and that little amendment of your own ..."

That was a conversation she was more than happy not to have with anyone else, ever. She was also perfectly happy to *pretend* to be his girlfriend. She had a feeling she was going to rather enjoy it.

Girlfriend. Her mind swooned at the word, spoken in his voice.

"Pretending it is," she agreed. "Does this mean I'll have to hold your hand in public? Or are we going to be one of those couples that show very little affection for each other?"

"Within reason."

His grumbled response warned her that a lecture was coming. *I don't date, don't let this go to your head, any romance is only for show, don't misinterpret this as you seem prone to do blah blah.* To save his breath – and her sanity – she decided it was a good place to end the conversation.

"I'll follow your lead then," she reassured, getting to her feet. "Anyway, I've got a lot to get on with seeing that I'm suddenly not going to be here at all for the next two weeks. Hmm ... Australia's pretty hot ... My summer wardrobe is less of a wardrobe and more like two old strappy tops and a pair of shorts. Do I even have swimwear? I'm going to have to find time to go shopping."

She was mostly talking to herself as she headed for the door, so it was almost a surprise to hear Max interject.

"Cathy, don't worry about it. I'll make sure you have everything you need."

Initially, she took that to mean *If you're stupid enough to forget something, I'll buy it for you at the airport or once we get there.* When she got home five hours later to Sara shouting her name, and a white and gold designer suitcase lying on the kitchen table that definitely *hadn't* been there yesterday, she realised he'd meant it much more literally.

"Cathy? What is this stuff?" Sara asked, her mouth hanging open as she gawped at the suitcase.

"I don't know," Cathy replied and, in that moment, she really didn't know. "Where did it come from?"

"A woman dropped it off like half an hour ago."

"For me?" Cathy reached a hand towards the suitcase, fighting against the impulse not to touch expensive, pristine things lest she leave so much as a fingerprint. Instead, she settled on the smooth white box tied with a black ribbon that sat unassumingly next to it. She pulled at the bow.

"That was what the card said."

"There's a card?"

Sara handed it over. It was small and square and matched the box. She knew she would have found it tucked under the ribbon, if not for her curious friend ...

Cathy,
Chocolates for this week.
Clothes for the next.
I hope it's all to your liking.
M

Shit.

"Did you look in the suitcase?" She asked slowly, as a cloud of panic settled over her brain.

"I just opened it up. I didn't touch anything," Sara muttered. "Cathy, I had no idea you and Mark were so serious already, *could* be so serious. I also had no idea scientists earnt so much! What's happening next week?"

"We're going away," Cathy replied, dazed, sliding the lid off the box, thanking the universe that Max and Mark started with the same letter.

"Really? You've only been on like two dates! Holy shit, they must be the poshest chocolates I've ever seen!"

They really were the poshest chocolates either of them had ever seen: a mix of white, milk and dark chocolate truffles decorated with all manner of toppings in a delicious explosion of colour. The smell alone was enough to make their mouths water.

"Is that ... gold?" Sara peered closer, fingers reaching for the perfectly smooth, mirror-glazed orb of dark chocolate topped with gold flakes.

Cathy slapped her hand away. "These aren't the kind of chocolates you can just help yourself to."

"You're not going to share?"

"Of course I'm going to share! But with a cup of tea after dinner." Cathy dropped the lid and her eyes hesitantly moved onto the suitcase. After the whole surprise wardrobe full of lingerie situation, she should have expected Max to do the exact same thing when it came to her holiday clothes. Hopefully, it wasn't just a suitcase full of skimpy bikinis ...

"Oh my God," she mumbled, as she tried to take it all in. There was everything she could possibly want: shorts, casual tops, maxi dresses, bikinis with floral cover-ups, sandals, trainers and, of course, two weeks' worth of matching underwear, most of which, she was happy to see, valued comfort over pure sex appeal.

"Exactly! What the actual fuck Cathy? A guy you've dated for like *a literal weekend* suddenly buys you Gucci's next summer collection? In December? And *underwear*?"

"We're going to Australia. For two weeks. He has family there."

Sara's eyes and nostrils flared. "I don't think you should go. You barely know the guy."

"I know him well enough," she half-heartedly reassured, distracted by the hollowing truth she'd known all along: *I never should have lied. I never should have lied. Why did I have to lie?*

"Really? You really know him 'well enough'?" Sara challenged, her eyes no longer warm like honey but sharp like a wasp's sting. "Because I can't believe it. Either you're an incredible fuck – you still need to tell me how last night went, by the way – or something freaky is going on."

"Nothing freaky is going on," Cathy laughed a little to hide her awkwardness. "And I do know him."

"Cathy—"

"I do!" It was too late to tell the truth, so she soldiered on, warming her voice and softening her expression. She let down her defences, filling her mind with Max in a way she knew was dangerous, losing herself to the limerence, and unleashed the infatuated idiot she really was. "And I know it's fast and a little scary – *I* find it scary – but it's different with him. Honestly, it was just ... instant connection. He adores me and I adore him. It's crazy but ... wonderful. Better than I ever could have imagined. And I promise I'll be safe. I'll give you the address of where we're staying. I'll call you every day. He won't hurt me, Sara."

Half-lies, half-truths, but convincing enough.

"I want to meet him first," her friend, her shieldmaiden, demanded. "Because he is waving so many red fucking flags."

"He'll be here on Saturday, for your birthday meal."

"He'd better be." Sara smoothed her frown and brightened her voice as she continued, but Cathy knew fury still bubbled beneath the surface. "Well, I guess for now there's nothing else except for you to try on these clothes. I'll put food on while you do. I still find it very weird he's buying clothes for you though."

Cathy took the temporary victory. After closing the suitcase, she headed towards her bedroom, wheeling her new summer wardrobe behind her.

"He knows I don't care all that much about how I look, and when I said I was seriously lacking in Australia-appropriate clothing, he offered to sort it. His mum has a personal shopper or something."

"How convenient ..." Sara observed with more than a hint of suspicion. "Anyway, you better show me how it all looks. And *you* can tell my parents on Thursday why you're not coming for Christmas anymore."

Oh God, more threads for my web of lies. How long until she tangled herself in them?

"Yeah, of course," she said with a contrite smile.

Once in the privacy of her own room, Cathy retrieved her phone and collapsed on the bed.

CATHY: A little extravagant, don't you think?

She lay still, breathing deeply while she waited for a response.

MAX: I said I'd sort it.

CATHY: I must have missed the part where you said you were buying me EVERYTHING.

MAX: I just wanted to make it as easy as possible for you. It's my fault it's all last minute, so I won't inconvenience you if I can help it.

CATHY: How did you even manage it?

MAX: Let's just say Sally had a busy afternoon.

CATHY: Poor Sally.

MAX: Not poor Sally. Lucky Sally. I spent almost as much on her as compensation as I did on you.

An uninvited smile crept onto her face. Suddenly, she felt like telling him about the mess she'd gotten herself into, but quickly decided against it. As good as he was at solving problems: it wasn't the kind of thing money could fix. She'd have to figure something out herself.

CATHY: Why the chocolates?

MAX: As an apology for my sternness earlier.

CATHY: An expensive apology.

MAX: You need to learn how to just say thank you.

CATHY: Thank you.

MAX: You're welcome.

She laid the phone down on her stomach and stared up at the ceiling. Butterflies mixed with nausea mixed with something unnameable, something that warmed from the inside out, something that made her want to smile and see him again; something she'd have to *pretend* to feel for two weeks as his 'girlfriend'.

It was going to be all too easy and, at the same time, impossible.

Chapter Nineteen

Sara's family were wonderful; perfectly, unfairly so. Her dad, Bo, had the visage of a Viking – tall, blonde, aging like fine whisky – and the golden soul of a true gentleman. Breadwinner, papa bear, and doting husband; the man was *goals*. He would have been an easy hire for the role of substitute father if Cathy hadn't found him slightly too attractive to think purely *fatherly* thoughts about him, and she wasn't about *that* kind of vibe. At some point they had mutually, silently, agreed to be polite, respectful, distant friends, whereas Sara's mum, Priya, could adopt her any day.

Priya was sunshine bottled, without a mean bone in her body and rose-tinted eyes that always saw the best in the world. While Bo was a senior civil servant (like *senior* senior) of some undisclosed ministry – honestly, the mystery only added to his allure – Priya had predominantly acted as housewife and homemaker, taking whatever little job piqued her fancy – cashier, receptionist, teaching assistant – moving on whenever they lost her interest, despite her masters in theoretical physics. Sara had always, and vocally, looked down on her mum for supporting the archaic gender divide, but Cathy thought there was something lovely about pottering through life, working a little, having time for hobbies, never missing a school pickup. No. If Bo was goals, Priya was *aspirations*.

Thursday evening, after an hour's Uber ride to Harrogate that Bo gracefully paid for, Cathy followed Sara into her middle-class childhood home – the private driveway, double garage, hot tub owning kind of middle-class – and into the arms of the family that was so perfect they welcomed her as a third child.

"Cathy! Welcome, welcome," Bo hugged her briefly, his touch firm, reassuring. The addition of a pat on her back maintained that she was very much the child in the relationship.

"Hi, Bo. Thanks for having me."

"Anytime."

The second she was released, Priya swooped in and held her tightly for a good minute, as if trying to heal all the pain she'd ever felt. For a moment, she almost managed it; Cathy always got a taste of that *coming home* feeling when the little woman wrapped her up in a blanket of selfless love, a feeling she didn't really get anywhere else anymore.

"Oh, Cathy. So lovely to see you," she said, utterly genuine. "Thank you for coming. Don't you look well? Doesn't she look well, Bo? Louis, come say hello."

Louis, Sara's adopted younger brother, raised his head to nod once in her vague direction before disappearing from the hallway.

"Don't mind him," Priya clucked. "Typical teenager."

Cathy smiled thinly. *Or maybe he's just remembering that horrendously awkward time Sara tried to set us up ...*

"Mum, you're smothering her." Sara pushed through into the entrance hall, planting a kiss on Bo's cheek before taking Cathy's hand and dragging her deeper into the house.

Priya tutted and followed them through into the farmhouse kitchen, with its olive-green cupboards and walnut countertops, a huge white aga oven the centrepiece, something warm and spicy simmering in a pot on the hotplate.

Perfect. And yes, she was jealous. But she was also glad for Sara. While her friend would never fully appreciate the middle-class comfort, the stable nuclear family, or having a supportive mum who had always *wanted* to be there; that was how it was meant to be. A child who grew up with the love they deserved would never know, could never know, just how lucky they were.

Sara grabbed a drink from the fridge, throwing a can of Diet Coke into Cathy's hands, before running into the lounge half of the room, flopping onto the sofa beside Louis to flick his nose and tease him mercilessly about his new girlfriend. Cathy smiled as she watched them, the can cold between her fingers, as cold as her heart at never experiencing anything even resembling affection with her two half-siblings.

"Congratulations on the new job," Priya said, bumping Cathy lightly with her shoulder before moving over to stir the food, releasing more spices into the air. "How are you finding it?"

Cathy turned to face her, leaning her hip against the kitchen island. "Good, thanks. It's a massive improvement."

"That's wonderful."

"My job's going great too, Mum. Thanks for asking," Sara shouted, not taking her eyes from Louis's phone as he showed her something. "You're lucky I took a night off to come here. Business is booming."

"That's great, Sara," Priya called back, before sighing under her breath.

Naturally, Sara hadn't hidden her chosen profession from her family and, equally naturally, her parents had not been particularly pleased about it. Unable to be vocally supportive, and never dreaming of being actively unsupportive, they maintained a polite indifference. Cathy wondered if a part of Sara's decision to first step into that controversial business had been to rebel against their pristine world and put a thorn in her mother's pride. And the fact Sara now insisted on doing everything on her own, when her parents had offered to fund her gallery? She definitely had a chip on her shoulder from growing up privileged.

"Erm, Priya?" Cathy asked, hoping to distract from Sara's acrimony whilst also getting a weight off her shoulders.

"Yes, deary?"

Cathy swallowed, bracing herself for more storytelling. "I really appreciated the invite, but I'm afraid I won't be able to come for Christmas anymore. I'm sorry. I had such a lovely time last year."

Concern softened Priya's brown eyes. "Oh, don't worry. Are you seeing family?"

She shook her head. "I, erm ... I've met someone, so I'm spending it with him. It's still new," she hastened to limit Priya's instant enthusiasm. "But it's going well so far."

"Well, if there was ever a better reason for changing plans ..." Priya flashed her a saucy little smile. "I hope you have a lovely time. Maybe you could bring him to the ceilidh in May?"

Cathy shrugged, hardly daring to think that far ahead. "How many years is it now?"

"Twenty-five! I can hardly believe it."

"That's impressive." Cathy's heart thawed a little at the thought of twenty-five years married and in love. Oh, to be so lucky. "I've always wondered, why ceilidhs?"

Priya chuckled as she waved her hands towards her face. "Well, definitely not because we're Scottish. But we did both go to St Andrews University as undergraduates. As a lonely, completely out of her depth, Indian girl far from home, I thought the ceilidh club would be the perfect place for me." She gave a wry frown. "Not really, but I was desperate to make some friends, and I've always loved dancing. As it turned out, at the very first session, I met Bo. He asked me to dance, and the rest is history."

"What a wonderful way to meet," Cathy said, starry-eyed at the romance of it all. Being asked to dance by a hot (*Don't tell Sara*), gentle Viking was definitely better than being subbed one by Mr Darcy. Whereas she got no dances, just an invite upstairs.

Before her mind could wander too far, Priya called everyone to the table, placing pots the size of cauldrons in the centre of the neatly laid table. Priya's food was always sublime; the fluffy rice, fragrant curry – she had made two, one for delicate taste buds and another for those who liked to sweat while they ate – and a variety of homemade naan breads did not disappoint. Cathy stayed mostly quiet while the Jefferies chatted like a real, cohesive family; a little bickering, a little banter seasoning the generally wholesome conversation.

Just as the plates were cleared and Articulate! placed on the table – because of course they were the kind of family that played games together, heck, they were the kind of family that still went on holiday together – a cry sounded from nowhere, startling only Cathy.

Bo picked up the baby monitor Cathy hadn't even noticed by his elbow. He watched the screen for a good minute before he smiled wearily.

"Robbie's awake."

"Let me go," Priya said, getting to her feet before Bo could.

He nodded. "I'll bring a bottle up."

"Can I come?" Cathy blurted, the words surprising her more than anyone else.

"Of course."

While the others returned to their easy chatter, Cathy followed Priya through the house and up the stairs, both their feet quiet on the carpet.

"You have a baby?" Cathy asked, unable to think of a better way to ask about the unexpected infant in the house.

Priya slowly opened the door into the pitch-black room. "Our latest foster."

Of course, how could she have forgotten the Jefferies were so perfect that they were emergency foster carers.

She'd never had anything to do with babies, never even held one, though something nestled deep inside her, something instinctive and probably mostly biological, told her she liked them. Fascinated, she watched as Priya changed their nappy, with only a tiny nightlight to brighten the darkness, and then reclined in the padded rocking chair to feed them the bottle Bo had snuck into the room. Cathy perched on the footstool nearby, watching the tiny human, feeling relief when their piercing cries petered out, soothed first by Priya's touch and then by warm milk.

"He's so little," she observed, keeping her voice low.

"He is," Priya acknowledged sadly. "He's very small for his age. Hasn't been getting enough milk."

Cathy's heart hollowed. "His parents weren't feeding him?"

"It would seem so."

It was sickening, horrifying. Priya must have noticed the abhorrence leak across her face, at her next words, spoken so calmly.

"There are many reasons why someone might be unable to care for a child: health, poverty, domestic abuse, to name a few. It's not always due to evil. But it does no good to dwell on it. He's safe now, and we'll give him everything he needs for as long as he's here."

Suitably humbled, Cathy watched as tiny hands pushed the bottle away and heavy eyes closed in sleep. "It's an amazing thing you do."

"After Sara tore her way out of me, so desperate to be her own person even then, it wasn't safe enough to me to carry another child," Priya reminisced. "So, we adopted Louis to complete our family. But as they've gotten older, as they've needed me less and less, I had to do something with all this love they didn't want anymore. I thought why not give it to the children that need it the most. I get to help so many, some for only days, some for weeks, but if I can be a little light in a darkness they never should have lived through, then it's all worth it."

There was something so terribly forlorn about it all, and yet still so hopeful.

If I could be half the woman she is ...

And despite it all, Priya smiled. "Would you like to hold him?"

"Can I?"

In reply, Priya carefully got to her feet, waiting until Cathy had taken the rocking chair before lowering a still sleeping Robbie into her arms. He stirred unhappily for a moment, his head resting in the crook of her arm – the fact he had known hunger before even being able to lift his head, made her eyes itch with tears. Little fingers found their way into his mouth and he sucked them vigorously, settling back into a deepening slumber. He felt so terribly light, so fragile, but more than that: precious. He was a little miracle, whether his parents wanted him or not, could care for him or not. As she placed a finger against the palm of his free hand, his grip tightening around it, she felt a categorical truth unfurl inside her.

The arrangement with Max, her additional clause; it had been a hasty, impulsive thing; a desperate attempt to make sure she came away with *something* after giving up so much of herself. But a part of her had known then, had always known, that children and motherhood would be part of her future. As much as she'd always dreamed of finding a lifelong partner, it wasn't as essential as creating a family of her own, whatever form it took.

If, at the end of it all, she didn't find a future in Max, maybe she could still come away with something to love.

Chapter Twenty

Considering nights out weren't really her thing, Cathy was actually rather enjoying herself. They'd had food followed by drinks at one bar, and were just heading over to bar number two when Alison decided it was time to sneak away.

"Do you want to leave too?" She asked, after hugging Sara goodbye and retreating to the back of the procession where Cathy dawdled on not-one-hundred-percent steady legs.

"Erm ..." Did she want to leave? Not really. She surprised herself with that thought, especially since they were out with Sara's friends who she didn't know particularly well and found slightly (highly) intimidating. "I think I might stay actually."

"You sure?"

"Yeah."

"Okay. I'll see you tomorrow then. Make sure Sara doesn't get too drunk."

"She can drink most men under the table."

"Just because she can, doesn't mean she should." Alison narrowed her eyes. "Do I have to tell you not to drink too much as well? Do I need to stay?"

"No, go! We'll be fine."

Cathy waved Alison goodbye and caught up with the rest of the group, that being Sara and her four other friends. She knew them a little, almost exclusively from Sara's previous birthday parties and, while they had always been nice enough to her, she still felt like she didn't quite fit in with them. She was just a little too awkward and drab in comparison, both in looks and in life. Ashley was a struggling musician with a passion for body positivity and feminist literature. Jaz was a primary school teacher, who spent her six-week summers travelling the world and competing in triathlons. Kanika, a young mother, whose family had deemed a failure when she became pregnant during her first year of university, who was now somehow managing to balance getting a medicine degree with solo parenthood. And finally, Gabrielle: Advertising Executive, freelance model, beauty influencer, almost a D-list celebrity, seen on TV that one time ...

Next to them all – and Sara, the most beautiful, confident, and talented woman she knew – Cathy had always felt rather inferior. She was a character drawn in 2D while they were 3D and fully animated. She'd always felt so ... boring. Tonight was different though. Even if they didn't know about her moonlighting as a millionaire's sex companion, and even if it wasn't something she was strictly proud of, she definitely thought it made her more interesting as an individual and, after three cocktails, she felt almost confident walking alongside animal-rights-activist, pole-dancing-for-exercise, this-is-my-real-nose-I-swear (Sara, a friend since childhood, had photographic evidence it wasn't her real nose), I-totally-kissed-Timothée-Chalamet-that-one-time, Gabrielle.

"I love your dress," Gabrielle complimented. Her voice was slightly nasally, which gave it a rather unfortunate, and permanent, disingenuous tone. Though, when paired with heavily mascaraed eyes that picked her little black dress apart stitch by stitch, Cathy felt it was rather authentically disingenuous that time.

"Thank you," she replied, wearing a fake smile of her own. "Sara gave it to me."

"It was one of my better charity shop finds," the birthday girl interjected. "I would have kept it for myself, but I don't have the tits to pull it off."

"I love thrifting," Ashley continued excitedly. She had the sweetest voice, the kind that belonged to an especially high-pitched ten-year-old girl; the multiple piercings, tattoo sleeves, and brightly coloured hair that changed every couple of months said otherwise. "There are so many hidden gems or things that just need a little altering."

"I'd still rather not wear other people's castoffs," Gabrielle said, nostrils flared with distaste.

"And I respect that as your choice. Though we really do need to address humanity's wasteful nature—"

"You know, Sara," Gabrielle interrupted to prevent one of Ashley's eco-warrior rants, "If you ever did want a boob job, I have the number of a great surgeon."

"Because plastic surgery is really more important than saving the planet we've fucked ..." Ashley muttered under her breath, falling back to walk with Kanika and Jaz in the hopes of finding more receptive ears.

"Is it the same guy that did your nose?" Sara retorted.

"*No*," Gabrielle replied testily. "He did my mum's boobs."

"Well, I'm happy for her, but my girls are perfect as they are." Sara flashed her sassiest smile. "Oh, here we are."

Rather than waiting in line, Sara strutted towards the bouncer that guarded the entrance.

"Hi Stan," she said, with a flirtatious lilt to her voice.

Stan's unimpressed scowl didn't waver. For a moment, he looked them over, bored eyes glancing at faces and handbags and questionable hemlines, as if he'd seen one too many skimpily clad young women to care anymore, and nodded at them to pass through. A ghost of a smile tugged at his lips as Sara blew him a kiss. It was for her eyes only and gone a second later, almost as if he didn't want people to know that under his tough exterior, he found plenty of amusement in the antics of his intoxicated patrons.

"Do you know him?" Cathy asked in a loud whisper as they stepped through into the stylish bar. The atmosphere was warm and sophisticated, the décor modern but with an alternative flair: leather seats with thin metal legs, lacquered oak tabletops, and jam jar chandeliers. Soft rock played in the background, barely audible over the layers of mumbled conversation and shrieking laughter.

"Stan? Yeah, he's great," Sara replied, effortlessly manoeuvring through the congestion by the entrance, while Cathy had to fight the impulse to apologise to every person whose elbow she bumped into. Sara had always moved more easily through the world than she did. "He's actually the guy that fixed the light last month, if you remember."

"Did he? I don't, but it's certainly nice of him to let us in ... and reserve us a table ..." She added hesitantly, as the woman at the bar smiled and waved Sara over to a nearby table, welcome tequila shots already waiting for them. "I didn't think they did this kind of thing."

"Not usually, but it helps when you're fucking the owner," Sara explained with her typical abrasive charm.

"You're sleeping with Stan?"

Sara gave her a sharp look. "No, not bouncer Stan. Stephen, the guy that owns the place. Are you feeling okay?"

"Great." Slightly embarrassed, Cathy plonked herself onto a chair and helped herself to a shot.

"I'm not quite drunk enough either," Kanika said, taking the next seat. "Got to make the most of a night out, rare as they are."

"No one ever said university *and* motherhood were easy, alone *or* together," Jaz sympathised, sitting next to Kanika, while Ashley, Sara, and Gabrielle shared the bench across the table, the birthday girl in the middle; the natural centre of attention and cohesive glue that made the group work.

There were cocktails and shots and conversation that became progressively lewder and, naturally, more amusing. Cathy worried for a moment they were being too loud but, after glancing around, she realised no one was paying them the slightest bit of attention; everyone else just as boisterous and carefree. *Just enjoy yourself*, she told herself firmly before turning back around and looking at Sara; eyes bright, smile easy. *I wish I could be more like her.* Sara always had, and probably always would, amaze her. The confidence, the candour, the natural expressiveness of her face; altogether it somehow managed to make the world shape to fit her rather than the other way around. She was animated, energising, and effortlessly enthusiastic, always livening up any situation she was in, just by being herself. That wholehearted, unassuming smile made Cathy forget for a moment her dislike of crowds and noise and strangers, made her realise just how much she adored her friend, and how, day by day, she was helping her to become a little freer too.

It was the reason she hadn't left early with Alison. She was braver now. She wanted to be braver still. So, she stopped shying away from the others, stopped being a passive listener, and joined in. Sure, she didn't have any scandalous stories she was at liberty to share, but she encouraged theirs and joined their chorus of laughter. She participated. With the alcohol warming her blood and the golden darkness wrapped around her skin, she felt ... happy. And as the sex anecdotes continued, more than a little aroused.

"Wait," Gabrielle gaped at Jaz, dazzlingly straight white teeth on show. "You broke up with someone—"

Jaz moaned as she hid behind her hands. "You don't have to say it again. I know it makes me a terrible person."

"Because she had an ugly cum face? That's wild."

"So mean," Ashley teased, giggling.

"It was really, really bad," Jaz justified quietly. "I couldn't stop laughing. So, it was kinder to end it."

"Did you ever tell her the reason?" Sara asked.

"Of course not! I told her I wasn't as over my last relationship as I thought I was."

"You martyr." Kanika wrapped a sympathetic arm around her still cringing friend.

Cathy had shared in their amusement, in their surprise, but it was shadowed a new fear, something she would never have thought to worry about: *Do I have an ugly cum face?*

Of course, there was only one person who knew the answer to that question, and as soon as her inebriated mind summoned his image, she could think of nothing else.

By the time Sara had decided they would have one more round of drinks before moving on to a club, Cathy was about ready to call it a night ... with the girls at least.

She got out her phone and paused for all of two seconds before sending a text sober-Cathy probably would have thought the better of.

CATHY: Wanna fuck?

She couldn't help but giggle to herself as she clutched the phone between her hands and imagined the sexy frown Max would pull when he read it. After a hectic week at work, she'd barely seen him, and the thought of waiting until Sunday to get her hands on him again felt unbearable. Luckily, her phone vibrated almost instantly.

MAX: Most of the time. I thought you had plans?

CATHY: I'm still out but about ready to head back, if you'd like to pick me up ...

MAX: Passive aggressive or actively suggestive ellipses, I wonder ...

MAX: Let me know where you are and I'll come get you.

CATHY: Thanks. We're at Babylon. Text me once you're outside and I'll come meet you.

Phew, at least drunk-Cathy was still intelligent enough to remember they couldn't be seen together.

"What are you smiling at, Cathy?" Jaz innocently enquired.

Luckily, Sara responded first, while Cathy's brain had a slight meltdown. Words, let alone lies, were suddenly impossible.

"It's probably just Mark texting her. She's been lovesick ever since they met all of a week ago, and they're already pretty serious."

"Wow, a week, huh?"

"Mhmm."

"That sounded rather judgemental," Cathy observed indignantly, her voice returning with attitude.

"A *week*, Cathy!" Sara exclaimed, banging a shot glass on the table like a gavel. "They're already going away together over Christmas. He bought her chocolates and clothes and I haven't even met the guy!"

"How's the sex?" Ashley asked, unabashedly revealing her priorities in a relationship.

"Erm ... there isn't any, yet."

"Exactly!" Sara shrieked. "He's bought her *underwear* before they've even slept together. It's fucking creepy."

She was getting fed up with this. Mark was definitely getting killed off (figuratively) after Australia.

"It does sound like you're moving pretty fast," Jaz said in what Cathy imagined was the concerned-teacher voice she used at naughty children's parents' evenings.

"Better than moving too slowly." Gabrielle gave a deliberate look in Sara's direction.

"What's that supposed to mean?" Sara snapped.

"You're having Jacob over tomorrow, aren't you?"

Cathy never thought she'd see the day where Gabrielle saved her ass.

"So?"

"*So*, you're still stringing him along as a friend when he's fancied you since secondary school."

There was an uncomfortable pause as Sara's scowl changed from incredulous to aggravated.

"Jacob does *not* fancy me. We're just good friends. And anyway, he's never dated anyone that I'm aware of, so I don't think he's into relationships. That, or he's closeted, but I think he would have told me if he was gay."

"Jacob's not gay, and he's not aromantic or asexual," Gabrielle dismissed. "He's never been with anyone because he's been pining after you for a *decade*."

"Then why would he never say anything?"

Even Cathy joined in with the others' guilty expressions.

"What?" Sara challenged.

"Well," Jaz began bravely. "It's always daunting to admit your feelings to someone else, especially when they're a friend and you don't want to risk the friendship ... and even more so when it's *you*."

"Is that your limp-dick way of calling me intimidating?" Sara looked between them all, anger ebbing slightly in the wake of disappointment.

Cathy gave her an apologetic smile. "But in a good kind of way. And Jacob is really, *painfully*, shy."

"You also don't have the kind of job many guys would be comfortable with their girlfriend doing," Gabrielle admitted, unusually pragmatic.

"No shit. There's a reason I gave up dating. Has he said anything about it?"

Gabrielle shook her head. "He wouldn't though. He respects you too much."

Sara appeared to mull the conversation over for a moment, before suddenly shaking herself, enchanting smile returning a second later.

"Well, I'm not changing my job for anyone, not until I have all the money I need. Not that it matters because we're just friends. Anyway, let's get these drinks." Her eyes turned towards the bar and widened. "Cathy ... isn't that Max?"

"Max?" Cathy turned around, eyes easily finding the man that always looked like a million dollars and knew it. "Oh, fuck."

Before she could run, or hide, or think of any other way to prevent him from spotting her, Sara got to her feet and waved to get his attention.

"Max!"

"Sara, stop!"

"Why? I want to know why he never made things happen with you."

"Sara, please don't! It's embarrassing. He's still my *boss*," she hissed.

But it was too late; he'd seen them.

He smiled at Sara before turning his attention on Cathy. At her obvious distress, he raised an eyebrow in question, and approached the table, two guys following closely behind him.

Shit shit shit.

"And what would bring Maximilian Cannavale to a place like this?" Sara saucily asked, as she sat back down and leaned forward on the table, looking playful and enticing and one wrong word away from becoming Cathy's worst nightmare.

Max's composure didn't falter under the scrutiny.

"It's one of the nicer bars in town. We thought we'd end the evening with a drink here," he said, indicating the two men behind him, one fair and blond, the other dark haired and coffee skinned. "This one," he nudged the blond man with his elbow, "Still thinks he can get lucky tonight."

After a moment, Cathy recognised him as Blonde Guy, the friend that had ditched Max during her last shift at the restaurant, the guy who would willingly run through a storm for sex.

"You two don't fancy your chances as well?" Sara pried with a suggestive smile.

"Not my style," Max easily replied. "And Myles is married."

"*Happily* married," Myles reaffirmed, as if to repel any women that were about to pounce on him.

"Well, you're welcome to join us, whatever you're here for, though I make no promises either way," Sara charmed, carrying on without giving them the space to refuse. "Jaz, Kanika; come out so Max can sit next to Cathy. Myles and ..."

"James," the blond man offered.

"*James.*" Sara thanked him with a smile that rarely failed to make people fall in love with her. "You can join on the end."

Cathy hadn't managed to raise her eyes by this point but, as she heard the strategic game of musical chairs being played around her, she finally looked up to watch Gabrielle, mouth open, expression vacant, as her eyes followed Max's every move. *Back off bitch,* Cathy thought to herself as she felt him take the seat beside her. She couldn't look at him, not when her body had started to hum with lust at the simple fact he was beside her; the scent of his aftershave turning her thoughts an erotic red. So, she switched her attention to Sara, who had Max straight across from her, right where she wanted him, and prayed the evening wasn't about to become the trainwreck it looked like it would.

"So, Max," Sara began, voice sickly sweet, eyes fiery. "What's your opinion of a couple who have only known each other for two weeks, dating for one, flying halfway around the world for a holiday together?"

"Is this about someone in particular?" Max calmly queried.

"Cathy. I, for one, think it's reckless."

"Sara, please," Cathy interrupted. "He doesn't need to know."

"If you don't mind, Cathy, I would like to know."

She finally looked at him, and sorely wished she hadn't. Underneath the external arrogance, concerns and questions simmered. At least he hadn't exposed her, at least not yet. If he did, the place would go up in flames, with a body or two left for dead on the floor. He had no idea about the bomb he held in his hands.

"As your employer, I care about your wellbeing," he expanded, perfectly at leisure. "And this explains the short notice with your recent holiday request."

He suddenly smiled and she realised, as much as he questioned her lies, he was enjoying the uncomfortable situation immensely.

"I also didn't know you were seeing someone," he added, looking directly at her.

She felt a blush rise in her already hot cheeks.

"His name is Mark," Sara answered for her. "A surprisingly wealthy scientist who thinks it's okay to buy her clothes and take her to the other side of the world barely a week after meeting her. I mean, the clothes thing is weird, right?"

"It is a little *familiar*," he acknowledged with a wryness Cathy's ears alone noticed.

"Exactly! And you can see why that's not the kind of guy I think my friend should be with?"

"I can but, ultimately, it's her decision. And, I would hope, she's taking reasonable precautions to minimise any potential danger."

"It is and I am," Cathy reaffirmed, heart fluttering as Sara's eyes narrowed. "Would you like a drink, Max?"

"No, thank you, I'm driving."

"Really? Why?"

"I joined the guys straight after work."

"How late did you stay at the office?"

"I left just after eight."

"Eight!"

He nodded, keen eyes looking her over, noticing the dilated pupils and pink cheeks. Oh, she wished she'd never lied because right then, she wanted to throw herself at him, especially since Gabrielle had never stopped gawping. It would have been nice to give them a story that was finally on a level with some of her lies.

Sara had watched their exchange with interest, noting their ease at conversation and the way their bodies leaned ever so slightly towards each other ... Was there something there?

"Well, I'm going to get myself a drink. Can I get anyone else one?" Myles asked, not quite prepared for the overlapping responses he received. As he and James headed to the bar, Sara gave her undivided attention to Max.

"So, is there a special lady in your life, Max? Or man, perhaps?"

His smile pulled to the side. "Neither."

"Oh, really? How surprising. Do you have a type?"

"Sara, stop," Cathy weakly complained.

Max shrugged. "I think most people have some preference."

Gabrielle suddenly lunged forward. "But you're not gay, are you?" She asked passionately.

Sara ignored her. "What do you think of Cathy?"

"I respect her highly."

"Do you find her attractive?"

"Sara!" Cathy exclaimed. "What are you doing?"

"Trying to help you find a decent man," her friend snapped back.

"I don't need you to! I don't want you to," she clarified meekly, suddenly deflated. "I'm going to get some air."

Cathy just glimpsed Sara's chagrined expression before she got to her feet and headed for the empty balcony. As she stepped outside, she immediately regretted not taking her coat with her, the late-night winter air wickedly cold, nibbling at her bare skin and quickly working its way under the thin layers of fabric she wore. Too late to go back, she clamped her chattering teeth together and stepped up to the railings, hands curling around the icy metal. She watched the lights over the river, the distant bodies crossing the bridge, and tried to forget about the annoyance that made her heart beat fast and the guilt that made her want to cry.

Why does Sara have to get so involved?

Because she cares about you.

What's going to happen tomorrow when there isn't a Mark?

Chaos. Catastrophe. Maybe you should just tell her the truth.

On her birthday? Do I really want to fall out with her on her birthday?

There will never be a good time to tell her you've been lying.

The door clicked softly open and closed behind her. Sighing, she took a deep lungful of ice, and prepared herself to tell the truth.

“Sara, I’m sorry—"

It wasn’t Sara but Max walking towards her. Wordlessly, he took off his jacket and placed it on her shoulders.

“Thank you,” she said as she slipped her arms into the sleeves. Max leaned forward on the railings beside her, tailored white shirt hugging that gorgeous torso. “Don’t look at me like that.”

“Like what?” He asked innocently, while wearing a very deliberate, very judgmental frown.

“This mess wouldn’t have happened if you’d just waited outside.”

“This mess wouldn’t have happened if you’d just told her the truth, even just a portion of it,” he retorted, frown softening at her wholly dejected expression. “Why wouldn’t you? Especially given her line of work.”

“It wouldn’t have made a difference. She never would have accepted it. She sees me as this fragile thing that needs protecting.” *And she, literally, said escorting wasn’t for me.*

“Then why didn’t you say we were together? Surely that would have been better than keeping an imaginary Mark around.”

“It would have been,” she acknowledged. “But the idea of it felt worse for some reason. I also didn’t want to involve you.”

“I would have played along.”

"I know."

But it would have felt too real. That was the reason. If he pretended to love her ... she would fall for the performance as much as anyone else. It was a boundary she needed. Sure, they could pretend for a couple of weeks in a different country, with people she'd never see again, but her everyday life, her little world; that had to stay authentic, or lies would mutate into delusions.

"I think it's time you went home," he said, his voice taking on a teasing tone. "Sad drunks don't make for very good company."

She suddenly remembered why he was there in the first place. The confrontation with Sara had dulled her lust, but alone, with him beside her, his jacket and cologne resting on her shoulders; it was eager to start building again.

"I'm not that drunk."

"Probably too drunk to consent," he countered.

"Haven't you already bought my consent?"

He scoffed. "Now there's an ethical dilemma. You can mull it over in the car," he ended with a tone of finality, and led the way back inside.

The others were downing their drinks and gathering their belongings, ready to move on. As they headed for the door, Sara brushed alongside Cathy.

"I'm sorry if I was out of line," she said, linking their arms together. "You know how loose my tongue can get after a few drinks. I'm sure I'll love Mark as much as you do when I meet him tomorrow."

"Yeah, probably," Cathy replied meekly, knowing full well there would be no Mark for anyone to love tomorrow.

Maybe she should have tried getting in touch with the real Mark, asked him to pretend to be her boyfriend like a bad Hollywood romcom. That thought was quickly dismissed at the image of Mark's guaranteed terrible acting (since he'd done a terrible job at *not* acting during their date), and that was assuming he didn't immediately block her at the suggestion after how despicably she'd treated him. No, using real Mark had never been an option. *Hire an amateur actor on Craigslist then? Is Craigslist still a thing?* Scrap that too – *her* acting skills weren't good enough either. She had no choice but to disappoint Sara.

She was startled from her ruminations as Sara turned away from the entrance, hand reaching for a door she hadn't even noticed.

"I thought you wanted to go to a club?"

"I do. It's downstairs." Sara took Cathy's hand and pulled her through into the black stairwell, music pulsing in the walls already. "Dance with me?"

She had to disappoint her tomorrow; she didn't want to start today. But ...

"Erm ..." She glanced back over her shoulder to see Max. Puzzled; he held her eye for a moment before sharing a word with his friends, and they all turned to follow.

Okay then.

"I should have drunk more if you wanted me to dance."

"We can chug some vodka," Sara giggled, beaming as she skipped down the stairs, Cathy just about managing not to tumble down after her.

Thumping music grew louder and louder until it was almost painful. The stairs opened into a packed basement club, a neon-lit bar on the wall nearest to them, the floor full of bodies dancing in the semi-darkness, colourful strobe lights illuminating their sweaty, intoxicated faces as they lost themselves in the music and each other.

Sara stepped behind the bar, whispering to one of the girls there before dumping coats and bags and helping herself to a bottle from the shelves.

"Happy birthday to me!" She cheered before taking a long swig from the bottle.

The bottle made its way around the group, James and Myles joining in while Max passed it over. It finally reached Cathy's hands, about a sixth of the clear liquid remaining.

"Cathy! Cathy! Cathy!" Sara started the chant, the other girls quickly joining in.

Cathy fumbled for a moment. It really wasn't her scene, but she wasn't ready to dull the joy on Sara's face just yet. She placed the glass to her lips and started to swallow.

"Cathy! Cathy! Cathy!"

It was foul. And it burned.

With a gasp, she came up for air, wincing at the poison stinging the back of her throat. She wiped her lips with the back of her hand before raising the empty bottle in the air. She couldn't help but smile at the cheers, at Sara wrapping her arms around her. Alcohol, old or new, hit her head. She wobbled. But then the bottle was gone and Sara was dragging her into the throng of bodies on the dancefloor.

"I don't know how to dance!" Cathy shouted as Sara started moving, shimmying her body to the music, oozing confidence and sensuality.

"No one does!" Sara grinned back, taking Cathy's hands and helping her move. "Don't think about it. Just feel it."

She closed her eyes, feeling her head spin. The music was so loud it vibrated the floor and pulsed in her brain like starbursts of colour. Floating in the darkness, she felt the music combine with the alcohol in her blood, the bass becoming her heartbeat, and she started to move.

Eyes open, she saw hazy air, flashing lights, warm bodies, and Sara's strawberry smile beaming at her.

Letting the alcohol take over, she danced, feeling loose and free, giddy almost. Sara's friends surrounded them, rocking on their feet and swaying their hips, dancing alone but together. All except Ashley, who was busy pushing her body up against James, dancing around him in some kind of modern mating ritual, which James was all for, given how his eyes clung to her, how his hands gravitated towards her generous hips. They wasted no time acquainting themselves with each other, hands roaming, hips rocking, until their mouths collided.

Oh ... Cathy watched them for a moment, feeling lustful heat spike in her cheeks, her hands itching to touch someone else's skin, too. Not just someone ...

She looked away, peering through the smoky darkness, barely making out the shape of two shadows by the bar. As a blue light flashed their way, it confirmed the shadows were Max and Myles; Myles watching the crowd, looking detached and ready for bed; Max with eyes only for her.

"Do you still like him?" Sara asked, noticing where her attention had wandered to.

"It's impossible," was all she could think to reply.

"He watches you like he wants to fuck you."

A laugh slipped through her lips. "I know, right?"

She continued dancing, enjoying the vibrations in her chest, closing her eyes to lose herself in the music. At some point, she lost Sara, lost the others completely, swallowedby the crowd. She didn't mind, just like how she didn't mind when unfamiliar arms brushed against her, or unknown shoulders bumped into her back. It didn't matter; it was just her, her body, and the music, basking in feeling weightless and free.

Something made her open her eyes. Maybe her body sensed him. Maybe it was the deliberate movement in a sea of chaos. Blinking back the darkness, she turned to see Max behind her, shoving another man away. The man stepped back in, so Max placed a firm hand on his chest whilst draping his other arm across her shoulders, tucking her in against his side in a way that clearly said *She's mine.* Hands held up in apology, the other man turned away, gone from sight a second later.

"What are you doing?" She shouted at Max, spinning out of his grasp to keep dancing.

"Stopping you from getting felt up by a stranger," he replied, placing his mouth close to her ear so that she could hear him.

Getting protective, are we, Max?

She scanned the bodies around them but there was no sign of anyone she knew, double-checking to make sure there was no Sara. They were more anonymous than ever.

A flirty, tipsy smile pulled at her lips as she shimmied in close to him, grazing him with her hips and then her bum as she spun around in front of him.

"Maybe I wanted to be felt up?" She suggested, pushing her back against his chest, peering up over her shoulder to see those hard eyes watching her. She grinded against him, watching the control slip from his face.

He didn't disappoint her. In that dark club, bodies all around them, his arms wrapped around her, stroking just under her boobs and down over her stomach, to rub against her thighs, teasing under the hem of her dress slightly. That was when she noticed how warm she felt and the fact she was still wearing his jacket.

"You're playing a dangerous game," he growled in her ear, as she rocked her body against his, feeling his erection digging into her ass.

She spun around, draping her arms around his neck, tipping back her head to offer her mouth to his, lips slightly parted against the hot, airless atmosphere. A second later his mouth found hers, hands pinching her waist before shamelessly grabbing her ass, pulling her closer, letting her feel his erection against her core. He moved his leg between hers, his thigh solid under her, and as his kisses deepened, she felt that firmness rub against her clit. She gasped at the sensation, at the friction that quickly sparked the fire in her, her clit suddenly a greedy thing. He clawed at her curves while she rubbed herself against his leg, unconcerned for the strangers around them. They were cloaked in shadows, in anonymity, just another couple in a mass of couples getting frisky under the effects of deafening dance music and too much alcohol, her moans silenced by the roaring all around her.

Maybe if Max had been drunk as well, they would have taken it further. Instead, he noticed her breathlessness, the desperation in her increasingly frantic movements, and removed his leg.

Her eyes snapped open.

"Time to go," he told her, a flicker of something playful softening his serious expression. "I have no plans to fuck you in a club, however tempting you're being."

"But you are going to fuck me?" She asked, desperate to rub herself against him again.

"Isn't that why I came to find you in the first place?"

Oh yeah, he had been her booty call tonight. The lucid part of her brain realised that probably wasn't right, but the drunk, horny part of her just shrugged. He made the rules and he'd answered her summons, so it must be okay.

"Come on," she saw him mouth before he reached for her hand and dragged her through the mayhem, shielding her with his body as much as he could.

"I have to say bye to Sara," she shouted at him, yanking at his arm a moment later when he hadn't heard her. From her wide eyes scanning the faceless crowd, he inferred her intentions. Pulling her flush against him, he searched from his vantage point of just being taller. *Hmm* ... she nuzzled his chest. She liked protective Max.

"I see her. Towards the bar." His voice vibrated by her ear. "I'll grab the guys and meet you by the door. Try not to get groped by anyone."

He gave her a gentle push in the right direction, her legs suddenly unsteady without him to hold onto. But she made it to Sara, flopping an arm around her shoulders as she felt the world spin.

"Cathy!" Sara cheered, pressing a kiss to her cheek.

"I think I'm done."

"Sure. Thanks for humouring me. Have you called an Uber?"

"Max is going to give me a lift home."

Sara's eyebrows shot up. "Really? You should totally invite him up for 'coffee' afterwards."

"Sara!" Cathy admonished before giggling.

"What! Mark never has to know. I wouldn't normally condone cheating but, after only a week, you're barely a couple anyway ... Come on, you know it's true. Plus, Max is gorgeous, and maybe it would lead to something ..."

Cathy swallowed her mirth. "Stop. You're terrible."

"Sorry, sorry! I'll see you tomorrow. Love you."

"Love you too."

An air kiss later, Sara headed back into the throng, finding her way to her friends, wrapping her arms around Kanika's and Gabrielle's waists as she claimed her place in the centre.

Cathy sobered a little as her eyes lingered on the back of Sara's head, until she was absorbed into the mosh pit, becoming another faceless member of the night-time crowd, and she wondered how their friendship would play out when her betrayal was inevitably uncovered.

She grabbed her coat and bag from behind the bar, dashing over to join Max by the doorway, where he watched Myles dragging James away from the dancefloor.

"She's lost interest, mate," she heard Myles shout.

"She'll come around!" James argued back.

With a nod towards the door, they all followed Max up the staircase, through the bar and out into the cold night. It was a bitter, sobering thing. Had she really been about to orgasm in public by grinding on Max's leg? If she'd been any less drunk, that thought would have had her curled up on the floor dying of embarrassment.

"That was a *fun* diversion," Max said next to her, breaking through her daze.

She might not have been embarrassed enough to die, but she was too embarrassed to look at him.

"It's only a short walk to the car," he continued at her silence, before leading the way. He wrapped an arm around her waist and pulled her into step beside him. "Can you manage a five-minute walk?" He asked, glancing down at her in concern as she half-limped, half-wobbled like baby Bambi.

She huffed, her breath visible in the icy air. "I'm really not that drunk. I'm just a novice at wearing heels and my feet hurt. Ah, sod it. Here." She shoved her coat in his hands to take off his jacket. "Sorry, I forgot I was still wearing it," she said, taking back her coat and returning his.

"I like you in it," he confessed, eyes scanning over her little black dress before slipping the jacket back onto his shoulders.

I like you in it more, she thought as she flung on her coat and stepped out of her shoes, sighing with relief as her blistered soles touched the cold pavement.

"Classy," he mumbled, flashing her a wry smile as he continued walking, James suddenly claiming his side.

"My Sal does that all the time," Myles said, waiting for her to pick up her shoes to walk with her.

"What's a Sal?" She asked, struggling to switch her mind off everything Max. It was probably a good idea to cool off a little whilst they had company.

He laughed to himself. It was a gentle sound and not at all malicious. Even though that would normally have been enough to make her insides flutter with embarrassment, she got nothing but positive vibes from Myles. He had a kind face, and a rough, gentle, voice that rumbled along at its own slow, unthreatening pace.

"Sally, my wife," he explained. "Rarely gets dressed up, but when she does; she puts in the effort. Half an hour in, the complaints about her feet start, and half an hour later she's walking around in the flats she brought as back-up."

"Sounds like a woman after my own heart, except I let my friend put the effort in for me. I really am quite useless at being glamorous," Cathy babbled while thinking about how Sally was a rather uncommon name these days. "Where is Sally tonight?"

"At home with the kids. We do take it in turns to have an evening off," he hastily reassured. "Tyler is no bother at all, but Abby is autistic, and we think she might have ADHD. She isn't comfortable with babysitters – strangers, you know – and we don't have much family nearby."

"That must be tough," Cathy acknowledged.

"Yeah, sometimes. Max gives us an evening out together about once a month, forks the bill as well, so I can't really complain."

"Max does?"

"The kids love him." Myles frowned to himself, finally remembering to share a vital bit of context. "Sal is his housekeeper, while I work in maintenance at the hotel. Over the years, I think he's become rather fond of us as a family."

Cathy couldn't help but smile, and that wasn't just because the thought of Max *babysitting* was kind of hilarious. "He has mentioned Sally a couple of times, and it's nothing but praise. I think he'd fall apart without her, or at least his house would."

"He'd fall apart without her; the house would fall apart without me," Myles clarified, eyes creased with amusement. "He has been good to us too though. When Sally had her cancer scare, he paid for all the tests and consultations; now the whole family has private healthcare – he added it to her contract so that we couldn't protest. And then at Christmas, it's him spoiling the kids rotten not us."

"Why are my ears burning?" Max suddenly asked, pausing his conversation with James and looking over his shoulder to glare at the two of them.

"I'm just learning that you fancy yourself a bit of a fairy godmother," she teased, looking at him in a new light. He had tried to tell her already that he wasn't purely selfish with his wealth, but she hadn't quite believed him. Hearing it from someone else's mouth was substantially more convincing.

"They do a lot for me; it's only fair I give them something back," he said, rather seriously.

"Why don't you spoil me at Christmas then?" James asked.

"We only play tennis with each other, which *I* pay for. You're not worth much more than that."

"Yeah, well, I let you win."

"Fuck off, no you don't," Max said, grinning at him.

They'd reached the car. When James instinctively sat himself down in the passenger seat, Max pulled him back out. "James, don't be a dick. Sweaty, drunk men in the back."

James just shrugged and clambered into the backseat. Max held the door open for Cathy. She brushed against his arm as she walked around him, pausing for a moment before getting in. She wanted to kiss him and confess she was more in awe of him than ever. Being rich and handsome was one thing; being down to earth and generous as well was another, and even sexier. But she refrained from any PDA, instead flashing him a saucy little smile and saying, "Thank you."

"It's more for me than you," he whispered back, eyes dipping to the generous neckline of her dress.

"What happened to all that talk about consent earlier?"

He smiled a little wickedly. "That's already gone out the window, don't you think?" He lowered his voice. "Around the time you were grinding your body on me."

Her skin grew warm – embarrassed, aroused – her clit wide awake and itchy as if saying *Time to go again?*

"You're easily persuaded," she observed, her voice soft, before she climbed into the passenger seat. Grace was not her forte, but giving him an eyeful of thigh and cleavage; that she easily achieved.

"I know when a battle isn't worth fighting—"

"Stop flirting and get in the fucking car," James called, his tone more humorous than annoyed.

Max leaned into the car to glare at James, his hand secretly sliding under Cathy's dress to stroke up her leg. As his hand wandered to her inner thigh, she clenched her legs together, trapping his hand against her sex. She looked up at him, wanting some smouldering eye-contact, but he kept himself expertly unaffected.

"I'll get in *my* fucking car when I want to," he retorted before moving away, pulling his hand free and shutting the door.

“They’re always like this,” Myles informed her. “It’s mostly good-natured.”

“It’s all good-natured until we’re on the court,” James chuckled, cracking his knuckles at the sight of Max getting into the car. Suddenly, he leaned forward, sour breath hot on her cheek. “Hey, Cathy, right? Could you give me that girl’s phone number?”

“Erm ... no?”

“James, you’re such an oaf,” Myles sighed, disgusted.

“What do you mean?”

“You don’t even know her name and you’re trying to get into her pants.”

“She was trying to get into mine too!”

Cathy saw Max roll his eyes as the dashboard came silently to life.

The guys talked quietly amongst themselves while Max drove. She was far too distracted thinking about the imminent sex she was about to have to pay attention to the conversation, and otherwise occupied by teasing Max – shifting her skirt an inch up her thighs, reclining against the seat to push her chest out, grazing a finger over her lips as if in thought. Through subtle glances at her, she knew he was paying attention. Where they were going to have sex was a bit of an issue though. She didn’t want him coming back to the flat, lest Sara return and find them, and she couldn’t really go back to his place because she needed to be home, lest Sara suspect something. They dropped James off outside of his flat first, followed by Myles outside his house, which was only ten minutes away from Max’s.

"He likes Sal to be nearby for any household *emergencies*," Myles joked. "Night Max. Nice to meet you, Cathy."

He waved goodbye and headed inside.

Max slid back into his seat after letting Myles out, quickly closing the door against the cold midnight air.

"Isn't it a bit tedious only having two doors?" She wondered aloud. It seemed a weird inconvenience for a rich person to have.

"I don't usually have a car full, so not really. It's hard enough finding a nice car with four seats let alone four doors."

They clearly had very different opinions about what constituted a *nice* car. But his car was very nice, she had to admit, very sexy, and it suited him.

"Do your friends know about me?" She asked, her voice just a whisper as she *felt* the fact they were now alone, her body humming in anticipation.

"Not exactly," Max replied rather unhelpfully. "So, am I taking you home?" He asked a heartbeat later, blatantly undressing her with his eyes.

"No. Drive somewhere quiet," she ordered and started shimmying out of her tights.

He didn't argue. After a couple of minutes, he turned the car down an empty street, the backs of houses on one side, a tall iron fence bordering a deserted park on the other. All was quiet, all was dark, not a streetlamp in sight to illuminate them. At least it was mildly less publicly indecent than a packed nightclub.

As soon as the engine powered down, she threw herself at him, or rather, awkwardly clambered over. It was a bit of a struggle, and not her sexiest moment, but eventually she managed to get comfortable straddling his thighs. An inelegant thirty seconds wasn't enough to dampen her desire, especially when it was fuelled by alcohol and two hours of closeness, by lust and secrets, near him but not *on* him. Now though ...

She pushed her body against his, while her hands stroked over the rough stubble along his jaw and burrowed into his hair, tugging slightly as their lips met. Their kisses were short and ferocious, like starved animals that had finally been allowed to feed. There was something savage in their movements too; in the fingers that clawed down her back, in the hot, heavy breathing that steamed up the windows. It was just him and her and the burning itch that needed satisfying. Nothing beyond their two bodies mattered.

"You drive me fucking crazy," he growled as the two buttons on the front of her dress were undone, breasts lifted out of their lace cups one by one to be admired and caressed. As his hands stroked over her bare skin and his lips kissed her neck, teeth sharp, grazing, biting, she gasped, losing the sliver of patience she'd been holding onto. There was no point drawing out the pleasure this time; she just wanted to come, deep and fast. Her hands explored under his untucked shirt to the leather belt that hid him from her. She struggled with the buckle for a moment; the chime of metal hitting metal as the strap pulled through like music to her ears. The rest was easier. A moment later, his erection was in her hand and, as she pulled her underwear to one side, in line with her cunt.

"Fuck," he hissed as she sharply lowered herself, taking all of him in one go.

"Finally," she breathed back, grazing her lips across his jaw.

Words were swapped for moans as their lips locked together again. For a moment, she just let him sit deep inside her, the tightness and fullness exactly what she wanted, before starting to move, just a little, just enough to rub her G-spot with his engorged head, while her clit brushed against the fabric of his shirt. It felt amazing. He felt amazing. Her orgasm was just waiting to be released, when an intrusive thought sashayed into her head, distracting her completely.

"Max?" She mewed.

"Cathy."

"When I ... finish? Is my expression ... ugly?"

A surprised huff escaped him, his fingers tightening their hold on her hips.

"No," he confirmed. "Quite the opposite."

The opposite being . . . *oh.*

This man was going to destroy her.

She kissed him to stop herself from asking any more dangerous questions, rocking her body against his to start the climb again. It didn't take long; her mind filled with the word he hadn't said. *Beautiful*. She was almost there, that delicious warmth beckoning. So, she moved faster, chasing it down, catching up with it a moment later as blissful heat consumed her.

"Oh ..." But there weren't any words. She was too distracted to do anything other than bite her lip and keepthe pressure where she needed it, savouring each delicious pulse. She barely heard Max's groan as he climaxed too, barely felt his desperate thrusts as he moved beneath her, riding out his orgasm.

She flattened herself against him, arms around his neck, her head using his shoulder as a pillow, and waited for him to still. It was dark and warm; she was drowsy and content. She could have easily drifted to sleep ...

"Hey," Max said, his voice unusually gentle, "I can't drive you home if you're asleep on me."

"Hmm? Oh ..." She woke up just enough to tumble off him, bruising her thigh on the central console as she went, and accepted the tissue he handed her. After half-heartedly making herself decent, she turned her head to the side and closed her eyes again, the purr of the car coming to life lulling her back into a stupor.

"Seatbelt please," a voice said.

She grumbled something incomprehensible back. The voice sighed before leaning over her, a metallic click following shortly after as her seatbelt was secured.

Black and orange flashed across her eyelids, like some kind of Morse code, until they came to a stop and there was just black.

"Cathy?"

"Hmmm?"

"We're here. Do you want me to come up with you?"

"Hmmm ..."

"I'm coming up with you."

A moment later, she was reluctantly pulled from the car and forced to walk through the terribly cold darkness.

"I'm tired," she muttered with great displeasure, as a strong arm wrapped around her waist and kept her upright. "And it's cold."

"I know. But you're nearly home."

"You smell nice." She curled in against his side, drinking in that intoxicating scent. "How much does it cost to smell like that?"

A tired chuckle was her only answer, which was a shame because she really was curious. If it hadn't been too expensive, she could have bought a bottle to sniff at when she missed him, sprayed it on her pillow to pretend he shared her bed ... Okay, she was definitely a little drunk.

"Thank you," she said as she reached the door to the flat. He let her struggle with her handbag for thirty seconds before reaching in to retrieve the keys himself. "Thank you," she repeated. "I'll see you Sunday."

"I'm not leaving just yet," he said firmly. "I'm going to make sure you reach your bed."

"You don't have to."

"I want to."

"Okay ..." She couldn't prevent the little leap her heart gave at his protectiveness. "I like your friends, by the way," she commented, opening the door and leading the way inside, feeling herself wake up a little as she stepped into the ordinary reality of her home.

"Yeah, they're good guys."

"It was nice to see you with them," she said, not quite casually, and disappeared into her room to grab her paisley pyjamas while he lingered in the living room.

"What do you mean?"

"It's nice to see you have normal friends."

"And by normal you mean ..."

She reappeared, walking past him to the bathroom. "Not filthy rich or pretentious. Nice, down-to-earth people."

"Are rich people only allowed to be friends with other rich people?" He teased, leaning against the wall beside the bathroom doorway she'd purposely left ajar. "Can't rich people be down-to-earth?"

"I'm sure they can be ..."

"Are you insinuating that I'm not?"

She poked her head around the door but kept her now naked body out of sight. "Actually, after seeing you with them, I think you're far more grounded and generous than I ever gave you credit for."

"Why are you looking at me like that?" He asked wryly, eyes catching on her bare shoulder.

"Like what?"

"Like you want to fuck again."

"I'm not." She deliberately bit her lip and pressed her body against the edge of the door. "I'm going to shower."

"Okay ..."

Smiling to herself, she turned the shower on, waiting thirty seconds for the water to warm up before stepping inside and washing the night off her.

"Does Myles know you fancy his wife?" She asked as she lathered the fruity body wash over her skin, cleaning away alcohol sweat and sex residue.

"I can't hear you," he called back.

She repeated her question.

"If you want to keep talking to me, I'll have to come in."

"Fine!"

He stepped through a second later, casually perching on the side of the bath, legs stretched out in front of him, to watch her in the shower.

Hmm, maybe I could go again, she thought as she stroked her hands over her stomach before dipping between her thighs. *Wait ... Shit. He wasn't meant to come in the flat! What if Sara comes back?*

"You were saying?" He asked, eyebrows raised in question as her sensual movements were morphed into efficient ones.

"I said, does Myles know how much you admire his wife."

"You said fancy the first time."

"I ... I thought you couldn't hear!" She spared a second to frown disapprovingly at him, before tipping her head back under the water and roughly rinsing her hair.

"Myles knows exactly how much I admire Sally, and him. They're decent, hardworking people who've had their fair share of difficulties, and I respect them both immensely."

"What do they know about me?" She asked, trying an open question this time after the closed one earlier had failed. While her tone was impressively offhanded, her ears pricked up, eager for answers. She turned the shower off and wrapped herself in a towel.

"Sally knows there's a woman in my life, not you specifically, but after Myles met you tonight, they'll probably put two and two together." He shrugged, raising his voice over the drone of her electric toothbrush. "Not that it really matters. They know I'm a private person, and they always keep everything between themselves."

She nodded, unable to prevent her mind from wondering about all the other *women* of his Sally had known about, dressed a bedroom for, bought clothes for, had sanitary products on standby for. *Did he treat them the same way he treats me? Gifts, holidays, genuine conversation? Did he make sure they got home safe?*

"Careful," he said, his stare suddenly firm, chiding.

"Hmmm?" She mumbled, feigning surprise, when really, she dreaded how well he seemed to read her.

"Whatever it was making your eyes sad. Careful. If this is causing you more harm than good, I'll—"

She turned on the tap and spat out the toothpaste. "You'll end it, I know. Don't worry, I don't love you, but that doesn't mean I like to be reminded I'm just the most recent in a long line of whores."

See, Max, I'm not scared of the L word, or the W word. I know what I am and I know what we're not.

She gasped as she felt his hands on her waist, forcing her to spin around and face him. He stepped in close, until the backs of her thighs touched the cool ceramic of the sink and her hands reached back to keep herself from falling. She wasn't sure what he intended to do (was she ever?): fuck her, intimidate her, humiliate her even – yet his next words still caught her slightly off guard.

"The line isn't that long," he murmured, leaning close to press a kiss to her still damp neck. "And you're not *just* anything."

She melted into the kiss, savouring the sensation that seemed to titillate more than just her neck, but her body stilled as she realised something.

"You enjoy it, don't you?" She whispered the accusation.

He leaned back, arrogant smile barely fading at her tone. "Like what?"

"This. This flirty game you play."

Making people fall in love with you, she elaborated in her head. *Do you like breaking their hearts as well?*

"Of course I do. You're enjoying it too," he replied, smile dying as he read her mind and realised the accusation was much more serious. His brow darkened. "Careful," he repeated, somehow making that single word impossibly heavy, sinking through her like an unwanted truth.

His hands snapped off her a moment later and he skulked from the room.

She took a minute to catch her breath. Another to change into her pyjamas. Stepping out, she found him stood in the kitchen, arms folded, surveying the new artwork on the fridge.

"I think I'll manage not to die on the way to my bed now," she said a little frostily.

"Good," he replied, his voice equally cool. "I'll see you Sunday. Bring your things; we fly on Monday."

"Yes, sir."

She just caught a glimpse of his exasperated yet amused smile, before she turned away and disappeared into her bedroom. It was pitch black but her feet easily found their way to the bed, her body sighing with relief as it collapsed and curled up; her mind following a second later at the sound of the Yale lock clanking shut as the front door closed. *At least he's gone*. She decided to stay awake for ten minutes to make sure Sara didn't cross his path, but with her tired head nestled in its favourite spot on the pillow, she immediately fell asleep instead.

Max had just reached his car when a taxi pulled up to the curb behind him. A rather unsteady Sara stepped out. Her balance returned in an instant as she stood up straight and watched a Maserati speed away down the street. There was only one dark silver Maserati she knew, and only one millionaire that seemed partial to driving to their shabby side of the city. Any immediate excitement was quickly lost under a cloud of suspicion. Cathy would never cheat; she was too much of a romantic. She might lie though ...

There was *definitely* something there.

Chapter TwentyOne

Cathy slept late into the morning. She had nothing to get up for and her bed had never felt more comfortable, so she was happy just to sleep the hours away. At some point, loud, metallic banging sounds started in the kitchen, followed by muffled pop song melodies as the radio was turned on and turned up. Groaning at the unfair state of the world, she patted her bedside table where her phone should have been, hand coming away empty. With more groaning, she forced herself out from under the covers, donned slippers and dressing gown, and followed the noises.

"Happy birthday!" She shouted at Sara as she entered the living room. The birthday girl was by the sink in the kitchen, briskly butchering vegetables before tossing their colourful carcasses into a giant casserole dish. "How many are you planning to feed tonight?"

"Thanks. Just six, but the leftovers will do me for ... the next week most likely," Sara replied, eyes locked on fingers and knife, no singing or dancing like she normally would while cooking. Perhaps she was still feeling the effects of the previous night.

Cathy had a quick scan of the room, looking for her wayward phone, before starting to search under books and cushions with increasing panic.

"You okay?" Sara asked, watching her frantic movements.

"Yeah, just trying to find my phone ..."

After another fruitless thirty seconds, she was about to check the bedroom and bathroom when Sara spoke again.

"Your coat was on the table when I got in, so I hung it up. Maybe it's there."

"Oh ..." Cathy dashed over to the coats hanging on the hooks by the front door, patting down pockets until she came away victorious. "There you are. Thank you," she said to Sara, joining her again in the kitchen. "I was so exhausted when I got back, I just crashed into bed. Phew ... there's no worse feeling than thinking you've lost your phone."

"I can think of a few."

Cathy paused in her gathering of breakfast, hand hovering over the granola jar. Sara sounded weird. Not angry or anything just ... not Sara. Her friend noticed her looking and finally smiled.

"You've obviously never thought you lost your passport, *that* is much worse," she teased, turning her attention back on the vegetables.

"I can imagine." Having successfully obtained bowl, granola, yoghurt, honey, and a sneaky handful of Sara's blueberries, Cathy sat down on one of the mismatched chairs at the kitchen table, spoon in one hand, phone in the other.

"Did you get back okay last night?" Sara asked.

"Yeah, fine. When did you get in?"

"Not sure." Sara continued after a slight pause, as if listening to the rhythmic *chop chop* of the knife on the wooden board. "How was Max? I didn't make things too awkward, did I?"

"No, he was fine, ever the professional. He took Myles and James home as well," Cathy replied distractedly, feeling a little deflated at the absence of new messages. "Do you want any help prepping?"

Sara kept her eyes down, her voice and manner still strangely neutral. "No, I'm all sorted. Once the stew's in, I'll make the kheer, and then make myself presentable. Actually, if you wouldn't mind tidying the place up a little ..."

"Yeah, sure. Let me know once you're done in the kitchen, so I can make your cake."

"You don't have to."

"I'd like to, especially since you're cooking your own birthday meal."

Sara eyed her over her shoulder. "That's because someone else never offered to."

"It would be awful! I'm a half-decent baker but a terrible cook. Unless you like soup. I got very good at making soup."

Sara rolled her eyes. "You're not a terrible cook, just a lazy one, hence the whole soup thing," she said, sounding more like her usual self.

They both knew that wasn't the real reason Cathy had acquired an impressive soup repertoire, but neither of them was going to mention terminally ill fathers just then.

"But I'll take a cake," Sara continued. "I'd also like to collect my present from you ..."

Cathy had almost forgotten. "Oh, my measurements."

"I want to make a start on the clothes. The designs are basically done."

"Okay. Probably best to get them now before I put on half a stone from tonight." Cathy dropped her spoon into the bowl with a resounding chink, before standing up to place it alongside the slightly intimidating stack of washing up on the counter. "Once I've gotten dressed, I'll tidy the flat, then you can measure me, and then I'll make your cake. How's that for being a great friend on your birthday?"

She was halfway across the room by the time Sara tossed the last handful of vegetables into the pot and turned around, an insincere smile stretching her lips. "Only finally sharing Mark with us will make you even better," she said, turning back again before Cathy could respond.

Oh boy, breaking the news later that Mark won't be attending is going to be apocalyptic, she thought to herself. But that could wait. She didn't plan on ruining any more of Sara's birthday than she had to.

*

"Jacob!" Sara exclaimed as she flung the door open to her oldest friend, hurling herself against him a second later. He was used to her violent attacks of affection, her enthusiasm for greetings and goodbyes, so he'd known to brace himself. His feet didn't move an inch on impact. His balance barely wavered as her arms wrapped around his neck. Only the quiet joy – the quiet despair – on his face gave away how much he loved the contact, how much it hurt him, and how he absolutely made the most of every second with her.

"Hey, Sara. Happy birthday," he replied softly, squeezing her back.

She stepped away a moment later, hands still on his arms, and beamed at him with that wholesome smile of hers. It had no effect on him since he was already hopelessly in love with her.

"Thank you. Please head through, I just need to finish up in the kitchen."

"Sure." Jacob stepped past her and headed towards the others, who had stood up at his arrival. "Hey, g-guys."

Cathy, Alison, and Dylan gave him a chorus of welcomes, followed by waves and one rejected handshake.

"Nah, man, come here," Dylan said, stepping past Jacob's outstretched hand for a brisk hug. Having only met Dylan a couple of times and being naturally shy, Jacob awkwardly went along with it, looking at Cathy with relief when it was her turn and she kept her hands to herself.

"Hey, Jacob. Want a drink?"

"Please."

"I'll show you what we have."

She led him over to the fridge to present their meagre alcohol collection, tactfully using her body to hide her and Sara's latest works of art.

"So, we have ... some beer that was on offer ... suspiciously cheap white wine ... one bottle of cider but that's Alison's ... and vodka. Sadly, all the rum's gone."

"Beer w-will be fine, thanks."

"Sure thing." Cathy grabbed him a bottle, prised off the cap and passed it to him. "So, how are things?"

"Err ... okay—"

"Why are you dressed like a waiter?" Sara interrupted as she carried the casserole dish from oven to table, large floral oven gloves covering her arms.

Cathy took a step back to look Jacob up and down. He was dressed in all black, even a black tie, shirt sleeves folded halfway up his forearms. Definite waiter-vibes.

"Oh ... w-well." Jacob scratched at the back of his neck. "I kind of am a w-waiter. I mmm-managed to squeeze in a lunch shift before d-d-driving here."

"What do you mean, 'you are a waiter'?" Sara challenged, a little aggressively. "Last I checked you were an IT prodigy up for promotion. And why is your stammer so bad? Are you okay?"

Jacob swallowed. "It's been a little stressful."

"Were you fired?"

"No. Redundancy," Jacob shrugged. "D ..." He struggled with the word for a moment. "D-downsizing, so they let me go."

Sara's face softened. "Oh, Jake, I'm so sorry. Was waiting tables the only job you could find at short-notice?"

He nodded.

"You must hate it."

He nodded again. "D-don't worry. I am looking for an IT job. It just mmm-might take some time."

"Hopefully not too long." Sara turned her attention on Cathy. "Food's ready. I don't think we can wait any longer for Mark. Is he on his way?"

"I'll try ringing him."

As Cathy skipped away into her bedroom, firmly shutting the door behind her, the others moved over to the table, taking their places and topping up drinks. Sara's eyes didn't move from the door, locking on Cathy as soon as she reappeared a minute later.

"So?" Sara asked.

Cathy grimaced. "He can't make it."

"Shocking."

Sara moved over to the table and started briskly dishing out the stew.

"Sara, I'm sorry—"

"Don't be," she muttered, not raising her eyes. "If you're happy being with the kind of guy who can't even make the time to meet your friends—" Coming to a sudden stop, her eyes homed in on Cathy and she gave an exasperated sigh. "Actually, do you know what? Fuck it. I'm not going to play along with this charade."

"What do you mean?" Cathy asked, dread washing over her, nailing her feet to the floor, keeping her centre stage.

"I was like, I can keep it in for a day, just one day, just for my birthday but, do you know what, Cathy, I can't. I just can't."

Oh God. She knows. She knows.

How does she know?

"What's going on?" Alison asked, looking between her two friends, concern and intrigue making her delicate features frown, while Dylan sat back in his chair, sipping his beer, ready for the show. Next to them, Jacob looked sadly at the food, then sadly up at Sara, and sadly back down again.

"What's going on?" Sara almost shouted before Cathy could figure out how to react. "There is no Mark, that's what."

"But they went on a date?"

Sara didn't take her eyes off Cathy. "Yes, one date. Everything else is utter bullshit. Isn't it, Cathy?"

"I ... " But she didn't know what to say, especially not when Alison turned wounded eyes on her too. "I ... "

"Jacob's the one with the fucking stammer, not you," Sara snapped. *Damn*. If Cathy was fragile like a flower; Sara was fragile like a bomb. "I'll make it easy for you then. I'll tell you what I know to save you the effort of having to think up more lies. Jacob, darling, stop staring at the food and just eat it. I think I've lost my appetite anyway."

"Sorry. I d-d-didn't have any time for lunch," Jacob said, gingerly picking up his fork and tucking in.

Sara carried on, almost talking over him. "So, Mark is a lie. You had one date with him then never saw him again. You never stayed over at his place and you're not going away with him next week."

"Is it true, Cathy?" Alison asked, also on her feet, as if ready to run to the most wounded of her friends. "What are you doing next week then?"

"Do you mind if I tell her?" Sara teased meanly, as if they were children in the playground sharing puerile secrets. She paused for dramatic effect. "She's going to Australia. With Max."

"Max? Cathy, why wouldn't you just tell us you're dating Max?"

Alison's earnest concern hurt far more than Sara's ire. Cathy closed her eyes as she heard Sara take the breath that would bring everything crashing down.

"That's the best bit," Sara continued. "They're not dating."

"What? So, you're going to Australia for work?"

Sara gave Alison a particularly withering look. "He's paying her to fuck him."

Alison's mouth dropped open but no words came out. *Here it is,* Cathy thought to herself, *the utter disbelief that I would do something like that. Not little Virgin Mary Cathy, who's never done anything untoward in her life.* She still shouldn't have lied, though, however much she'd wanted to avoid their judgement.

"I'm sorry I didn't tell you," she said to both of them.

"Are you okay? He didn't force you or ..." Alison; all-caring, all-forgiving.

"No, no, it was my choice." *I just wish I could have done it all for free*, she caveated in her head.

"Am I the only one that's actually worried about this?" Sara roared as Alison nodded at Cathy, as if confirmation of her intent put the matter to rest. "Cathy, he's *paying* you to sleep with him. You do realise what that makes you? You were meant to find your first boyfriend, not your first fucking client!"

Cathy took a steadying breath. She wished she had something to hold onto, like how Sara gripped the back of the chair she was stood behind. But she had nothing.

"It's not that different from what you do," she justified, Sara's eyes widening and nostrils flaring immediately in response. "So, if it's okay for you to do it, why isn't it okay for me?"

"Because you're different."

"I know what I'm doing."

"No, you don't. You really don't," Sara muttered, becoming stern; the parent that knew best. "Sex isn't that straightforward. It messes with your emotions whether you like it or not. I'm detached from it now but you; you're a romantic and you always have been. You're going to fall for him."

"I won't."

Liar.

"Cathy, you've been in a relationship with Mr Darcy for as long as I've known you. No real man could ever compare. Obviously, Max is the first that can. He's rich, attractive, powerful, mysterious – mix sex in with all that and you *are* going to fall for him, if you haven't already."

"Fine," she gave up. "Maybe I have. Maybe I will. But it doesn't matter."

"He won't love you back."

Those words were cutting. They were meant to be.

"He might."

"Then why aren't you dating?"

Cathy looked at the floor. "He said he doesn't date."

"Then he won't fall for you. Who was it?"

"Who was what?"

"Well, a man like him doesn't have commitment issues for no reason. Someone broke his heart." In a breath, her voice changed from reasonable to malicious. "He probably thinks of her whilst fucking you."

"You didn't have to say that," Cathy spat back. "I'm sorry you don't agree with what I'm doing, I'm sorry I lied to you, even though *this* is the *exact* reason why I did, but you don't have to attack me."

"You're setting yourself up to get hurt. If me saying some harsh truths would help you get out early and spare you some of the pain, then I'll say everything I have to."

"I don't need you to!" Cathy protested. "I don't need you to protect me! I can make my own decisions, and if I get hurt, then I'll get hurt, and one day, I'll get over it. But right now, I'm enjoying myself and making money while I do. So, if you don't mind, I'm going to carry on." She saw Sara open her mouth to retort but she spoke first, finally asking the question she'd wanted to ten minutes ago. "How did you find out?"

It was Sara's turn to look uncomfortable. "I saw Max's car when I got back last night. It doesn't take the best part of two hours to drive someone home. I knew you would never actually cheat on 'Mark' so ... I looked through your phone."

"Sara!" Alison chided.

"You looked at my phone!"

"Mhmm. And it told me everything I needed to know," Sara continued, no longer apologetic. "You texted him last night at the bar. Rule two: the escort *never* asks the client for sex. That's how I know you're in over your head."

Cathy waited a moment, tried to digest it all, tried to calm her frantic heart. She was hot, sweaty, and furious, and she knew Sara wouldn't stop.

"You want him more than he wants you. That's—"

"That's enough," she declared. "I don't want to hear any more."

"You need to—"

"No, I *really* don't."

Cathy turned away, getting out her phone as she headed towards her bedroom. The door slammed shut behind her, shaking the pictures on the wall.

CATHY: Hey, so, shit's hit the fan. Would you mind if I came over tonight?

She'd just started booking an Uber when she got a reply.

MAX: Sure, I'll come get you.

CATHY: Thank you. DO NOT come upstairs. Sara might kill you. Just let me know when you're outside.

MAX: That bad?

CATHY: That bad.

Excellent. Pissed best friend, birthday dinner party ruined, ride booked; everything according to plan. She just needed to finish packing.

Hairbrush, Kindle, deodorant—

There was a knock at the door, followed by Alison tentatively letting herself in.

"Hey," she said, looking miserable.

"Hey," Cathy acknowledged before checking over her bags. "Please say you haven't come to lecture me?"

Alison shook her head as she perched on the end of the bed. "I came to see if you're okay."

"I'm fine, or at least I will be."

"She's only like this because she cares. Once she's calmed down a little, she'll realise she's being too aggressive with her opinions."

"Aggressive; more like lethal," Cathy joked half-heartedly, before sighing. "But, yeah, I know she will. I just can't be attacked any more right now. She needs to learn the difference between being concerned and being spiteful."

"She does."

"And I don't need protecting." Cathy shook her head in dismay. "I'm an adult, I'm somewhat emotionally mature, and I mostly know what I'm doing. I could have a go at her about poor Jacob but I don't."

"He adores her."

"And I think they could be genuinely happy together. I think he wouldn't even make a fuss about her job." Cathy held up her hands. "But, hey, it's not for me to give her relationship advice without her asking for it." She zipped up her rucksack, flung it on her back and started heading towards the door, wheeling the obnoxious designer suitcase behind her.

Alison followed her to her feet, voice cracking as she asked with genuine concern: "Are you sure this is the right thing for you, Cathy? I'm not judging, I just ... never pictured you doing this kind of thing."

Cathy had to bite down on the wave of annoyance that moved through her. She couldn't get upset with Alison though; she never meant any harm.

"I'm sure," she repeated, turning back so that Alison could see how honest she was being. "And I know it will probably all end in tears but ... I like him," she confessed, feeling a blush rise in her cheeks. "I've never liked anyone the way I like him ... and this was the only way I could have him. I haven't been coerced or manipulated. It's a mutual agreement and he couldn't have been more transparent about it. I know it won't last forever, but I plan on enjoying the time I have with him and, afterwards ... Well, I'll probably have earnt enough to take a year off and actually focus on trying to write, see if it's what I really want to do, or if I'm any good at it ..."

Alison smiled. "That sounds like a great idea. At the very least, you could write a story about the whole experience."

"Exactly!" Cathy laughed, leaving the suitcase behind to give her friend a hug. "Thank you for being understanding."

Alison squeezed her back. "You're welcome. I'll try to work on Sara while you're away. Enjoy Australia." She leaned back, frowning slightly. "But you better stay safe."

"Yes, Mum."

"And I'm disappointed you didn't have a password on your phone. I would strongly advise you use one."

"I do have one," Cathy replied, feeling the outrage at the invasion of her privacy return. Thank God their texts hadn't said anything about the fact the sex was *unprotected.* "I guess she knew it."

"How?" Alison asked, noting something in her tone.

Cathy shrugged. "It's Dad's birthday."

"Oh ..."

She turned away from Alison's sad frown, ready to run from the whole unpleasant ordeal, when she heard the buzz of the doorbell.

"Oh shit," she muttered under her breath, dashing out of the room. "I told him not to come up ..."

But Sara was already by the front door, finger on the buzzer to let him into the building. Furious eyes turned on Cathy, immediately noting the rucksack and suitcase.

"Are you seriously still going to Australia?" She accused. "Did you seriously ask your *client* to come pick you up?"

"He offered," Cathy replied surprisingly composed. "And you finding out doesn't change anything."

Sara looked like she'd just been slapped; cheeks pinched pink, eyes wide, lips pursed.

"So, what? You're leaving now and not coming back for two weeks? Is this how you want to leave things?"

"You haven't really given me a choice," Cathy replied, bitterness like salt on her tongue. She jumped at the sound of a knock at the door, panic sending sparks through her limbs at the sight of Sara approaching the source of the sound. “Sara, don’t!”

“Oh man,” Dylan said to himself, already on his third beer and second helping of casserole, as he prepared himself for further drama. Jacob set down his cutlery and slowly got to his feet.

Sara opened the door, slapped an attitude-fuelled smile on her face, and addressed the unwelcome visitor.

“Well, if it isn’t the asshole in question?” She said brightly, as if the comment was a complement and not blatantly laced with derision.

“Is that how you talk to your clients?” Max retorted, his expression serious, that teasingly confident smile nowhere to be seen. Cathy could just see him past Sara, in a dark grey woollen coat over a jumper and slightly distressed jeans; relaxed yet somehow perfectly put together, as if he was always ready to rescue his distressed whores. He kept talking, his voice calm but with a harsh undertone. “Cathy is always so polite. Looks like I made the right choice.”

“You bastard—" Sara jumped forward, whether to attack or just intimidate, Cathy didn’t know, as Jacob immediately rushed past to stop her. He didn’t need sharp words or physical restraints, just a gentle hand on her arm and a whisper in her ear to make her take a step back. Though her eyes never moved from Max.

“I don’t see how you of all people could judge me, or her,” Max said levelly, eyebrows raised as if he was genuinely intrigued in her reasoning. He took a step into the flat, but stopped as Jacob moved to stand in front of him.

"You're not welcome in here," he said, with no hint of a stutter on any syllable.

Max held up his hands and stepped back. "I'm not here to cause a scene. I just came to pick up Cathy."

"I told you to wait outside," Cathy said meekly.

Sara scoffed. "You don't get paid to tell him what to do."

"I wanted to know why she's being so hypocritical," Max explained, turning his attention back on Sara. "So?"

"Let's just go." Cathy made to move, but stopped again as Sara spoke.

"You're too close," she told him unflinchingly. "Working together, sleeping together, spending whole nights together: it's nothing like what I do. What I do has boundaries. You're not paying for an escort to keep you company once a week, or even once a month, for a few hours. You're paying to pretend you're in a relationship, a perfect relationship *for you*: full control, sex on demand and exactly how you want it, and you can call the whole thing off whenever you feel like it. A wholly selfish relationship. And I can't help but wonder what kind of man you must be under this calculated exterior to want that over something genuine."

Max gave nothing away as he listened to her unflattering analysis. Once she'd finished, he inclined his head to her.

"Well, thank you, now I understand." He smiled sarcastically. "I'm the selfish villain and Cathy has no autonomy; no wonder the situation appears so abhorrent to you. I would, however, ask that you consider the possibility that it's actually a mutually beneficial arrangement between two consenting adults. At least, thinking of it that way helps me sleep at night," he added darkly.

She sneered at him; face twisted with revulsion. "You're her boss on two accounts. Does it make you feel like a big man having all that power over one person?"

"Not at all," he replied blandly, as if suddenly bored, before turning his attention to Cathy. "Are you ready?"

"Erm ... yes." Cathy looked over her shoulder at Alison, where she'd been stood frozen the entire time. Her apologetic grimace moved onto Dylan and Jacob, and finally Sara as she walked past and out the door, Max immediately taking the suitcase from her. They had just started moving down the corridor when Sara leaned out of the doorway.

"Cathy," she said, her expression frosty, eyes glazed. "Do you want to know what the first rule of being an escort is?"

She waited barely a breath before telling her, though Cathy was pretty sure she already knew the answer. It still felt like a bead of ice slipping down her spine as she heard it spoken aloud.

"Don't fall in love with the clients. It doesn't matter how good a fuck you are; they're not going to leave their wives for you ..."

She didn't say the last part and she didn't have to. Cathy hadn't known why Max chose to do things this way, but it had been blindingly obvious when Sara said it.

They're not going to leave their wives for you ... or their ghosts.

A man like him doesn't have commitment issues for no reason. Someone broke his heart.

It meant someone still owned his heart.

If you got to the end, thank you so much!

And if you enjoyed the ride, please leave an enthusiastic review anywhere and everywhere.

It really makes all the difference.

If you'd like to read a bonus chapter from Max's perspective, please sign up to my newsletter at www.sophieoswald.com

♡ See you for the next one ♡

Acknowledgements

All the Words has been in the works for about seven years. It may have been seven more if not for the following people.

Anna for her generosity that enabled me to print words on paper (and ePaper), and make my dream of holding my very own book a reality. Steph for her guidance and advice around self-publishing, making a daunting process a little less daunting. My wonderful friends and family who acted as my beta readers; I'm sure you'll never be able to look at me the same way again.

Zoe, the mum friend, for being just that; a companion through the messiest, hardest time of my life, looking after other little lives. Amy, the school friend, for being the best first reader anyone could hope for: your enthusiasm made me believe that I hadn't written a story only I could love. Jamie, the gay best friend, for being the amazing editor I really needed – the Mean Girls reference is for you (I hope I got away with it!) – and for your willingness to read heterosexual sex scenes.

And finally, to Tom, the husband, for your unending support, infinite patience, and for saving the day by making the beautiful cover. How are you so good at everything?

Printed in Dunstable, United Kingdom

79003202R00201